BEYOND LIFE WITHOUT PURPOSE

THE SUMMERS CHRONICLE   BOOK FOUR

PHILLIP ROSEWARNE

Published in Australia by Sid Harta Books & Print Pty Ltd,
ABN: 34632585293
23 Stirling Crescent, Glen Waverley, Victoria 3150 Australia
Telephone: +61 3 9560 9920, Facsimile: +61 3 9545 1742
E-mail: author@sidharta.com.au

First published in Australia 2024
This edition published 2024
Copyright © Phillip Rosewarne 2024
Cover design, typesetting: WorkingType (www.workingtype.com.au)

The right of Phillip Rosewarne to be identified as the Author of the Work
has been asserted in accordance with the Copyright, Designs and Patents Act 1988.

This book is a work of fiction. Any similarities to that of people living
or dead are purely coincidental.

All rights reserved. No part of this publication may be reproduced,
stored in a retrieval system, or transmitted, in any form or by any means without the prior
written permission of the publisher, nor be otherwise circulated in any form of binding or cover
other than that in which it is published and without a similar condition being imposed on the
subsequent purchaser.

Phillip Rosewarne
Beyond Life Without Purpose
Book Four
ISBN: 978-1-922958-75-4

ABOUT THE AUTHOR

Phillip Rosewarne has lived and worked in various places on the east coast of Australia, his first job being for a shipping company. After working in New Guinea, Phillip was a project clerk for the Australian Government in Canberra and the Northern  Territory, where he worked in Darwin and Katherine, initially for the Commonwealth Department of Works and then for three years as head storeman for Woolworths in the Darwin area, two years either side of Cyclone Tracy. Phillip then bought a cattle property in Queensland, which he operated for four years.

After returning to Canberra, he initially worked at Mount Stromlo Observatory as a groundsman. It was in Canberra that he obtained a Certificate of Horticulture from TAFE. He then spent the next twenty-five years at the Commonwealth Department of Primary Industries, as it was then known. During this time, he worked in a science bureau within several primary industry sections and gained an Applied Science Degree from the University of Canberra.

Phillip always had a desire to write novels as opposed to scientific papers. He began writing after leaving school, and the passion to write never left him. It was only later in life that he had the opportunity to write fiction on a more permanent basis.

Phillip is currently retired and lives on the northern beaches of Sydney.

OTHER BOOKS BY THE AUTHOR
The Summers Chronicle
Book 1: Beyond His Station (Sid Harta)
Book 2: Growing Wings (Sid Harta)
Book 3: Looking Back at a Stranger (Sid Harta)

This story is the fourth in the Summers Chronicle. It is again dedicated to my wife Patricia to whom I owe all that I am. Her struggles and sacrifice have allowed me to indulge in the creation of this saga.

PROLOGUE

Graham Richard Longley's connection to the Summers Chronicle is a tenuous and belated one. It is arrived at via a tortuous and complex amalgam of seemingly unrelated events occurring in a totally different environment. He is, however, drawn inevitably into the maelstrom of the dramatic lives of the two main characters. He also contributes unintentionally to the advancement of the circumstances surrounding both of their complex and intertwined lives through the connections bequeathed to him on the death of a distant relative.

The Summers Chronicle is a collection of disparate stories of apparent disconnection that come together to form a saga of some considerable magnitude that combines the sweep of the vast Australian wilderness with the isolation of rural and outback existence.

In Book One we meet John Wesley Summers, the central figure in this unfolding saga. After the death of his parents as a baby, he is brought up in a rural setting in western New South Wales. He purloins a considerable sum of money from his disingenuous adoptive family, most of which, unbeknown to him, is possibly his anyway. He manages to do this when he is a very young man. This changes everything, and his life is set off in an unplanned direction that devolves into an accumulation of vast wealth and hidden secrets that haunt him all his days. His cautious and miserly accumulation of assets all lead to the unfolding of events and to the circumstances for all that follows.

John, almost inadvertently and against his planning, manages to marry a wonderful woman who bequeaths to him five children, one of whom dies aged ten. The others contribute to his entangled life in various ways, resulting in disparate outcomes, chief of which is Thomas, his first and unintended grandson, who introduces into the life of John the most amazing personage. This is because Thomas will be the catalyst for John's life to become entangled with the astonishing Jessie MacIntyre.

In Book Two we meet Jessie MacIntyre. Jessie was not meant to be. Her arrival, and indeed her survival, were unplanned and accompanied with much outside assistance. Her latent rebellious and tenacious spirit is awakened and aroused in a series of devious manoeuvres brought about by unusual circumstances. In the immense isolation of the real outback, she encounters a motley crew of souls of ancient vintage, one of whom is a controversial aristocrat from Britain, long-thought lost but all with vast experience of bygone days of a now departed early Australia. These elderly bushmen slowly succumb to her natural aura and begin to pass on their disappearing wisdom and knowledge, all of which helps to mould her into the person she becomes.

It also arouses in her the insatiable and compulsive desire to create, and her life force transcends all obstacles until she finally impacts unintentionally on those about her, achieving enormous fame, and infamy, through deeds perpetrated on her by others, and by her own often secretly compulsive activities. Jessie befriends the local Aboriginal people who live on her isolated Kimberley station, many of whom still follow their traditional ways. She learns all their customs, and masters their language. She dispenses their knowledge in some of her texts that create for her considerable fame.

Jessie's own saga evolves from intense isolation in the Kimberley region into the naked public glare of a sensational court appearance and revelations pertaining to multifarious matters that lead her into much heartache and discomfort. This leaves her with a legacy of disrespect for authority and the possessor of much knowledge about the perpetrators of evil who now wish her gone. She lives in fear of retribution.

Book Three brought these two disparate people and their unrelated stories together in a rare alignment of forces with enormous impacts on all around them through the medium of the asset-accumulating John Summers. Their secretive and controversial lives collide in a confusion of incidents and actions that strain their existence.

Book Four is the latest story and begins with a man whom life seems to have dismissed as redundant. As a consequence of his apparent failings in life, real or perceived, a caring and concerned distant relative bequeaths to him a small cottage in a secluded and remote village that has connected to it some considerable unintended encumbrances – or were they so unintended? This gift comes with attachments, many of which lead eventually to the culmination of the Summers Chronicle. His own hidden inner strength and his real character emerge as a series of events unfold about him in his new existence which impacts hugely on those with whom he interacts. This apparently disconnected story then morphs into a culminating addition and refinement to the Summers Chronicle. It turned out that Graham Longley had inherited far more than just a cottage in a remote village.

CHAPTER ONE

The telephone rang, loudly. Mrs Longley answered as usual, as most calls were for her, despite the undoubtedly suspect nature of her hearing. She was an avid user of the telephone, utilising it incessantly.

It was a decidedly officious, or was that just efficient, young female voice. She was enquiring if that were the home of Mr Graham Richard Longley of Palindue Street, Mooloolaba. The caller was advised that this was indeed his residence but that he was not available at present. On enquiring as to the nature of the call, Mrs Longley was requested simply to ask Graham to contact a number in Queanbeyan during office hours and ask for Mr Deane. The caller hung up the telephone.

Graham worked odd hours, usually starting late in the evening and finishing often after midnight, depending on circumstances. He worked four or five days on and then had two or maybe three days off. He usually arrived home about one or two o'clock. This day, tired and dirty from the day, he arrived home very late, or rather very early, in the morning. It was still hot and humid, which was not unusual for this time of year on the coast, so close to the water.

His mother was keen to tell him of the call, and curiosity was killing her to know what it was about. She would try not to show it as she treated her son with as much respect and dignity as she could muster to assuage any traumatic feelings remaining in his battered personage. The morning would have to do. Unfortunately for Mrs Longley, Graham would not rise until quite late next morning after the late-night stacking of shelves at the large supermarket located in the next suburban centre to where they lived. Mrs Longley racked her brains to determine what the mysterious call could be about.

The Longleys knew exactly where Queanbeyan was, because that was near where one of her aunties lived whom she occasionally called and to whom she sent the odd card. Mrs Longley tried to ring her aunty immediately she hung up from the call but there was no answer. That was not that unusual as she knew that her aunty, though getting on now, was still very active and kept busy out at the village located near Queanbeyan.

Graham arose late in the morning to be accosted immediately by his anxious mother. She called from the lounge for him to come to her. He did not answer immediately as he knew she would probably mishear any reply he made until he was much closer to her.

Chapter One

'Are you coming in here, dear?' she yelled out again, still fiddling with things on her lap.

Mrs Longley was nervously awaiting his entry into the lounge and trying not to appear too concerned about talking to him. She had by now been harbouring the knowledge of the telephone call for many hours and was beside herself with curiosity. Her husband had been absolutely no comfort at all to her as he was a very pragmatic and sensible man who had long ago refused to indulge her in her endless concerns for the feelings and complexities of all and sundry of their acquaintances. She tried to wheedle out of him some thoughts or at least entice him into a discussion on the possibilities. The only thing she could surmise was its concerning in some way her treasured aunty. She certainly thought it could not possibly concern anything relating to that witch of a woman who was his former wife and who had made all their lives a misery. Besides, as far as they all knew, she still lived in Sydney.

Finally, he entered the room in a state of semi-undress and headed for the dresser bench carrying a long glass of some concoction his doting mother prepared for him at the beginning of every day that he was working. Mrs Longley anxiously awaited his entry. She felt she had no more need of niceties this morning and launched straight into the prime centre of her particular concern at this moment, the earlier telephone call from the previous day.

'Graham, dear,' she blurted out, 'you had a call yesterday afternoon from a number in Queanbeyan, you know, near where Aunty Alice lives. They want you to call them back. What's that about, do you think?'

He looked puzzled for a moment. He did not like any form of mystery or contacts as they had invariably meant disaster for him in the past.

'I don't know.' he answered. 'What could that possibly be? And whose Aunty Alice again?' he simply asked.

'You know, Aunty Alice. I ring her occasionally. She's a lovely lady.'

There was a momentary silence. 'I suppose I'd better ring them then. But not till I've had some breakfast.'

Mrs Longley understood. She left him be as he wandered off to the bathroom. She still had been unable to raise her aunty on the telephone.

It was now about midday. He returned to the lounge and picked up the piece of paper on which his mother had written the number. He looked at it for some time.

'Is it all right if I ring on your phone?' he enquired.

'Of course, dear,' she responded emphatically.

He picked up the receiver and began to dial. Mrs Longley listened intently, but Graham stood by the phone desk transfixed, concentrating earnestly, barely speaking but grunting appropriately. It was a short call. Graham replaced the receiver and stood staring deeply straight ahead at the wall.

'Well?' asked Mrs Longley.

Graham turned to peer at his mother. There was silence.

'What is it then?' she asked again.

Finally, he responded. 'Aunty Alice has just died and left

her place in Captains Flat to me.' he announced, almost exclaimed. Another interlude of stony silence.

'What do you mean?' asked his mother, perplexed.

'That was a solicitor's office in ...' He paused, looking down at the piece of paper on which he had jotted a few scribblings. 'Queanbeyan, is it? Anyway, apparently Aunty Alice died recently. How come we didn't know about that? Wouldn't you've gone to the funeral? Aunty Alice has left her property in Captains Flat to me. Why would she do that?' he asked in total confusion. He was deep in thought. 'Where's Captains Flat again?'

Mrs Longley was more concerned about the death of her aunty and that she did not even know about it. She began to cry a little and rushed out to the back to call her husband. Mrs Longley was mortified that she had not known about this death. It was a wonder some other family members had not informed her. Aunty Alice was always fairly circumspect, so maybe no one else knew of it yet. She took some moments to recover. Then her attention turned back to her confused son.

'Aunty Alice always liked you,' she said sadly.

Graham stood by the phone desk still deep in thought. He fondly but dimly recalled in his early childhood, visiting Aunty Alice and Uncle Tom, who lived, as he remembered it, in an idyllic rustic cottage that sat close to what was rather a discoloured and degraded little stream, a little creek really, in a steep gully. He had not visited for ages, and up until this recent news of the passing of Aunty Alice, whom he recalled must have been very ancient by now, had not given them much thought. He did recollect that for many years as a child, and before life beat it out of him through incessant rebuffs, that he always sent her a card for her birthday and Christmas and always dutifully replied to any she sent to him. Surely that was not sufficient reason to bestow on him the honour, or was it the burden of bequeathing the last morsels of her earthly possessions to him of all people, whom the world currently seemed to despise, however so slightly.

Graham tried to bring to mind any memories he had of those far distant past events when he was very small. He could visualise the treasure trove that seemed to comprise the largish back yard that was Uncle Tom's place in this quiet secluded little rural village. He also recalled that it was quite some distance from civilisation as he clearly remembered much open countryside associated with his visits.

Graham was jolted out of these daydreaming reminiscences by the increasing loudness of his approaching father. He was now a stately and reticent man by nature and was married to a woman who could communicate sufficiently to suffice for the both of them, so he usually let his wife conduct most occasions that involved any activity of a loquacious nature. Graham's domestic affairs had inflicted considerable collateral damage on his father, and this had affected his demeanour. Mr Longley severely felt Graham's pain, as he had a rather unfulfilled life – at least he saw it that way – and had placed a lot of his fulfilment on the once considerable success of his only child, Graham. His son's family disintegration was sorely felt by Mr Longley, to the detriment of his now slowly failing health.

'Tell your father what you just told me,' she said, wringing her hands in proud excitement and confusing fondness for her son.

'Aunty Alice has recently died and left me her place in Captains Flat,' he calmly announced.

They sat down in the lounge to discuss the shattering news, for it was shattering news to all, especially for Graham.

Graham was thirty-five years old. He was a late child, a sort of unexpected belated gift to Mr and Mrs Longley. He had been quite a bright child. He succeeded well at school and moved into a successful career in a major bank. When he was in his early twenties, he married a woman who would turn out to be every bit the very disaster his parents had hoped would never happen to them.

She was a pretty woman, almost beautiful, but with a slightly haughty personality. In the beginning, all went well. Graham moved into an expensive property in Dover Heights with a commanding view and a huge mortgage. Not to worry though, as he was very successful in the bank and moved rapidly up the pay scale and managed his finances admirably. His wife was similarly placed, and together they had it all planned out.

The problems arose after the three children arrived and she had too much time on her hands. She began mixing with the coffee set and found a taste for the high life, which preferably might not include the encumbrance of a husband; at least not one in her nice home. The company she kept comprised divorced, or preferably widowed, women of considerable means. Graham's wife decided, after much goading from her friends, she did not now need a man in her life, just his remotely supplied and abundant income. Unfortunately for Graham, the then current legal and social mores contemporaneous with these circumstances conspired to align with her wishes, not his and certainly not with the children's.

In the end, she made little effort to disguise the new intent of her liaisons, which had changed from the formerly mutually agreed married bliss. Her new goal became to abandon the suitably compliant person and jettison him now that he had provided her with her new requirements, which were, in this case, three lovely children and an exquisite, expensive house in a ritzy suburb.

After a suitably brief time together, she then abandoned him without a backward glance, leaving him with nothing and certainly no access to any offspring. He was devastatingly cut by this turn of events, not least at the way she had gone about the process. To ensure he was completely out of their lives, she had even hinted at molestation of her children, an accusation that so deeply cut him that he almost departed this realm with heartbreak.

The trouble was that Graham did not hate his wife. He knew that she had been directed by her female company, and especially her own parents, notably her freedom-loving feminist mother. He could still love her and wished for it all to be returned to normal.

Alas, he finally concluded that that was not going to

happen. What he did conclude was that if his wife and her cohorts thought that his career was going to be solely for her sustenance while he eked out a miserable existence in some hovel, she had been sadly mistaken.

Once all the legals were out of the way and he had been cut adrift to supply her and their Dover Heights property with all she desired, he made a dramatic, uncharacteristic and totally unforeseen decision: he simply resigned. Moreover, as he had to support her with a large percentage of his salary, he now simply was earning far too little, in fact almost none, to supply her any income. He moved from Sydney and in with his shattered parents who had by then moved to the warmer climes of the Sunshine Coast in Queensland.

It took Graham many months to gather some semblance of rationale and he drifted aimlessly about the Sunshine Coast picking up odd jobs occasionally. This went on for several years, he essentially sponging on his compliant parents. For the last few months or so, he had finally secured a semi-permanent position with evening work. This near meaningless pastime suited his new paradigm, all earthly ambition having now been well and truly driven out of him completely.

Graham had resigned himself to the fact of being alone, a fact that appeared to be decreed by fate rather than what he himself wished for. He was of medium build but had put on a lot of weight as slothfulness, neglect and acquiescence had led to indolence. He enjoyed a few beers and usually accompanied his father in an afternoon imbibe or two before going to work.

Graham was blessed with two caring parents who did all at

their disposal to accommodate their cruelly treated offspring. Graham appeared to be a loser in life's race. Why then, unexpectedly, did this totally astonishing event suddenly present itself to him? He was travelling along relatively happily now, despite all that had happened to him. His first inclination was to dispose of this offering as quickly and as painlessly as possible to revert to his quiet life subjugated in the world of dark nights and sleepy days. Graham looked at his parents. *Would they wish him to move on*, he wondered.

Mrs Longley was also wondering. She recalled that she had discussed at length over the years the circumstances of Graham's family demise, as Alice was one of the few distant relatives that she could chat to in confidence, and she had poured her aching heart out to the compliant, understanding and sympathetic Alice. Had all this family talk persuaded Alice, being childless herself, that she could contribute to her niece's family rehabilitation by this gesture?

The solicitor had requested that he attend to matters as soon as possible, preferably, but not necessarily, by attending himself in person at their address in Queanbeyan. This presented a not so small a problem. Graham owned a twenty-five-year-old car that had spent its entire life sitting by the beach. It did not inspire one with its capabilities, let alone embarking on a long trip from Queensland to the 'wilds' of southern New South Wales. What to do? Graham would do what he was now accustomed to do: he would think about it and above all, he would not be rushed. He did not think he was in the slightest bit interested in any form of responsibility or accountability or anything that involved care or dependence. Besides, there might be implications for his child maintenance responsibilities involved with all this. He would have to contact his divorce solicitor, again!

One thing was for sure, however, and that was that he was not in the mood to be involved again with solicitors, even those bearing good news, if there were such a thing from solicitors. The solicitor in Queanbeyan had intimated that, if he so desired, they could arrange to dispose of the property from their office – he need not even travel down, if he really preferred that option.

Graham finally got some private time alone in the lounge. Time to think, an activity with which he was not overly familiar and one he desperately attempted to avoid at every turn. If he sat alone too long, all the bad memories flooded back and he would dwell on all his misfortunes. Best not to think but to confuse the heartaches and keep them at bay by maintaining a mildly inebriated state with occasional beers and nightcaps. Not this time, though. He tried to fight it but really wanted to think about his distant relative.

Aunty Alice was his grandfather's sister. His grandfather had come, unusually, from a large country family, very large, numbering twelve. Alice had been one of the last sisters, so was much younger than his grandfather. She had married a rather nice bloke called Tom but, for some reason, they had no children. Graham spent his very early childhood visiting them at some vaguely idyllic, illusionary fantastic nirvana. He had no knowledge why this occurred, but he clearly recalled the dreamy illusion through the misty recollections of retrospective fondness of childhood. He had some vague hints that the connection was more through his own father and Tom being very good mates, something to do with hunting and fishing, a pastime in which his father had, up until recently, indulged copiously.

Aunty Alice was already ancient to him then. She was a kindly, caring figure, drifting mystically through his vague memories of her and her fantastic surroundings. Tom was even more formless and indistinct, a towering presence necessary only for the completeness of the picture. He died years ago – Graham recalled the time – but he was too young and too remote to be attending any funerals. Poor Alice had soldiered on alone in isolation, growing, he did recall, less lucid or at least more mentally suspect as she aged. At least, that was what the family held in respect of her, an incorrect view as Graham would learn soon enough. That might account, Graham supposed, why she might have rather eccentrically, and possibly unconventionally, devolved to him her meagre worldly goods, consisting, he assumed at this point, mostly of this small derelict cottage, as the solicitor described it, also passing some obtuse demeaning aspersions on the village, as he called it.

The Longley's lounge room was tawdry and dull, the furniture well-worn and a reflection of the age and circumstances of his aging parents. They had struggled valiantly through life, striving to bequeath to their only child all the requirements for success that they, through circumstance and the period of national conditions, had not had the opportunity to aspire to or achieve themselves. The Longleys sold their unpretentious little Sydney house for a considerable amount, enough to buy a nice modern town house in rural coastal Queensland with a modest surplus to assist with their retirement expenses.

Graham had finally settled down into an uneventful and lonely life living with his parents and contributing towards their care with really what was insufficient input but well-meaning attendance.

Why would someone now suddenly attempt to dislodge him from this morbid existence where he was coping and thrust him into one where he just knew he would not succeed? What to do?

Graham's mother was now aging and not doing that well at it. She was starting to feel the effects of a hard life and constant housework as well as the great disappointments associated with just living. His father was trying to pass through his retirement years with as little as possible of the family troubles that seemed to attend that establishment. Graham had been a burden to them now for years, but they felt responsible for attending to his psychological needs as he had suffered severely from several life events that really seemed to be not of his own making. It would be with some trepidation that he would even consider the implications of this rather unwelcome eventuality.

CHAPTER TWO

Graham had two days of thinking about it all. He dwelt considerably on his aunty. He began to realise that, as she had done him the honour of leaving her modest estate to him, the least he could do was to show her the courtesy of attending to it in person. The property in Captains Flat was actually not worth very much, as the solicitor in Queanbeyan kept reiterating, and he was advised by his divorce lawyer it would not impact on his situation in any way as there was no income. He would travel down to see what it was all about. Besides, it would be a change from his humdrum existence at home.

Graham had almost no money, so asked if he could borrow a little from his parents to tide him over. Then he decided to drive his old Mazda slowly down to Queanbeyan, taking two or three days to get there. On the third day, he stayed a night in Goulburn and rang Mr Deane from there, tentatively arranging to meet him midday the next day.

Mr Deane met him effusively, Graham thought, especially as Graham disrespectfully, and with a touch of disingenuousness towards his country cousins, made little effort to present himself with any style. Graham felt a little sheepish about the whole affair, as none of his family even knew his aunt had died, let alone attended the funeral. He was actually embarrassed that he should inherit her property, however small that may be.

Mr Deane was a large, gregarious man, well dressed and quite extrovert. He seemed to possess a permanent smile, almost laughing, and appeared to Graham, initially anyway, that little would faze him. His joviality and cheerfulness were slightly distasteful to Graham as his interactions with solicitors and lawyers to date had always been very unpleasant.

Mr Deane began by instantly going directly to finances. With a pleasant smile, he stated that his firm had so far incurred some considerable cost involved with attending to Mrs Butler's affairs, not the least being the costs of the funeral. She had been buried as per instructions in her will in the Queanbeyan Cemetery in a plot beside her long-dead husband. There had also been ongoing expenses associated with her will and probate. He hoped all this attention to her affairs met with his approval and casually handed over to Graham some papers which he said detailed their services to date all the while talking away as if discussing the weather.

Graham glanced at the sheets and noted with some internal

horror that the costs to date appeared to amount to nearly fifteen thousand dollars. Graham intimated reluctantly that he was rather short of cash at present and that he might need some time to attend to these matters. Mr Deane smiled knowingly.

Mr Deane cheerfully announced that he had compiled a thorough list of all the items that Graham would need to attend to and passed that over. Top of the list was to change all the banking details over to his name and then he could, if he so desired, attend to the costs owing to the firm. He hoped that this was helpful to his new client. Graham was not entirely sure whether all this endeavour by Mr Deane was not a disguised attempt to intimidate and confuse him with the hope of possibly taking control of the whole affair, with all the pecuniary advantages that might entail. Graham realised that he did not present, at this moment, a reassuring and competent personality.

That was, however, still a little more reassuring for Graham, so he quickly glanced down the remainder of what he thought was a rather long list of matters. There in neatly numbered sequence were items such as changing the title deeds, changing over to his name all the utilities, the telephone, banking details, the lands boards, the licence and car registration and so on. Mr Deane kindly advised again that maybe the first item might be the bank. Graham was struck at the enthusiasm with which Mr Deane seemed to constantly revert back to references to the bank for some reason.

Mr Deane now turned his attention to other matters.

To begin with, he was in possession of the keys to the house in Captains Flat. These he promptly handed over to Graham. He also handed to him a map of the district and a plan of the village showing Graham where the house was located. All the while, he casually explained in a matter-of-fact way that the little old house was sadly not particularly valuable. He gave casual directions to the village and cheerfully pointed out that the house was on a relatively large block, and conveniently, he noted with undisguised glee, was located almost opposite the hotel that had the longest bar in New South Wales. He hoped Graham would find that comfortable. There was then a noticeable pause in proceedings, Graham noted.

Then Mr Deane said, slightly more seriously, 'Now to another matter. As you are aware, Mrs Butler owned a small grazing block out of town.'

Graham indeed was not aware of this fact. This was undeniably stunningly worrying news to Graham; he was not aware that she owned such a thing and expressed his considerable surprise at this information. That was the first real break in the incessant cheeriness of Mr Deane. Mr Deane found that detail an unusually sobering fact. For the first time, Mr Deane slowed the frantic pace at which he was devolving information to his bewildered new client. This particular piece of information was rather central to the entire affairs of his late client.

Mr Deane sat slowly back in his large leather chair and looked earnestly at Graham. He then slowly and deliberately began to explain that Mrs Butler owned a three-thousand-hectare grazing block to the east of Captains Flat towards Braidwood. These names meant little to Graham and the size of the place did not register with him as either favourable or not – it was all a blur.

The reason Mr Deane was at such pains to cover this topic, he explained, was that Mrs Butler had been agisting a neighbour's sheep on the place for years now and it afforded her quite a reasonable income – hence, the cash in the bank.

'What cash in the bank would that be?' asked Graham more in confused hope rather than in expectation of any substantial amount. *First, there's this farm thing, now cash in the bank!* He thought he was only dealing with an insubstantial hovel in some distant village in the bush – no other complications.

'Why, there's rather a large sum of money in her bank accounts. She in fact has two separate accounts in two banks,' stated a slightly more serious Mr Deane.

Graham suddenly perked up his interest, not in the sums of money but rather that there was such a thing and why Mr Deane seemed so keen and eager for Graham to attend to what he, Graham, thought was rather a large outstanding account owing to the solicitor already. Mr Deane then advised Graham, however, that this aspect of her affairs was not his domain. He suggested that Graham wander around to Mrs Butler's accountant located just two streets away and discuss these matters with him, preferably sooner rather than later. He leaned around in his chair and produced a large rolled-up plan that he handed over to Graham. He stated that he had taken the opportunity to acquire for Graham a plan from council of the grazing property boundary.

'Oh, by the way,' said Mr Deane almost as an aside, 'this farm also has a small irrigation licence for, I think, ten hectares. That would be from the Shoalhaven River, I believe. Not much I know, but better than nothing, eh?'

Mr Deane then asked which of these matters his firm could take on board and which Graham wished to attend to himself. That could all be put in abeyance momentarily while Graham thought about things. Armed with this flurry of information and advice, Graham was eagerly shunted out of the office with friendly guidance that he return as often as he desired while attending to these matters.

Graham sat in the cool and rather elegantly attired waiting area of Mr Deane's office while he digested all these matters. What a shock it all was. He had better see the accountant immediately. He would also visit his aunt's grave out of respect as soon as possible. His father had not mentioned anything about a grazing block out of town. Maybe he had forgotten about it after all these years.

The accountant's name was George Dukakis. Graham found his office upstairs in a quiet side street surrounded by associated kinds of businesses. George was with a client but, Graham was assured, would be free shortly and keen to meet with him, so he waited.

It was now approaching mid-afternoon and Graham was wishing for some quiet time, but that was unlikely just yet. Finally, George was free. He ushered Graham into his spacious office and sat down. George was obviously Greek, but born here as he spoke with a pure Australian accent. He was rotund and not that young, but well dressed.

George explained Mrs Butler's affairs succinctly and expertly. He described in detail how it arose. His firm had been the Butler's accountants for years. When Mr Butler died many years ago, Mrs Butler got out of sheep completely and reverted to agisting sheep from her neighbours. Her property was quite large and of good quality but there was no dwelling on it. It was originally part of a huge grazing property that had been subdivided into four or five smaller blocks comprising mostly about five to ten thousand acres each. One retained the original homestead; that was his immediate neighbour on the left. His block was about seven thousand acres but contained the shearing shed. The neighbour on the right had about the same but they had built a house on it years ago. The Shoalhaven River ran right through these properties.

When it was first subdivided, the Butlers bought the block with the shearing shed on it and a small cottage in Captains Flat as it was only thirty-five to forty kilometres away. They had hoped to build a place on it but Tom got ill before they could do that.

George explained in some detail the finances of these arrangements, the tax implications and the gross income as opposed to any net income that could be derived. He pointed out that he would be delighted to remain the accountant for the new owner if that so suited him.

'And there are two bank accounts, I understand?' asked

Graham. He was now thinking for the first time that all this may impact on him and his child maintenance responsibilities.

'Yes.' responded George. 'At present, there is approximately fifty-one thousand dollars in total in both.' Graham was stunned into complete silence and some trepidation.

'Why would she have two?' asked Graham innocently.

'Well, one for the property here in Captains Flat and one for Cobar,' replied George.

'What is a Cobar?' asked Graham.

'What do you mean, what is a Cobar?' responded a puzzled George.

'Well, that is the first I've heard of a Cobar.'

George sat back bewildered and confused. He studied his opposite carefully. Then he said, 'Didn't Mr Deane explain about Cobar?'

'No. This is the first I've heard of it,' reiterated Graham, almost cranky. He was now becoming irritated.

George Dukakis slowly leaned forward again. He sighed audibly.

'Mr Longley, your aunt also had an interest in a bush block, as she called it, near a place called Cobar. Maybe Mr Deane is not aware of it.'

'Where the bloody hell is Cobar?' asked a fractious Graham.

'Somewhere back o' Bourke,' responded an amused George. 'Let me explain. Tom Butler came from a family of western graziers and cattlemen who owned considerable land holdings in the far western parts of New South Wales. It was hard country, and you usually needed a lot of it just to make a living.

Tom had a half-interest in a family property out from Cobar in the far west. Its income was, to say the least, spasmodic and minimal. The other half was owned by one of Tom's brothers, but Tom kept its existence quiet for tax reasons and as a proposed source of avoiding tax on what he hoped would be a successful enterprise here in Captains Flat.'

Graham was again dumbfounded. This revelation was particularly disturbing. The whole thing was getting out of hand. How come no one knew any of this? Graham was overwhelmed with this deluge. He left George Dukakis with a heavy heart. He had no mind to attend to any of these items but decided before he went out to the house and tried to find the place, the only thing he had better do was visit the banks. He would try and change the accounts and then reimburse the solicitor and the accountant as soon as possible and also his obliging parents. Now he knew why Mr Deane was so enamoured of his new client and kept alluding to the finances. He had also better contact his divorce lawyer in Sydney, again!

Late in the afternoon, Graham bought a few supplies and headed out along the coast road before turning south towards the village of Captains Flat. It was a winding narrow road that traversed hilly country, some of it good grazing, some of it shaly rock, especially nearer Captains Flat as the old mining sites came into view.

It was a moderate-sized village sunk in among steep hills right on top of the old mine sites. The main street was as much as Mr Deane had described, with an enormous hotel in surprisingly good shape and obviously still in use. That was the landmark he desired because his aunt's property was not far off being opposite that place. That made it easy for him to find the house, which he did with little trouble.

The old house was not quite as dilapidated as he had been led to believe. It needed some attention – painting, tidying up and resurrecting some moderately neglected front fencing. The lawns were surprisingly well maintained, and somebody was obviously still mowing them. It presented quite well, fitting in with the streetscape in which it was placed, with at least two large brick chimneys prominently visible from the street on each side of the house. It was painted a shabby faded white and the weatherboards all appeared to be in reasonable condition. The corrugated iron roof looked serviceable, with little rust, and all the gutters were in place. It was all rather picturesque to Graham. He drove onto the driveway in front of the house as his aunt's car was still in the driveway blocking complete entry beyond where it lay. He got out of the car and fumbled for the keys the solicitor had given him and headed for the back door.

It was rather creepy for Graham to be standing at the back door of a house that he could not really remember being in, and that belonged to his aunt but now was entirely his through no effort on his part. It was getting gloomy now. He looked furtively into the quickly darkening dullness that embraced what he thought was rather a large and very untidy accumulation of material comprising the back yard. What a mess, he thought it looked. Still, that was for another day. There were remnants of a functional long-abandoned fowl yard, and an equally long unused pen that was probably used for any dogs they might have had.

The village was nestled snugly within the craggy hills that contained the assorted mined substances it was founded on, ensuring that the sun was late arriving and early departing the cold little gorge. He studied the door in the dim light and inspected the small bunch of keys and selected the appropriate looking one to insert into the shabby, heavy, wooden door. The house was cold and dark inside. It had a strange aroma. He quickly wandered through the small cottage to inspect the three small bedrooms and the other facilities and checked all the lights and taps. He would sleep in the small back room that appeared unused for many years.

He rang his parents in Mooloolaba that evening. They had never heard of Cobar either, nor had they ever met any of Tom Butler's family. He ate a meagre dinner in the cool kitchen.

Next morning, Graham needed to return to town to continue on with his affairs, so little could be done about the house. He again returned to the house almost in the dark. He rang his parents again. This time he wandered over to the grandiose hotel not far from his front door and tried the counter meal.

The next day was Saturday. He could at last explore the substance of his inheritance. He still had not done much in the house, so he had little idea of its contents. He was, however, at this stage more eager to drive out to this huge acreage he supposedly owned about forty kilometres from here, and much the same distance from Braidwood.

He still had not moved his aunt's car from the front driveway, so was using his old Mazda. Before driving out, he decided to go via the mess that was the backyard to ascertain its contents briefly. It was dark and dusty in the depths of the 'shed', a misnomer for this construction. It was difficult to weave his way through the confusion and muddle of items that lay in every space.

Graham finally decided he had deciphered the layout enough to satisfy his immediate curiosity as he was keen to progress his acreage inspection. He determined that in some far distant past, there had been a reasonably well-constructed wooden shed located in the far corner. However, there had been numerous additional lean-tos added over the years, so the shed grew topsy-turvy into this final conglomeration of sagging ancient wooden poles and leaning, suspect rusting, corrugated iron roofing. It now covered almost half the sizable yard.

Into this assemblage had been crammed so much material that this veritable Aladdin's cave was going to require some considerable effort to sort. There were mounds of tools of all sorts and equipment of a farming nature. Small machinery abounded with fencing gear in every nook. Some of the larger pieces were covered in dusty, fading, torn remnants of canvas tarpaulins and sheeting. It was a long time since some loving owner attended to anything in this pile. Still, that would all have to wait.

He went out to the front of the property and started up his faithful old Mazda. This was a new road for Graham as he headed east towards the coast. The road wound its way quickly and steeply out of the village and almost immediately turned into rough gravel. The directions were good and he found the turnoffs all right until he was finally heading south towards Numeralla and Cooma.

According to the plan he was given, the property began approximately five kilometres from the last turnoff. He found the neighbour's place easily and then what he hoped was the boundary fence. As his place was supposed to have a shearing shed on it visible from the road, it should be easy enough to locate. This he finally did. He followed the road down for nearly four kilometres, as that was how far his front boundary was supposed to go. Then he turned around and headed back towards the shearing shed.

The shearing shed was set back about five hundred metres from the road and positioned among towering and ancient gum trees that proliferated throughout this particular paddock. It was an untidy paddock with fallen branches, long grass and small scrubby growths scattered among the timber. It was incongruous, as the entire rest of the surrounding country was basically bare of any timber and consisted entirely of grassed paddocks dotted with white specks of sheep.

The track in was rough gravel but easily traversed and obviously well used. Graham drove across the rather generous iron grid at the front entrance tentatively as he still was not entirely sure all this was his. The shed was large and set high on stumps and contained many wooden and iron yards, with fences going off in all directions. There were also several other buildings associated with this building and a line of power poles leading from the road into the shed.

Graham parked under a large and spreading gum and alighted the car, and stood peering at this huge edifice. He still could not believe all this could possibly be his. It was all so alien to him. Graham came from a long line of strictly urban dwellers on his father's side going back, as far as he knew, many generations. He was totally unfamiliar with anything rural. It was his mother's family who had the bucolic roots. Many of his mother's distant relatives, and there were many of them, still had rural interests around the Goulburn and Yass area where they had originally come from.

Finally, he walked over to the shed. Inside was a foreign world of stock pens, equipment and strange and exotic odours and an atmosphere of unfamiliarity so overpowering that he was daunted considerably by the whole thought. He wandered about in a kind of daze.

He stepped outside to explore the complex of out-buildings and yards. Astonishingly, there was a very presentable accommodation block comprising six separate sleeping rooms and a sizable kitchen with multifarious cooking equipment and cold storage facilities, including a respectable ablution block. None of the power points or light switches seemed to work anywhere in any of the buildings but they were everywhere, so there must be a master switch somewhere. He would check into that later.

Graham found all this rather enervating. He decided to go for a short walk down towards where he assumed the river was located. The block sloped gently away from the road and sheds into the distance. Away on the horizon, he could see tree-lined hills and cleared paddocks all the way in every direction. There were sheep in the near distance, and he presumed they were the neighbour's agisted sheep.

After a gentle and pleasant stroll over the grassy paddocks and negotiating a couple of fences, Graham came to a creek. Well, he assumed it was a creek. It was rather non-descript and barely a trickle, though the water was cool and clear as it gently gurgled through enormous rocks and its stone-strewn bed, much wider and far more extensive than this little creek seemed to need. Despite the astonishingly huge and wide river course, surely this was not the supposedly mighty Shoalhaven River, Graham surmised.

He wandered along the creek for some time and found what he assumed were the remains of a long-abandoned irrigation paddock where the river presented a raised, solid rock bar that impounded a large natural pool. It had clearly, in some dark distant past, been quite an exercise as there were remains of dilapidated fences and evidence of pumping and pumps long neglected.

It was now getting late in the afternoon, so he turned and headed across the paddocks back towards the distant sheds that he could clearly see even from this distance. As he wandered deep in thought, he disturbed some plump sheep that scattered at his approach. He contemplated how little he knew about anything out here. He was slightly despondent.

The next day was a Sunday. He would try and spend some time in the sheds in the back yard. He spent the morning sitting at what appeared to be Alice's office desk or workspace in the corner of a weirdly arranged hallway. She appeared to be rather thorough and organised with folders covering all manner of her affairs. One of them was marked Cobar. He would explore that one as soon as he could. In the second drawer, he found a collection of keys. Most were unmarked but a small bunch had a tag that read 'electric box'. He hoped this one would apply to the shearing shed. He would test it next time he went out. The other keys were a mystery, but he hoped some would fit her Subaru Forrester parked in the driveway. It was a much better car than his old Mazda.

This was exactly the case. He spent some time trying to start it and eventually it fired up and seemed fine once it was warmed up. He was impressed that his old aunty was able to drive this more suitable vehicle and that it had a manual gearbox. He now turned his attention to the shed. There were tools everywhere. After a morning rummaging through the contents, the real surprise to him was the two old vehicles covered over with rotting tarps in the far recesses of one of the add-ons attending the original shed. One was an early Land Rover short wheelbase ute with no tarpaulin covering for the frame. The other was the first model Holden ute. Both still had original and early NSW number plates and were covered in grime and dust, despite the coverings. There were to be many more startling discoveries in these sheds, but those would turn up as time progressed.

In the early afternoon, Graham felt he would rather like to find out more about the Cobar file, so he removed himself from the shed and returned to the house. He retrieved the Cobar folder that he had left on top of Alice's desk. He glanced through the rather ponderous file with earnest interest. Alice was nothing if not thorough. This exercise might require a little more attention than he felt it would receive at this particular time of day. As it was only midafternoon, he felt he had better allocate some time to a more important assignment – that of meeting his two immediate neighbours.

This was not a prospect that Graham held with any enthusiasm, as he was not the people person he once was, and he feared the response he might receive from people who probably held his late aunt in some respect. They may not appreciate his swanning in undeservedly with little effort and assuming her place in their sedate lives.

Graham ventured next door to the cottage on his left and knocked on the door. A pleasant elderly woman answered. He introduced himself, and her husband, an elderly unkempt, thinnish man, wandered to the door and they chattered momentarily. Graham then ventured the question was it they who were maintaining his front lawn so fastidiously, to which they replied, no, it was Tony on the other side. He was then invited in if he wished, but he declined their kind offer this time in order to speak to Tony as well, if they did not mind. They seemed fine with that arrangement, so he departed reasonably happy with that outcome. He would come to learn more about them in due course.

Graham then anxiously moved to the house that was his

right-side neighbour. His house was larger than the cottage of the other neighbour's and well maintained and neatly presented. He knocked on the door. Another elderly man answered, sheepishly peering out from behind the dark heavy, rather ornate front door. Graham introduced himself and the man opened the door wider and sauntered out onto the small front veranda. He was gaunt and sported a well-established beard. He struck Graham as foreign, possibly Italian as his name hinted, but he was not entirely sure.

They spoke for some time, Tony finally inviting him in. Graham again declined the kind offer, and after thanking him profusely for his kind attention to his late aunt's property, said he had a few things to do but would like to accept at a later date. Tony was an intriguing person to Graham; there was something fascinating about him that Graham thought might reveal some interesting details later on. As there was no mention of a woman, Graham assumed Tony lived alone. He was not wrong about Tony, as he would learn in due course.

Graham then went back to the Cobar file. The file contained some ancient papers, maps and plans and a few photographs. It appeared to Graham that Tom had come by the interest many years ago and it entailed little effort on his part to keep it current. It was to Graham an enormous property of many, many hundreds, if not thousands, of acres, translating into many thousands of hectares these days. It seemed to be rather barren and foreboding and appeared to Graham as semi-desert. There was, however, a name and contact number in the folder which Graham would attempt to contact in the evening. There were two names listed, one Frank Butler and a Sid.

That evening about eight o'clock, Graham rang the number listed on the paperwork. A man answered. It was Sid. Frank Butler was Tom Butler's brother, and he was now long dead. Sid was Frank's son. He now ran the place. Graham had a long talk to Sid. He sounded very pleasant on the phone. Even he was not aware that Alice was dead. From this conversation Graham learned many things.

The property was an extensive acreage in a semi-arid area devoid of much development. The country was depauperate and habitually dry. It had run very little in the way of stock that was of any commercial value in the past. However, of late, the place, having always been heavily infested with feral goats that thrived out there, was now using this resource for meatworks or re-selling for domestic use. It was now turning into a more profitable enterprise. The establishment costs of suitable yards, and musterers if required, were an outlay, but on the whole, Sid could handle most of it himself. Of course, he could always use some assistance from the other part-owner anytime he was available. There were some financial implications for Graham, but on the whole he would turn a handsome little dividend. The entire thing was intriguing to Graham. He finally found an old map of the state and located Cobar. Mr Dukakis was right, it was 'back o' Bourke', but he noted, it could have been worse. He would dearly love to go out and investigate this new enterprise that he apparently also owned. This he would do in due course, but firstly, things closer to home needed attention.

CHAPTER THREE

It was a dismal and cold day on the Tablelands, with scudding showers and a heavy misty feel. It was the sort of day that was not conducive to much other than melancholia. Graham did not need much to induce him to that state. He was finding all these new experiences and the people he was meeting not to his liking. He had been used to mixing with a more vibrant and worldly crowd that was a little more informed. His immediate neighbours were very friendly and caring and really missed old Alice. He thought they viewed him with some misgivings, a reserve, a coolness. He realised that his battered persona would not help in his ability to integrate.

He sat at an old wooden table in a room crowded with an unfamiliar and esoteric collection of ancient, dishevelled furniture. It had more of a make-do feel about it rather than any sense of planning. In fact, the whole house was in this state, almost a time warp of a long-past existence that, somehow, he had entered and was suddenly reawakened by new circumstances. This all was totally alien to him, a foreign country – he felt a stranger here. The house was full to the brim with early rustic furniture strewn in every nook and cranny. He found it heartily discouraging.

He had retrieved two large photographs of his departed uncle and aunt and put them in the kitchen to keep reminding him of their benevolence towards him, but the magnitude of this gift, if it were indeed such a thing, was escaping him at this present moment. He peered at the pictures, particularly his aunt. She was portrayed as well dressed, though informal, with a gentle, thin face, short brown hair and dark caring eyes. There was just a wispy hint of a sad little smile on her slightly strained looking face. *What would she think of me?* he wondered.

He turned from her portrait to look out the curtained window. Then there was the issue of the locals. The word 'yokel' leapt into his mind; he was almost ashamed of himself. Nevertheless, he found them dim-witted and parochial, not at all like the former sharp minds he had once worked alongside. Their interests were blinkered and their conversation uninspiring. What on earth did his aunt find in them and what possessed her to aspire to this sinkhole of an existence cast off in the wilderness of the remote and isolated Southern Tablelands? Had his existence really potentially descended to this?

Trouble was, Graham did not need much to trigger his

journey back into his problems and he would quickly dwell on all his grievances with little prompting if left unattended for too long. He agonised incessantly over where it all went wrong, when it began and why it had happened to him.

Graham sorely missed his children. He had romanticised his erstwhile existence and had only the fondest memories of all the good times he had remembered. Graham had been a very successful banking executive, highly paid and well respected. It was widely known that he was a man destined for great things in his chosen field. He was smart, sharp-witted and stylish. The girls found him very attractive. He fell for a lovely woman, Jenny, who was uncannily similar in many facets of her personality to him, though much more assertive, and together they planned out a wonderful life together in the dynamic world of high finance.

Jenny's parents were weird. There was no other way to describe them. They were basically alternatives: vegan, left wing and greenies. This in itself was not an issue for either of them, though Jenny was sometimes slightly tainted with some of this attitude on some matters, but not to the point that it grated.

Graham and Jenny married and moved to an expensive property in Dover Heights. They took out a large mortgage; together, on high salaries, they expected to cover this burden with little problem. Things were going swimmingly, and in due course three children were conceived and the family begun. Sally was first, followed in due course by Sam and then Ben. The children were aged about six, three and two when the bomb hit his life.

Jenny had found childcare an onerous affair and not to her liking at all. To ease her discomfort and tedium with family concerns while her husband was off earning copiously, she had taken to fraternising with a local push consisting entirely of other young widows or divorcees, sipping coffees and generally finding fault with the world, especially that world before their present state. Raising children alone with substantial outside income from ex-husbands was rather a divine way to exist.

Unfortunately for Graham, Jenny was beginning to find this idea rather attractive too. One day, without any warning, she announced that she had decided to end the relationship, he could find himself some new accommodation and her lawyer would be finalising all the details about her future income.

This was an unexpected shock, and one for which he was totally unprepared. He was so bewildered and astounded that he became incompetent and almost incapable of preparing any defence for himself. Besides, he soon discovered that the current communal attitudes aligned themselves with the desires of the woman, no matter how wrong she might be, let alone any consideration for what the children might want.

Graham was shattered. He let the dust settle, thought about things and then promptly resigned from his employment, a direction Jenny had never contemplated. Graham then moved in with his parents who had moved up to the Sunshine Coast after their retirement from Sydney.

The hurt he felt derived from several aspects of this occurrence, and it festered almost interminably. Firstly,

Graham was caught completely unawares by all this. He had no inkling of its impending arrival, or even its possibility. That still haunted him, that he could be so naïve and gullible and deceived by someone he loved and truly trusted.

Secondly, he was traumatised by the severity and ruthlessness with which the process was conducted and how the outcome was attained. No issue was too trivial, no lies about him were challenged; the worst she could make him out the better her chances of attaining her goal.

Thirdly, he was astounded that he, a hard-working, ambitious and caring husband, could so easily be imposed upon to provide his now ex-wife with the extravagant revenue and major share of his substantial income, not to mention the detail of retaining the house, along with total control of the children.

Fourthly, he was embittered and damaged that the vow of marriage that he had taken so seriously could be so flippantly discarded and cast to the dust. That hurt him the most, especially considering the huge battle it had taken to get his wife to even agree to such an outdated concept as 'marriage'. Maybe there were warning signs even then that he had overlooked.

Fifthly, he agonised for his lovely children. They were little angels to him, innocent, caring and a joy. They had shared many precious moments together as a family; he could not understand how that could be taken from him permanently and at the discretion of total strangers.

Sixthly, he wondered incessantly where he had gone so wrong.

What was it that had turned him into such a failure, because that is how he saw himself – a complete failure. His friends abandoned him in his predicament, and he became reclusive. His pain was increased considerably as he saw his parents suffer with him at the instant loss of their only grandchildren.

To add more hurt to his pain, some of his friends berated him at the callous way he had abandoned his responsibility to his offspring on resigning. His rather terse and angry retort to them, if it were any of their business, was that the State of New South Wales had decided what was best for him and his family; therefore, the State of New South Wales could also now provide for them as it knew best!

He had plenty to dwell on in his misery. In addition, there was this great pub just over the road, not an auspicious amalgam of circumstances. Another thing worried him. He was constantly and readily transferred back to this morbid state, and little seemed to remove him from it for any length of time. He at least realised all this. If he were ever going to recover any form of new life, it was going to be up to him alone, especially now he was down here.

Graham cast his mind back to the traumatic courthouse theatre. The only weird aspect of the whole drama that had raised any acknowledgement of support for him was the uncanny way his defence had been arranged. He had had no idea, and was in no condition, to go about such a thing. One day, very shortly after the whole thing was set in motion, Graham was contacted by a young woman representing a law firm that specialised in this form of defence. She handed him a card and sympathetically suggested that, if he so desired, they may be able to assist him. As he and his parents were so confused, they just acquiesced feebly to the unsolicited offer.

Graham had presented himself to the law firm in the city with little confidence in any outcome. The receptionist was another very agreeable young woman, who advised that the main partner and founder would see him herself, as she did with all potential new clients.

Graham was ushered into a large and spacious office and pointed to a chair in front of the large desk. There sat an elegant and attractive middle-aged woman of some charisma. She introduced herself as Dr Leslie Charmers. She explained that, despite being a woman, she was distressed at the way modern society was demeaning both men and the institution of marriage and decided to try to fight this deteriorating aspect of life by attending to the needs of an increasingly battered male population.

Graham's spirits began to lift the more she spoke, and his demeanour improved. They spoke for some time. She emphasised that the prospects were not good, but they would do their best. She would allocate to him the services of one of their very competent male attorneys for his exclusive attention, if he so desired. Graham quietly agreed. She buzzed an outside line and, after a few words, asked Graham to follow her out to the man she had in mind.

Graham was taken to another office and introduced to a young man of medium height, well-built, neatly dressed and espousing an air of total competence and ability. His name was

Peter Knuckey. He was a sympathetic and tolerant exponent of the details and made no effort to hide the difficulties ahead. Graham sat in sad melancholia as the system was explained and the prognosis discussed. During the discourse, Graham had a sense that the name 'Knuckey' was vaguely familiar but could not ascertain exactly why. Its relevance would arise in due course with dramatic consequences into the future.

His mind returned to the present state in the old kitchen of his late aunt. Graham looked again at the two photographs on the table of his aunt and uncle. He really knew neither of them at all. He stared for a long time. He was trying to think how he could change.

He had a sudden thought while staring at his aunt. It was still drizzling and morbid outside, a perfect time to visit his new neighbours out at the block. As it was so inclement, he figured, they probably would also be indoors out at the farm. The thought cheered him slightly.

He gathered a few things and went out to his aunt's old car to head off to the east on what was really a crook and muddy dirt road, especially in the wet. The time was just after one; they would have finished lunch by now, he figured.

The road wound out of the village and quickly became gravel all the way to either Braidwood or Numeralla. He turned off into his new road at the turnoff and headed south. At the shearing shed, Graham followed the road slowly to the end of his property and then turned around. He retraced his steps back to the shed. Just past the shed was the entry to the neighbour's place, the Wheatleys.

He could see where the homestead was located, about half a mile in from the road, but the house was completely concealed from view by the excess of exuberant growth that had been there for decades, probably for that very purpose. He followed the road in and entered the gridded compound that was the rather extensive garden surrounds of the house. He pulled up near the house and looked at it.

Graham was not particularly observant; being a city child, he never had that much need to note anything pastoral. The house was large, brick and neatly maintained with manicured lawns and well-kept gardens. If it were set in Sydney, with a harbour view, it would be worth squillions.

He walked over to the front door and knocked with the ornate and oversized brass knocker. It banged out loudly so anyone nearby would hear. Shortly after, an elderly lady opened the heavy wooden door and peered out.

'Yes?' was all she said on seeing a complete stranger.

'Hi, Mrs Wheatley, is it?'

'Yes.'

'My name's Graham Longley.' he said. 'Alice Butler was my aunt.'

There was a slight delay, then Mrs Wheatley opened the door with a little animation and replied, 'Yes, Graham. My name's Gloria. Alice was a dear friend to us. I miss her already. Would you care to come in?'

Gloria ushered Graham into the parlour and indicated that he could wait there while she retrieved her husband. John Wheatley soon entered the parlour and they sat down to talk.

Graham began by asking, 'Is it true that the shearing shed is on my property, that is, the property that my aunt left to me?'

'Yes, that's correct.' answered John, his eyebrows rising slightly at that revelation.

They conversed for over an hour, discussing finances, history and ongoing arrangements regarding agistment, payment methods and shearing agreements with the shed, and life on the land. All Graham could do was ask questions and listen, intently.

Finally, he said, 'Thanks for your time. I'll try to find my boundary sometime.'

With that, John got up and said that if Graham would wait a minute, he would retrieve some plans that show the entire layout of the original place and the subdivisions. In fact, if Graham were so inclined, John was prepared to drive him around the boundaries to show him where they all were. Graham was awestruck at the kindness and agreed, almost embarrassed. That event showed Graham his entire place and the extent of the holding. He was very grateful.

On the lonely slow drive back to his cottage, Graham suddenly realised something new. John Wheatley was a cut above the other natives he had encountered. He was erudite, knowledgeable within his field and content in his aged-gained worldly view. Abruptly, it hit him, coldly and brutally. John Wheatley was not a cut above the other locals he had encountered at all. John Wheatley was more typical of the locals than Graham was. In other words, he realised, the predominantly rural folks he had suddenly been immersed into were all just like John – he, Graham, was the fish out of water. He cringed at the thoughts that he had of the locals and the demeaning way in which he had initially held them, still did to some extent. That attitude must change, he reasoned, and soon.

Graham realised that he was the stranger here and not they. These people did not rule their lives by the contents of the *7.30 Report* but rather through the real and brutal reality of semi-isolation that was Captains Flat and its surrounds. He must adapt his attitude to suit a new paradigm. He was deep in thought indeed. He made a serious decision on that drive home.

Graham thought about himself. If he were going to fit in here, he had better make more of an effort. He needed to make a few changes. For a start, the sandshoes could go. He noticed all the locals wore very sturdy boots, hats and decent clothes that could withstand rough treatment; he would look into that as well.

Lastly, he might have to upgrade from his twenty-five-year-old beach car to something more suitable. Even his aunt's Subaru was a bit of a toy compared to the Land Cruisers most seemed to drive. His aunty had left a substantial monetary legacy to him; he had dissipated a sizable chunk on necessary expenses, but it was time to use some of it on himself.

He was wary of incurring child maintenance responsibilities. On his return home, Graham rang Peter Knuckey. They had a long chat about his new conditions and the implications for himself of this sudden inheritance. He thought of his children. He knew that deep down they probably did not miss him as his estranged wife would be enthralled with her new existence, heavily supported by government assistance, a high paying job and a supportive gaggle of like-minded associates. It saddened him. He was not enamoured of the idea of his contributing towards her treachery.

CHAPTER FOUR

Next morning, Graham rang the solicitor in Queanbeyan and made an appointment. That afternoon he was able to see him. Graham sat down in the office of Mr Deane and sat calmly for a long time, gathering his thoughts.

He thanked Mr Deane for seeing him at such short notice and then he asked, 'Mr Deane, are you sure all this property you assigned to me is really mine? Are you sure no one can claim it from me?'

There was a small delay. The ever-smiling Mr Deane leaned back in his chair. Graham had the feeling that this was not the reason Mr Deane assumed the appointment had been made. In fact, Graham had had the impression most of the time that Mr Deane and the accountant, Mr Dukakis, were of the notion that Graham was an unsophisticated, unworldly Queensland urban dolt who would wish to unload all this unfamiliar remote property at his earliest opportunity. Graham realised that he would have contributed to this impression by his tawdry and unkempt appearance and the initial bewilderment engendered in him at such an impressive conglomeration of landholdings being offered to him at his first encounter.

Mr Deane now stared at Graham differently. He finally said in a more serious tone, 'Well, Graham, probate is proceeding and we expect no issues to arise. I cannot with total surety guarantee outcomes, but there are no issues I am aware of. What is your concern?'

'I have, in my short time here, made a considerable effort to ascertain all the facts pertaining to the acquisition of the properties, especially the grazing block on the Cooma Road. I am of the mind to continue on as things stand at present, with a view to accepting more responsibility for the running of the farm myself. I do not wish to undertake considerable effort only to have all that taken from me ...' there followed a small pause before he continued tersely with disdainful sarcasm in his tone '... especially at the behest of some total arbitrary and contrary personage with altogether ulterior motives promulgating other agendas.'

The bitter and hidden deeper meaning of that sentence was totally missed by Mr Deane, but the intent was not. Mr Deane had been scrutinising Graham intensely while he spoke. This was not quite the bumpkin he thought he had been dealing with. He spoke more lucidly than before, and the content of his conversation showed a deeper and sharper intellect than he might have initially surmised.

The two men conversed for some time more after this initial starter, but things were panning out differently from Mr Deane's early prospects. He had had inquiries from several interested parties about the grazing block as there was much interest in its potential if it were to come onto the market. That might now not be the case. Graham discussed several other issues, including a survey of the property. The freehold was to be transferred into Graham's name as soon as probate was completed.

Graham asked, 'Mr Deane, have you had any dealings with a property at Cobar?'

Mr Deane looked askance at Graham. He simply replied, 'No.'

'You've never heard of it?'

'No. Not in connection with you at all. Why do you ask?'

'Oh, no reason.'

He thanked Mr Deane for his time and left.

The next day Graham drove out again to the block. His first port of call was the neighbour, John Wheatley. They stood outside in the manicured front lawns and Graham had a serious conversation with him. His request was that when John next mustered the sheep on Graham's block, could he be advised and be able to assist with the task and be as helpful as was possible for a novice. It was agreed.

Graham rang his parents often to assuage his feelings of isolation and ineptitude and to mull over the contents of the house. His mother rather eagerly offered to come down and assist with the sorting, an offer he willingly accepted. It would be nice for him to have the company in his isolation and shock of his new circumstances. Besides, he and his father could explore the full attributes of the rather grandiose hotel almost opposite his new domicile.

This eventuality had several advantages for him and his parents. Graham's mother was ecstatic at the prospect of sorting out the potentially historic artefacts and records old Mrs Butler had accumulated. His father was also enthralled at sorting a huge shed full of tools and old equipment. Graham's father could have kleptomaniac tendencies given the right circumstances, and finding so much good matter was likely to trigger them. He was especially enamoured of fishing gear; old Tom Butler and he were avid fly fishermen in their day and the sight of tons of this equipment was beyond his control to leave. In the end, Graham was only too pleased for his father to take anything he desired.

The arrival of his parents had several advantages all round. The only major drawbacks were twofold. One was the relative isolation of the old house, but Queanbeyan was not that far away for people who were not tied down by time and commitments. The only other real issue was the temperamental vagaries of the climate in a secluded hill-bound village in the snow-prone mountainous Southern Tablelands. It was bitterly cold and sunless in winter and dry and hot in summer. Captains Flat sat at quite a high elevation; it was prone to all sorts of nasties, especially in winter.

Apart from these concerns, the Longleys could play happy families with more determination and commitment thanks to the benevolence of a distant aunt. Graham and especially his father, Richard, spent much time sorting the sheds. Richard had had a relatively deprived upbringing and had always hankered after a better life. Sadly, this was never supplied, but nevertheless he had inherent good taste and appreciated quality and workmanship. This he instantly recognised in much of the shed contents, but to him the two outstanding items worthy of much praise and admiration were the two emerging ancient vehicles slowly evolving from within the mess that was the inner shed.

They had obviously been unattended for decades but were in rather good condition. Richard took it upon himself to wander about the village familiarising himself with its layout and potential contacts it might present. Richard, though normally taciturn and distant, could be much more garrulous than his brow-beaten son in the right circumstances and he felt no feelings whatsoever of inferiority regarding the locals, and the new existence was reawakening within him a revitalised sense of purpose. He could be of little use in hard physical activity, but he was no slouch at smooching up assistance where other matters existed.

He located several locals who had known the Butlers well and had useful skills such as mechanics and auto-electricians. He would be able to use much of their latent skills in returning the old vehicles to their usefulness, to the point that they could eventually be used to travel to the farm. Richard was enthralled at the discovery that his new neighbour on Graham's right, Tony, was a retired panel beater-spray painter and competent amateur mechanic. He and Richard spent much time together.

Richard, though totally from an urban background, found the farm an attractive activity. He bemoaned the sad but obvious fact that his energetic and productive days were well behind him. He nevertheless found the whole idea of the rural block an extremely attractive proposition. He accompanied Graham at every opportunity out to the place. The huge shearing shed was a particular favourite of his.

As alluded to before, attendant to this shed was an accommodation block consisting of six individually lockable small sleeping rooms accompanied by a rather grandiose kitchen affair and ablution block that was totally self-contained. In the short time that Graham had had access to this facility, he had purloined for his own exclusive use the far end little room and kept a few personal items there for the times he stayed out at the property rather than going back into the village. When there, Graham did not use any of the facilities other than the generous supply of free water available from the ubiquitous water tanks scattered about the abundant buildings. He was rather proficient at attending to an open fire generously supplied with unlimited firewood from the mature gum trees scattered about the home paddock. While his parents were there with him, he did not use this facility as his aged mother was not so enamoured of roughing it in the bush, especially when she had 'a perfectly adequate little cottage in the nice little town', as she continually reminded them.

Graham had shown a strangely unexpected and growing empathy with all things rural, a talent he was till then unaware of possessing. He was not entirely sure whether this was the result of having such an enterprise thrust upon him unencumbered or whether this latent aptitude had always lain dormant.

To this end, he had wandered far and wide over his new possession and ascertained in great detail all the foibles and vagaries of the extensive boundary fences, the internal layout, the irrigation allocation, the carrying capacity, the better country, the extent of the massive Shoalhaven River that traversed his property for some distance and assorted other matters pertaining to his territory.

The Shoalhaven River was quite voluminous in its prime and could flood rapidly. It was, however, often just a trickle this far inland but was normally permanent. It was quite an asset. He often wandered out among the sheep that grazed extensively all over his property. These all belonged to his aging neighbour, John Wheatley. Graham would often peer at them in a kind of wonderment and perplexity at their anomalous existence in his own world. He gazed at them in the sure knowledge that he knew absolutely nothing about them. He wondered how he could rectify this issue or whether indeed he had the ability to achieve this. It daunted him considerably, but he was developing a desire to try and accomplish this somehow.

Graham took every opportunity offered to him to assist

the Wheatleys and any other of his immediate neighbours who found out that he was prepared to assist in any tasks as long as he could learn. John and the others taught Graham all the finer points of fencing, mustering, training puppies and dogs, sheep husbandry, paddock control and rotation, tractors and trail bikes and yard building, even cattle work. The only aspect he felt unable to attack was horse riding; that was definitely beyond his capability and desire to master.

After a year or so of first arriving, Graham came out especially to see the Wheatleys at their homestead to discuss some financial aspects. Graham had been giving it a lot of thought. His banking background gave him considerable ability to peruse this subject.

Graham began by stating, 'John, I've been giving this some thought. I wondered if we could come to some arrangement whereby, instead of paying me agistment as at present, would it be possible to sell me some of your sheep that are on my place? That way I can ease my way into becoming a fair dinkum grazier like the rest of you are. If I do it a little at a time, any mistakes I make will be relatively small.'

John Wheatley gazed at Graham. He was taken aback by this request. He had no illusions about himself. He knew he was getting on and that his two sons, though helpful about the place when they were there, held no desire to follow in their father's footsteps. He found himself contemplating life after health dictated his inability to carry on such physically demanding work. This unexpected development could be the initiating of that anticipated wind down.

The two men had a long chat. They came to an agreement that suited and Graham started on the road to becoming a fully-fledged grazier. Graham would begin to attend sales and buy a few expensive rams with John's advice and begin to breed his own sheep instead of just agisting someone else's. It would be a steep learning curve, but he would have good support. This advent had a twofold aspect: one was a genuine desire to become more involved with his new paradigm, and he was conscious that he needed to rein in his income to avoid any involvement with the legal system regarding his children. His solicitor, Peter Knuckey, advised him that, as long as his income remained low, or he disposed of excess appropriately, he would incur no obligation. He maintained a constant rapport with his friendly legal connections. He quickly learnt that a rural property was a bottomless pit of need for upkeep.

Graham often thought of his children, how they were going, if they ever thought of him, what they thought of him. It was easier now to think of them, now that he had something to divert his energy and immerse himself in, something to divert the pain. He was bitter and envious of what had been taken from him. Not hatred, not loathing, just bitterness. He contemplated their lovely home. No doubt Jenny would have gone back to her high-flying job. She was ambitious and talented – she would be raking it in, sending the kids to boarding school and mixing with others of prodigious success. They would not need access to his meagre resources available from this agrarian backwater, no matter how modest. He was ashamed of his failings. It saddened him.

On one of his early visits to John Wheatley, after some more financial dealings and advice about sheep breeding, John had raised a delicate issue with the man about whom he really knew very little. All John knew about Graham was that he had once been a banker in Sydney when his aunty passed away, leaving him all her property. He had finally settled into a lifestyle with the rest of the local community that was successfully transitioning him to rural existence. Graham never mentioned any family, though John knew Graham had parents who regularly attended his property. John was wondering if Graham had any ideas about his future, especially as it might affect his own property.

John asked, 'You're not married then, Graham? I was just wondering what plans you might have for the future of your place and any impact it might have on me.'

That is a rather indelicate question, Graham thought. But he had too much respect for the Wheatleys to be overly offended by it. He realised that John would not ask idle questions without a serious reason. He simply replied with a sheepish 'no', disguising his deeply hidden hurt. As to the future, Graham simply replied with an obtusely vague comment, dismissing the subject as of no consequence at this time. John was now still none the wiser. They chattered on for some time then Graham bid his farewell.

He drove out of the Wheatleys' and around to his shearing shed. That query had reawakened some deep hidden secrets that he kept deeply caged. He got out of the car and went into the shed. He sat on a long wooden bench and thought. He was surrounded by the now familiar all-pervading aroma of a seriously used shearing shed. He aroused old fears that he had long held buried.

Graham thought of Jenny. He wondered what she was doing and the children, what of them, after all, it had not been all that long ago. He somehow still felt he loved her. It pained him so, to have been discarded so easily. In his pain and anguish, he had acquiesced to all her demands, most of which were imposed on him anyway. The one and only request over which he had had any control was her appeal for a divorce. He held his marriage vow as sacred. He would not consent. Peter Knuckey advised him copiously on this topic.

Sitting there in his new province, Graham realised that he truly did love Jenny. She had been his first and only true love. He had never even dated another girl in his youth, and he had experienced only the once that true, devastating, euphoric and ecstatic sense of blissful devotion that came maybe once in a man's life, either with his first love or when he encountered the real one for him. His brief encounter with the potential joys of marriage and fatherhood were cruelly and prematurely removed from his domain by conditions and settings that he still did not understand. He knew he still fondly loved her.

Graham's mother descended from a large family of rural background. The previous generations were staunch Protestant adherents – stern, teetotal, God-fearing, strict believers in Sabbath observance. There was still some evidence in the remainders of the life of Alice. His parents had drifted into mild apostasy and by the time of Graham's generation, the zeal and adherence were well and truly gone. But deep inside him there laid this dimly smouldering remnant of the early learning. He truly did believe that a vow before God was sacrosanct. She would get no divorce, at least not from his initiating. It was the one tangible fact onto which he could tenuously cling that pertained to his now disappeared love.

In Graham's new world, he knew very few women. Those he did associate with were nearly all married or committed, so the issue was irrelevant. He now carried deep scars of the hurt and damage to his persona from the episode of his separation. He, rather gladly, found most of the females he encountered were not entirely to his liking, especially after the city girls who had some sophisticated worldliness about them and an air of gentility and glamour.

He now carried a morbid fear of them and the potential trauma they could inflict on him after the court system deprived him of everything. He had no real desire to retrace that dangerous track. With all this baggage, the final reassurance that he would not again succumb was the comforting certainty of his married status, however tenuous. No – no divorce would emanate from his hand.

From inside the deep recesses of his shearing shed, he felt he had begun to take up the challenge of his new life. The next thing was to be in on the whole aim of the business, the shearing. He would attend that event when next it arose.

Graham drove into the shearing shed compound very early, just as light was breaking. He was nervous about this as it was the first time he was going to attend such a pivotal aspect of the sheep industry that had been so unexpectedly thrust upon him. It already was a hive of activity as there were by now about a dozen utes and trucks there and people milling about in the cool air. He was the only participant whose practical knowledge of this activity was absolutely nil and he was conscious of that encumbrance.

There seemed to be two distinct groups at this early stage. One contained mostly familiar faces, those of his three neighbours he already knew, though not very well, plus one or two more who were probably also neighbours. The other group which was busier, he deduced, would belong to the contractor.

He drove up in his aunt's Subaru wagon and parked near what was a large collection of serious farm vehicles, making him feel already at a disadvantage and out of place. He wandered over to the familiar neighbours, he wearing casual town gear, not working clobber. His arrival seemed to ignite an amalgamation of the disparate groups and they congregated at the spot where the neighbours were standing.

A large overweight and unhealthy-looking man sauntered over. He was obviously the boss; everyone just called him Snow. His impression on Graham was that he was slightly bellicose and jarring but also efficient. He took charge of affairs, and no one seemed to object. There was a short conversation that appeared that all was in order. All seemed in readiness, and activities were agreed on and about to be implemented.

As Snow turned towards the shed and the huge collection of bleating sheep, Graham made his only contribution by stating, almost as an aside and basically to Snow and his troupe, 'I'll be inside in a few minutes.'

There was a momentary stunned silence as the neighbours looked at each other sheepishly, as if to say 'What!'

Snow stopped in his tracks and wheeled around, looking almost disdainfully at Graham and said gruffly, 'Ah, there'll be no one else in the sheds while we are shearing. Them's the rules.'

Then he turned towards the sheds, the others of his crew following. Graham was taken aback severely by this seemingly innocuous occurrence. Something in him snapped.

Graham had only been here now at this point for a matter of months. He was a complete fish out of water but he was trying to learn all the ropes that to these people were their bread and butter. He, however, owned this whole scene and no upstart blow-in was going to deprive him of his chance to accumulate more knowledge. Some of the old fire from back in his banking days, and the managerial spats that had been dormantly lurking within him still, was suddenly rekindled.

Graham abruptly blurted out rather loudly, not fully realising how out of place it appeared, 'Now listen here, sport. I don't give a rat's what rules or protocols or etiquette you make up. Round here, mate, there's only one rule: that's the golden rule.'

There was a shuddering silence. Everyone was stony-faced

and silent. Apparently, Snow had never been spoken to like that, or if so, he quickly and viciously quelled it.

Graham, still having the upper hand, continued, staring straight at Snow, and speaking clearly and slowly, 'The man who owns the gold makes the rules.'

There was a momentary stand-off, then Graham continued while all the others were diverted by this unexpected outburst.

'That's how it's goin' to be. And if you don't like it, you can lump it.' Graham paused slightly. 'And if you don't like it,' he repeated, 'there's the bloody gate,' he said, raising his left arm and pointing with a backwards jerk of his thumb.

Silence, except for the bleating and the odd bird. Then Snow regained his composure and replied rather sneeringly to whom he thought of as a novice, 'You've got thousands o' sheep standing there ready to be shorn. Where just exactly you gonna get another shearer for that lot in a hurry?'

Graham had done a lot of research before coming there that morning and not just so he could outwit anyone but for his own edification. Graham was finally feeling for the first time as an equal to the yokels that were the community out here. Dealing with confrontation and harassment from opponents on matters that he was really conversant with was his turf. He had at least done some homework.

'Now listen here, sport. I can get any number of contractors to come here by tomorrow morning. I know contractors who'd give their left little finger to come to a job like this. We have thousands of sheep, a run of weeks, permanent, onsite accommodation, twenty minutes to the nearest pub, no travelling, better rates.'

Snow hesitated. He was thinking, *this job was a cushy little number.* He had enough wit to realise that maybe this bloke knew a thing or two. He had not bargained on that. This bloke was not the complete fool he had thought he was.

Graham intervened quickly. Having belittled his opponent unintentionally but effectively, he came from a conciliatory approach while Snow was still digesting the unexpected.

'You know a lotta stuff, mate,' he said. 'If I ask you a question, I expect a sensible answer. Is that clear?'

Snow twisted his face. That last comment was actually a compliment to him and he knew it. He just nodded his head.

'Good,' said Graham, 'as long as we understand each other. Is that perfectly clear?' he repeated.

Snow was cranky. He turned and stormed off to the shed. His retinue quickly followed in submissive silence. The neighbours stood in stunned awe at the unfolding events. Then, one of them turned to head for the vehicles.

Graham yelled out to him in a loud voice, 'Can I see you before you go, mate?'

Graham headed for the sheds briefly then returned to the collection of five neighbours whose sheep would be shorn in his shed over the next couple of weeks. They were standing huddled together under one of the very large eucalyptus trees that were generously scattered about the large shed paddock.

'Has he been comin' here long?' Graham asked.

'For many years,' stated John.

'Any good?' asked Graham.

'He's okay.' They all agreed, some just nodding with a muffled yes.

'Well, I don't mean to interfere with things, but I will be payin' attention to what he does and how he does it and why. That okay?'

'Yes.' came their collective, rapid and emphatic agreement.

They returned to their respective vehicles in bewildered silence.

For the first time in a very long time, Graham felt a tinge of self-worth. He had finally begun to embrace this new existence that was thrust upon him by the gift from his distant aunt. This unexpected minor moral victory this morning was the first time he had held the upper hand among this band of cohorts. He was under no illusions, however. All this had done was open the door to an entirely new and extensive learning experience where he was still at a huge disadvantage. All he could do was ask, observe and learn – fast.

Now every time shearing occurred, Graham turned up to participate. He had a frigid relationship with Snow and terse words were sometimes exchanged. However, Graham was always found treading the boards and contributing where and when he could, much to the chagrin of Snow. Graham often thought of changing contractors but was wary of rocking the boat too much – better the devil you know, at least for now.

CHAPTER FIVE

The first year or so flew by. Graham settled into a rhythm of attending to the small house and the shed contents and spending vast amounts of time out at the farm, as his father called it. Graham's parents made frequent visits for short periods which they thoroughly enjoyed, but the rural setting had a lot of challenges for them, not the least being seasonal extremes. It was a very long way, in every sense of that word, from the Sunshine Coast to the Southern Tablelands.

Graham got to know more people in the community as time went by. It was a community there, even though many of the inhabitants commuted to bigger towns for work or to local properties scattered in all directions. Captains Flat was quite a vibrant little place. It possessed a rather ornate police station and courthouse, the afore-mentioned expansive hotel, a post office, churches, a school or two and sundry other little outlets.

Graham had noticed on his many trips into Queanbeyan that he often crossed or ran alongside a now long-abandoned railway line. *Surely*, he thought, *this discarded and derelict expensive line with all its cuttings and bridges did not have the sole purpose of arriving at disconnected Captains Flat in the middle of nowhere.* It transpired, on enquiry, that that was indeed the case, to service the once thriving mines. *It must have once been quite a scene*, he thought. That would explain why this outcast, isolated village possessed such a grandiose and imposing police station and courthouse, not to mention the still magnificent hotel and so many still presentable houses in so isolated a district.

Graham started to fit in better with the locals once he adjusted to the rhythm of the lifestyle. He finally disposed of both the vehicles that he originally owned or inherited and bought himself a Toyota Land Cruiser ute, more appropriate for his needs. He had plans to use this vehicle to travel eventually out to Cobar one day.

Despite slowly immersing himself into his new surroundings, Graham still often thought of his children, but the pain was subsiding as that whole experience was further removed in time. He so engrossed himself in his new occupation that that memory was fading, though not the trauma. He hoped they were all doing well and living comfortably on Jenny's abundant income. He tried not to contemplate that she would ever take up with another man in their lives, especially the children's.

A couple of interesting things happened over the next few

months. One involved an incident on the rugged, isolated track that led to his farm. Graham had taken to occasionally driving long distances around his district to see what was about. He traversed different kinds of country, including some rather good grazing land. Even in this sparsely settled and remote part of the state, there existed quality properties, some with stately old homesteads on them. He became familiar with some of the more prominent family names but of course never became acquainted with any of them personally. These sorts of people would not move in his lowly circle.

About eighteen months after his arrival, something occurred that jangled with him slightly at the time but would have major repercussions later on. It was a coolish day with scudding grey-black clouds whirling across the windy sky and coolness in the air from the southerly breeze. Graham was a relatively sedate driver with his still unfamiliar heavy Land Cruiser, and his constant awareness that these were tricky rural roads to drive on, at least for him, often in poor condition and prone to rapid deterioration constantly. Besides, he was normally not in any hurry to get anywhere. Half the pleasure was in the journey.

About mid-morning on this day, he was ascending a mild, narrow climb terminating in a gentle right-hand curve down the other side of a small rise when he espied a vehicle stationary on the road ahead. It was stopped in the middle of the road so as to preclude passing in any direction. This in itself was not that much of an issue, as this was a remote and challenging area with little traffic.

Graham slowed his driving to a crawl as he approached and took in the scene. There was an upmarket, rather expensive, dull-coloured Land Rover Discovery towing behind it a large double-width horse float. The vehicle's doors were open and the tailgate was up: obviously car trouble. Graham was no mechanic – in fact it was one of the things that concerned him a little, his inability at anything mechanical – so potentially he would be of little assistance here. As the road was already blocked and a little narrow just there, he pulled up in front of the Rover and alighted.

The sole occupant, on hearing his approaching, peered out from behind the horse float to see who it was. Graham was taken aback at what he saw. There, as she removed herself from behind the float, was a woman whom Graham had difficulty in placing in this scene.

He approached her gingerly and she said, 'Hello. I am sorry for blocking the road.'

She was so elegantly attired and sophisticatedly refined in her manner and speech that he thought her totally out of place. He had not seen such class, such refined poise, not even in Sydney, at least not in his circles. He was momentarily slightly astonished, and paused before he could speak.

Finally, he acknowledged her in saying, 'That's all right. Not sure I can help.'

She looked at him. She was shortish, slim, her pale hair carefully and neatly placed in a bun affair behind her head. Her clothes were immaculate. Again, she spoke.

'I am sorry but I have blown a rear tyre on the near side of the float. I can't seem to loosen the nuts.'

Graham walked around behind the rear of the float to inspect the scene. As he passed the rear of the float, the single occupant, a massive, huge brown rump, began clattering and banging the floor with startlingly loud noises such that it alarmed the inexperienced Graham. She issued some rather authoritative commands and soothing comments which seemed to quieten the huge occupant, whose name apparently was Starlight.

He could see the second tyre of the float was indeed flat and partially off its rim. There were some tools strewn about the gravel. She pointed at the offending mess and intimated she seemed to lack the strength and knowledge to remove it.

Graham had little experience with cars and had never actually changed a tyre before. He was not all that sure he knew how. He asked her how far she had got. He asked her if the float should not be jacked up first. She responded that, no, they needed to loosen the nuts while the weight was on the road, then jack it up. She was unable to loosen the nuts. Maybe Graham could achieve that.

Graham picked up the wheel brace and found the end that fitted these nuts. She was right – it was immovable. He suddenly remembered his father's tools. He always carried a length of pipe to fit the brace to add leverage. Graham had such a thing in his ute; he had never used it but it was there. He retrieved the pipe and, magic, it fitted! This manoeuvre might assuage the delightful apparition before him that he was not a complete imbecile and go some way to reverse his now acknowledged *faux pas* regarding jacking up the float. The other item he always carried, another hang-over from his father, was a can of RP7 or WD 40, just in case. He retrieved that as well.

The upshot was that, with her guidance and his brawn plus his add-ons, he managed to remove the offending wheel and replace it with the float's spare. He tried to appear conversant with this affair; he learnt a lot that day about changing tyres that he never knew. More importantly, he spent some drawn-out time with what he could only describe as an exceedingly graceful, stylish and charming creature. Her manner of speaking reeked of class and refinement and education way beyond his limited experience.

She was so grateful for his timely intervention that she delayed her departure beyond a courteous moment and spoke to him for some time. Graham was desperate to comprehend her personality that he compromised his manners between small talk and plain interrogation. She was just so out of his ken. He was not entirely sure whether this was just because of the incongruous location or whether she really was just so superior, so sophisticated.

It transpired that she was indeed a local. Her family had been in the area since the 1850s but he did not recognise the name. She introduced herself as Sophia. He would never forget her. He wondered how many other glamorous beings lay hidden in this wilderness. Maybe it was not such a desolate wayside as he imagined.

He removed his vehicle to the side as far as he could and she gingerly navigated the large encumbrance past him and out of his life. He sat momentarily alone in the silent, isolated remoteness of the bush, thinking, his large diesel engine throbbing gently above the otherwise all-pervading stillness.

However, the episode was materially disturbing for him. Graham had some time ago dispensed with any thought of the opposite sex in any form of contact after society's disposing of his contribution to his now lost family. This encounter with a rather delectable being stirred his soul. He was still not sure whether it was the incongruous setting inconsistent with this crossing of paths (she would not give him a second glance normally) or whether he just found her particularly attractive. He tormented himself momentarily over the whole incident, then rationality slowly reasserted itself.

Firstly, she was simply way out of his league. What would she find in an upstart, crude ex-high-flying bank executive now turned peasant farmer? Secondly, he consoled himself with his fallback position of maintaining his married status by refusing Jenny's many requests for a divorce, his complete trump card. He smiled inwardly.

This incident, however, was not quite finished with Graham's emotions. It had a couple of consequential followings. The first occurred many months later. Graham had been exploring his new habitat with some intensity. He was becoming familiar with some of the more prominent names of the district, and in his wanderings discovered that there were some very large landholdings in the area, particularly further south. Some of the more prominent families owned many thousands of hectares stretching over many, often contiguous properties in large swathes of high tableland grazing country. Sophia Faulkner's family was just such an example.

A year or so later, on about the third episode of his attending the shearing process at his shed, he received an unexpected and unanticipated visitor. Sophia was driving past the scene and recognised the distinctive Land Cruiser parked under the nearby tree. The main giveaway was the one mismatching front left mud guard, slightly off colour with the rest of the vehicle. She recalled he had intimated that he was involved with the shearing game in their chance meeting on the road.

She stopped the Rover and reversed back enough to enter the grid and parked near to his Cruiser. She wandered over to the melee and asked for Graham, as she did not know his last name. She was directed into the shed. Her entrance into this hive of action was greeted with some momentary amazement and a minor cessation of activity as all surveyed this attractive intruder. She looked about and they spied each other at the same time. Some eyebrows were raised that Graham would be receiving, or even know, such an elegant being.

He came bounding over, saying with some enthusiasm, 'Hi, Sophia.'

She acknowledged him with a smile and they departed the hectic scene to a quieter area away from all the hubbub.

She said, 'Hello, Graham. When I saw your truck, I

thought I might drop in and see how you were going after all your kind assistance some months ago.'

'I'm fine. Nice to see you again. Come over here away from the noise.'

They walked away from the shed and into a more open area where the vista of all he owned was more visible and conditions were more conducive to conversation. They chattered briefly, discussing rural matters in general.

Then Graham nervously ventured, 'Sophie, may I ask you something?'

'Sure.' she replied.

'You may have gathered that I'm not altogether that familiar with all this business at our last encounter.'

She hummed in a non-committal fashion.

'I know your family has been in this game for generations and was wondering if I might just ask you a thing or two.'

'Certainly,' she replied reassuringly.

'May I ask you how you go about your shearing, as I gather you would have thousands of sheep to do.'

Sophia explained in some detail the operation of their properties and the timing and procedures they all followed. She was thorough and comprehensive in her coverage. Graham listened intently, making many mental notes of their system.

Finally, he asked, 'And who do you use for a shearing contractor?'

She explained that JJ Faulkner had used the same shearers for decades now and they were obviously very good and reliable. Graham asked for their name. Sophia ventured that they would be commencing in a few weeks and would he like to meet them. Graham wondered whether such a big organisation would be interested in his little operation. She invited him to visit during the procedure. Her father's name was Jackson. She would alert him to his possible visit. Graham was enthusiastic and keen to attend.

During the allotted period, Graham nervously ventured over to the enormous enterprise that was the JJ Faulkner operation. He gingerly negotiated the well-maintained tree-lined entrance road that led to the enormous blue granite, two-storied homestead. Graham was particularly struck by the massive complex of horse-related buildings that comprised many well-built and some rather ornate stables, along with several riding and exercising yards. The whole affair covered an area much larger than his own shearing complex. It must be worth a fortune, he surmised.

He drove on to the shearing compound further away from the horse yards and homestead. It was an organised bedlam of activity on a scale he was unaware was even possible. Sadly, Sophie was not there but her father, ever grateful for the assistance Graham had rendered to his stricken daughter that day on the road, was ready to devote some time to her benefactor.

They had a quick chat and Graham was given a brief tour of the enterprise. He intimated that he was interested in the shearing details, so was introduced to the boss of the shearers, Billy Sergeant. Together they discussed some matters. Then

Jackson suggested he needed to go, so left them to it. He had a good look at Graham. He figured he would be about twice the age of Sophia. He hoped his interest did not extend beyond the stated shearing matters he purported to be the reason for his visit to the complex.

Graham asked Billy if he would be interested in his small enterprise some miles further down the river. Billy would not commit to anything but agreed to visit Graham next Sunday, the shearer's traditional day off. Graham departed the property rather despondent at the understated enormousness of what he had just witnessed, its wealth, its gravitas, the overwhelming sense of its mere presence. He was feeling slightly inadequate.

Billy turned up on the appointed day right on time. They had a quick look about.

Then Graham said, 'I know this is not on the scale of your other operations, but would you be at all interested?'

'Oh, we do all sizes of jobs. This is a nice little number, especially if we could rearrange your timing to fit in with the Faulkners and others around here a bit better.'

'That would not be a problem, I'm sure,' replied Graham. 'There's one thing though that I need from you,' he said nervously.

'Oh, what's that?' replied Billy.'

'I'm new to this game. I want from you complete access to all you are doing at all times, and I might be a pest with questions.'

'That sounds okay. I have no issues if clients wish to be

about the site.'

'Good,' said Graham. 'The current guy here is a proper bastard. He doesn't want anybody on the boards anytime and it is a real standoff for me to get access to my own damned shed,' said an annoyed Graham.

'That right,' responded Billy. 'An' who's your current guy?'

'I only know him as Snow. A big bloke with a cranky outlook.'

'Yeah, I know him well. Well, I'm nothing like that.'

'Can you give me your card and I'll try to arrange for you to fit in next time around,' said Graham.

With that, Billy gave him his details and left the arranging to Graham.

After Billy departed, Graham went around to John Wheatley's place next door to discuss matters. As it was usually John who organised all the shearing with the neighbours, Graham gave him all the details and asked if he could smooth it all out with the rest of them if possible and get back to him.

In the end, all the neighbours were prepared to fit in with the new scheduling and arrangements that Graham had set in train. The benefits from this transition were manifold. Graham got to deal with a much more obliging shearing team. He was able to socialise readily and have a beer with them at the end of each day. He was able to assist where he could and participate in all the activities. In due course, even his father Richard was able to instil his not so small garrulousness into the scene and eventually, far into the future, other family members would come to be involved as well. All in all, a very successful outcome, all down to the kind and unexpected intervention of the delightful Sophia.

Another incident emanating from the encounter on the road occurred sometime after all the above transpired. It happened in town one afternoon when Graham chanced to run into Jackson Faulkner accidently.

'Hi, Mr Faulkner.'

He was not sure why he referred to him in that manner. It was almost a reflex out of respect for such a towering character in the otherwise small rural community of this part of the world.

'How's life?' asked Graham.

'Fine, thanks. Graham, isn't it?'

'Yes,' said Graham. 'Would you mind thanking Sophia profusely for her assistance with the introductions to Billy and his troupe? That has all worked out very well for me now. I am most grateful.'

'Yeah, no worries. Glad to be of assistance, mate. Is it all going well now?'

'Yes, thank you and her for me, please.'

'Sure. Nice to see you again. Any time I can be of assistance, don't hesitate to contact me.'

'Thank you, Jackson. Nice to see you again too.'

Graham was rather pleased with how that had all panned out. If not for that flat tyre, he would never have had the minor brush with such rural aristocracy.

Graham had spoken several times to Sid on the property out near Cobar. He had ascertained that he was married with a nice wife and a couple of older children. The finances were a bit nebulous to all concerned but that could eventually all be sorted out together. He was anxious to see his other inheritance which, apparently, involved little input from him with regards to expenses and labour, but income was in low supply, input and income not impinging on him greatly. That eliminated most of his child maintenance concerns – at least the income side did – but he could always dispose of any amount of excess income to the bottomless pit that was a rural holding, which was apparently Tom Butler's thinking in keeping that family asset.

To get to Cobar from Queanbeyan, there were several ways to go. It was a long way there no matter which way was chosen. The longest way, staying on the main roads and highways and travelling at a high speed, was quite circuitous. To travel there in an almost straight line involved using rough, gravel back roads through small, isolated localities. Either way, it was at least seven or eight hundred kilometres to get there.

Graham waited a few years, from first moving south and being able to use his by now more familiar and much more appropriate diesel Land Cruiser, before attempting to go there. From his research into travelling way out there, he decided to upgrade his Land Cruiser ute to accommodate long-range fuel tanks and strengthen the sizable bull bar.

It already had an oversized prominent snorkel protruding demonstrably high up to the roofline, useful for the dusty conditions he would encounter. It also came with a winch, but he had no idea how to use it. He added two large spotlights on the bull bar to allow for night driving while going out west.

When he finally roused up the courage to attempt the arduous trip to the near outback, he gathered Aunty Alice's neat folder on the topic, and after arranging to be able to stay with Sid and his family on the property, contacted Sid to agree to a date and a stay of maybe a week or so.

The trip to the Cobar property was an arduous one for Graham. He had done very little travelling within Australia and was inexperienced at such undertakings. Another rapid learning exercise for the innocent and unproven former city dweller, it took him almost two days of constant travel to get to his final destination.

Cobar was, to say the least, an eye-opener for Graham. Surprisingly, it was a lot like Captains Flat in that it was mostly a mining town. Unlike Captains Flat, however, it was still active in that pursuit all around the rather attractive, though isolated, little town. In an ironic turn of fate, Cobar boasted several fine hotels, one of which apparently possessed the longest veranda in New South Wales, or Australia, or the world, or something. What was it with himself and unique hotels in the villages with which he became involved? Graham's interest was nevertheless, not in the town, but in the property of which he apparently also owned an interest. After wandering down some narrow, gravel back roads following directions, he finally found his goal.

He negotiated a rather rough, neglected and dilapidated iron grid to enter the place and meandered down the long entrance road until he came to the unpretentious but adequate homestead sitting in a modicum of greenery in the otherwise drab, dusty, arid landscape.

On arrival, Sid Butler came out to meet him. Sid was a lanky, taciturn character, thin, tall and tanned and partly unshaven. He greeted Graham warmly but with little display. They entered the large mostly unpainted weatherboard homestead which possessed a silvery coloured, dappled iron roof surrounded by numerous large water tanks. Graham later learned that, as it rarely rained out here and the climate was very dry, nothing much ever rotted or rusted in the low humidity.

Inside the surprisingly cooler house, Graham met Sid's wife, Fiona, and his two young teenage sons. Fiona was a particularly pleasant and gregarious woman in her late thirties, appearing to be slightly younger than Sid. She had gone to some trouble to ensure Graham was welcomed, he surmising that she would probably receive very few visitors way out here. They spent a pleasant afternoon getting to know each other while the heat of the late day slowly dissipated into a cooler evening.

Graham was surprised at the maturity of the two Butler boys. They were fourteen and twelve. He was astounded at how competent and proficient they were at absolutely every aspect of rural life in so isolated an area. Their skill at bike riding and fencing, mustering and machinery maintenance as well as hunting gave him a serious sense of inadequacy and inferiority. They were, in every sense of the word, young adults.

Sid spent much time and endeavour in explaining the operations of the property to Graham, of course, another completely foreign field to the inexpert new chum to the rural scene. He thought that learning the ropes of the relatively gentrified Southern Tablelands sheep industry was a challenge. This was another dimension to him, and one he was not sure that he wished to master or even had the wit to do so. Captains Flat was looking rather more appealing and attractive right now.

Graham was keen to clear up the rather nebulous financial position as soon as he could. His banking background was uneasy with what appeared to him to be merely a 'gentleman's agreement' as far as that was concerned here. He retrieved his aunt's file and he and Sid compared notes. Graham explained the position as he understood it, which, according to his records, was as follows.

Alice Butler was on the title deeds as joint tenant with a Frank Butler. Apparently, Alice contributed to the expenses from a separate account in her name in Captains Flat. Was this the case?

Sid then began the long and involved sage of the Cobar enterprise. Yes, it was true that Alice and Frank were joint owners of the property. Graham hastily explained to Sid and

Fiona that there was a big difference between 'joint tenants' and 'tenants-in-common'. This was a nuance to which Sid was totally unfamiliar. It did rather have a seriously significant bearing on matters. Graham would attend to that issue shortly.

Sid continued. His father Frank and Alice's husband Tom were brothers. On the death of their father, the property was willed to Frank and Tom. For some reason, Tom had had the title deeds altered on their father's death to include Alice's name instead of Tom's. On the death of Sid's father, Frank, nothing was ever done to alter the names on the deeds as all continued on as normal with Sid now running the place and Alice carrying on as before. She probably did not know that the deeds were never corrected. The authorities would not be aroused to anything untoward as they both shared a common surname. Graham showed Sid letters in Alice's file from such entities as the Rural Lands Protection Board and the Bush Fire Brigade, water authorities and so on, clearly addressed to Frank and Alice Butler.

Graham surmised that it was a wonder Alice did not seek to correct this slight anomaly. It was a simple matter to do this process and Graham volunteered to achieve that end, and he would cover all the minor costs involved if Sid agreed to the correction.

Graham looked at Sid and Fiona across the paper-strewn table and said, 'I assume, Sid, you would want Fiona here to inherit your half of the property if you were to die, and vice versa?'

'Of course,' agreed a confused Sid.

'Then I will have to make a change to the deeds to reflect that fact,' said Graham. 'At present, if you die, I get it all. Not a good prospect.'

'No.' agreed Sid. 'How come?'

'Well, we will have to alter it to read as Sidney James Butler and Fiona Butler on one hand and Graham Richard Longley on the other hand as joint tenants, so the survivor gets the proper share. Do you understand what that means?'

'I think so,' nodded both of the Butlers.

'Good. Then I will arrange it all with my solicitor in Queanbeyan.'

Of slightly less import to Graham was the issue of the property's operations. This was a field so foreign to Graham that he would have to be thoroughly guided by the expertise of the apparently capable Sid and his wife.

Over the next few days, Sid drove Graham around parts of the extensive and sprawling property, showing him what fencing there was, the bores, watercourses that ran in the rain, earth dams that were graded out, and the numerous yards for the dwindling sheep and the ever-increasing feral goat herds. The prognosis was rather promising for the goat industry, and they required very little input from the property management. Plus, they thrived out here in what was really their ideal habitat.

Graham proposed to continue with the previous arrangements as operated with Alice. He would maintain the Cobar account with Sid having depositor access for any income and reciprocate with any expenses occurring with an account in

Sid's name that he could direct deposit to as well. The balance appeared to be slightly on the income side and projected to grow. Graham was advised that his participation in this joint exercise was appreciated, and his visitations would also be most welcomed at any time. Graham was so fascinated by the whole atmosphere of this intriguing endeavour that he would try and devote some of his dwindling precious time to visitations to the place as long as Sid provided all the management expertise, as Graham had almost none in this weird adventure.

On his initial return to Captains Flat from Cobar, Graham promptly requested an appointment with his solicitor in Queanbeyan, Mr Deane. He explained the situation to him of the intricacies of the Cobar property and instructed Mr Deane to do all the necessary paper and legal work to correct the long-neglected oversight of the title deed names. This he promptly did.

Graham's father was beside himself with excitement at the new life of his once morose and gloomy son. All these developments were affecting great improvements on his own once also miserable and pessimistic outlook. Mrs Longley even made contact with Fiona out at Cobar and made another garrulous companion to add to her small list of correspondents accumulating in their new life. She became most fond of the elderly couple next door to Graham and also to the shy and lonely old Tony on the other side.

Cobar, though, would play some prominence in the developing life cycle of the once desolate existence of all the Longleys, some beginning very soon.

CHAPTER SIX

Graham saw the familiar dull-coloured Land Rover Discovery of Sophia drive into the paddock that contained the shearing shed and a superfluity of vegetation. She seemed to place the vehicle in an unobtrusive a position as possible. He was puzzled. He was some distance away in the clearer parts of the place, so began the trek back across the browning grassy paddocks. As he approached, he thought he heard her softly sobbing. He was wary.

He came around to the back of the sheds and found her seated in a huddle on the grassy verge with her arms tucked closely around her bent-up legs. She was indeed softly sobbing into her clutched knees. He was mortified at the sight.

'Sophie, what's up?' he enquired.

'Oh, Graham,' she stated, struggling to stand. 'I don't know what to do. I'm sorry to bother you, but I'm so scared.'

'Why, what's happened?'

'Oh, Graham, I'm in big trouble.'

'Tell me what's happened.'

'I'm sorry to bother you,' she said again, 'but I don't know what to do or where to go.'

She stood gazing up at him, the terror in her face obvious. She exhibited some bruising and cuts on her face and her clothing was slightly dishevelled. He had never seen her in any condition other than immaculately attired. She was shaking a little.

'You all right?' he asked.

'No … I mean, yes. I'm okay, but I'm worried about …' She tapered off abruptly.

'Tell me what has happened,' he said again.

Sophia tried to explain as best she could. Graham listened intently as she unfolded the saga of disintegrating relationships and human failings. It seemed that Sophia had been seeing a man she had known now for about three years, despite her young age. He turned out to be a possessive and jealous man who had slowly tried to take over her life and confine her to himself alone. He was ex-army and a former mounted policeman who was also a proficient bushman.

He became more demanding and controlling and finally began to turn violent towards her, and when she decided to discontinue the relationship, he became threatening. He was now after her to do her harm as he stated that if he could not have her, no one was going to. Her parents were away in Queensland at present and she was at home alone when he turned up and began to hit her. One of the farmhands was luckily there and distracted him briefly. That was when she made her escape. Now she was here.

Graham comforted her as best he could while he thought about it all. Was this an issue that he needed right now in his hectic little life? They went inside the shed while he thought about it. She was distraught and shaking with fright and nerves.

He asked, 'Can't you go to your parents?'

'No,' she replied. 'And he knows all our property hideouts.'

'What about the police? Surely they can help.'

'They can't do much unless they catch him. He's already out on bail, I discovered, for other violent crimes.'

'That figures!' snorted an irritated Graham.

Graham was thinking that he was no fighter and that he was inexperienced with competently violent people, so he would have to remove her and himself from the trouble. He was thinking he would hide her vehicle in the small garage shed near the yards and take her back in his ute.

Then he asked, 'What about your parents? Won't they need to know about all this?'

'No, not yet. I need to be safe first. Oh, Graham, I didn't know who to turn to who is unknown to him, somebody he doesn't know about.'

'Right, well, let's get you out of here.'

He moved her car into the now emptied shed and closed the door and secured it. Then he gathered a few things, grabbed the dogs, and they got into his ute and he drove off

Chapter Six

back to Captains Flat.

On the way she asked, 'Don't you live close by, Graham?'

'No,' he simply answered. He was deep in thought.

Meanwhile, the station hand at Faulkners had contacted the police and the manager there had contacted her parents. There was now a flurry of activity. The man they sought was a known criminal with violent tendencies and was being hunted far and wide. He was known to frequent the local area often and was a competent and capable survival expert. They expected some difficulty in apprehending him.

Graham took her to his small cottage in Captains Flat. She was unaware that he lived there. He drove right inside the yard as close to the door as he could. He put the dogs into their yard. Once inside, he attended to her needs and said she should be contacting someone. She insisted that that would not be a good idea, at the moment anyway. She needed to hide, preferably right away from here. Graham had a thought. He rang Sid in Cobar but did not mention her especially. They would never look for her there.

Graham made some arrangements. The neighbour Tony would feed the dogs again. Then he told her to prepare for a long trip. She had nothing with her, but would comply. That evening, they departed for the long difficult trip to Cobar. Once he was well clear of civilisation, he would be able to travel in daylight. It would take two days at least to travel there, depending on how she coped. Smoothing it all over with Sid and Fiona was going to be a tricky manoeuvre; he would cross that bridge when he came to it. He would have plenty of time to prepare a reason. Plus, he could learn more about the situation while they drove along. She seemed to slowly revert to her more normal self the further they got from her problem.

Graham did not wish to pry too much into her privacy but felt a few more enquiries would be appropriate. He learned that they had met at a large horse show in Sydney, she apparently being a show standard dressage performer and show jumper of note. He was at first most amenable but over time developed a more possessive attitude towards her. She subsequently learnt that he had had failed relationships before with women who proved to be non-compliant to his chauvinistic ways and expectations.

They finally arrived at the entrance to Wilingubra early in the afternoon. Graham was uneasy at how he was going to explain this unannounced arrival accompanied by a complete stranger, one who was in trouble to boot. As they crossed the unkempt cattle grid, Sophia looked about the alien countryside through which she had been seemingly interminably traversing, thinking that no one would find her here. They drove on for some time before arriving at the only sign of civilisation she had seen for miles, the ramshackle weatherboard homestead of the Butlers. *Now for the hard part*, he thought.

Sid was not at home and the two boys were still in town at school, but Fiona was there about the house. She was surprised to see a vehicle turn up at her home and more so to recognise an unusually unannounced Graham. She was puzzled. Sid had not mentioned anything about his coming.

Chapter Six

Fiona came out to meet them when no one exited the vehicle. She was more surprised to see a stranger with Graham. Graham introduced her and apologised profusely for turning up unannounced. They were invited inside by a very accommodating and obliging Fiona. She could see that his companion was a little dishevelled and sporting some damage to her body. She wondered at the sight. Graham enquired after Sid. He would be back probably about sundown.

Fiona was a gentle and tender person, sympathetic, taciturn and lonely. If Graham explained this the right way, she might be conducive to the proposal he had in mind, that Sophia could hibernate there for a short time while her domestic situation was sorted. It all hinged on the acceptability to both Sid and Fiona; after all, they had themselves and their children to consider.

Graham explained the position as briefly as he could, alerting her to the potential danger. Fiona was all the time appraising Sophia. She appeared to Fiona as a petite, gentle soul of rather elegant demeanour, sophisticated and timid, not the sort to cause trouble. She could see why any man would want to possess her. Her sympathies were rising.

The two boys arrived home quite late from their long school bus trip and Sid arrived, as predicted, just before sundown. There was a long discussion. Sid also could see that Sophia was a graceful and refined young woman. He was inclined to concur with his wife that they could agree to Graham's request to harbour her here for a short time. Graham assured them that Sophia's family would be very grateful. Graham would contribute substantially towards her attendance while at the Butlers. All was finally agreed and Graham remained a few more days then left her there, he hoped, in safety. Sophia requested that no one, not even her parents, be told of her whereabouts. She feared her tormentor would extract any information about her from them.

Graham drove back home alone. He had a lot to think about. He followed what little there was said about the manhunt in the media, and no mention was made of the Faulkner involvement.

A few days later, Graham ventured over to see Jackson Faulkner. He pulled up at the imposing and ornate Faulkner mansion in the impressive grounds, again marvelling at the sumptuousness of the enormous horse complex nearby the house. There were many vehicles in and around the homestead. He parked the Cruiser near the front and went to the door. He knocked several times.

Finally, Jackson appeared at the door. He said 'G'day, Graham, isn't it?'

'Yes,' replied Graham.

'Look, Graham, Sophia's not here at present. I'm afraid this is not a good time to visit. Could you come back later?'

'I think you'd like to talk to me, mate,' said Graham.

'Oh, why's that, then?' said a slightly anxious Jackson.

'May I come in and talk – in private?'

'Well, okay, if it's that important,' said a rather dejected Jackson with no real conviction. 'Come on through to my office.'

There were many people throughout the extensive interior of the place. They entered a small office close to the front. He shut the door. Graham was shown a chair.

'Mr Faulkner, I have some news for you about your daughter.'

Jackson perked up noticeably. 'What's that then?' he asked eagerly. 'Is she all right? Where is she, do you know?'

'Sophia came to me a few days ago over this affair, not knowing where to go. She is at present at a safe location far from here.'

'Where is she? Is she all right?' he asked again.

'She's fine. She's a long way from here, Mr Faulkner.'

'Can you hang on a minute while I get my wife?' asked a more animated Jackson.

'Sure,' answered Graham.

Jackson got up from behind the desk and scurried hurriedly across the floor to the doorway. He scampered out the door and Graham heard him calling out for Edith to come in quickly. Jackson returned and shortly after, a classy and stylish older woman entered rather eagerly. Jackson introduced her as Edith, Sophia's mother, and Graham to Edith as the nice young man who had helped Sophie that day on the road. Mrs Faulkner nodded politely and acknowledged Graham with a courteous hello.

Jackson then said to his wife, 'Edith, this man has some news on Sophie.'

'What is it?' she blurted.

Graham repeated his former comment, saying, 'Sophia is

fine, Mrs Faulkner. She is at present a long way from here and quite safe. She actually asked me not to divulge her whereabouts, but I think you deserve to know she's all right.'

'But how come? What does this all mean?' she asked.

Graham explained his part in the whole sorry saga to the troubled couple. He assumed they knew of this man's existence in her life and possibly of his demeanour towards her; this proved mostly the case. They were extremely relieved to have this news. Graham promised he would try and convince Sophia to contact them via his equipment in case this man had access to advanced listening apparatus, as intimated by his background. Graham refused to divulge her location; that way, no one else could discover it in any manner. He asked them to please keep all this information a close secret. This they promised to do for the moment. The police were still hunting for the man who caused all this, and for Sophia for that matter.

Ten days later, Graham rang the Butlers out west and requested could he bring Sophia's parents out there to see her. They acquiesced immediately. Graham returned to the Faulkner's homestead the next day. He asked if they would like to go to see Sophia, to which they agreed also immediately. They would drive out at once. No, indeed not, indicated a brusque Graham. They would accompany him alone in his own inadequate Land Cruiser, that way avoiding any suspicion if they happened to be observed. All this cloak-and-dagger stuff was starting to wear thinly with Jackson. Nevertheless, they agreed readily.

Chapter Six

Graham warned them they would be travelling for a few days on rough and dusty tracks and to take a few things with that in mind. Also, as Sophia at this point had nothing of her own with her, could they gather a few things for her as well? They departed very early in the morning. They would arrive very late, hopefully on the second day.

Graham normally travelled to the property near Cobar by the most direct route, which entailed mostly gravel roads. It was shorter, it allowed him to survey the intricacies of the new industry that was suddenly thrust upon him by allowing him to stop as often as he wished and it was much less wear on his knobbly tyres. He usually stayed about one night at any old small-town motel or pub. This time, however, as he had a more elderly and traumatised couple with him who might not have been so used to slumming it, he chose a bigger country city to find a suitable place.

They arrived at what Graham judged to be a suitable venue at a sizable city about five-thirty, and Graham booked in under the name of Longley. When Jackson tried to pay the bill, Graham stopped him severely by pointing out that his name must not be traceable. Jackson half-understood.

It was during the course of the unsettling dinner at a close-by restaurant that Jackson asked, 'You mentioned that you were new to the game, Graham. What did you mean?'

'You must have gathered, Jackson, that I'm not as familiar with this industry as the rest of you.'

'Not noticeably. What did you do before then?'

'I worked in a bank in the city.'

'I see. What, as an accountant or so? And what did you do there?'

'No, not an accountant. I was in foreign exchange and commercial conveyance, mostly in Asia.'

'You must need good quals for that, then.'

'Yes, I guess so. I have a Masters in Economics and diplomas in commerce and admin.'

'That's impressive.'

'It doesn't help me in the shed, Jackson,' responded Graham, a little tersely.

'Well, it must have been interesting, then,' replied Jackson.

'In its context, Jackson, it was.'

That was all Graham wanted to say on that topic. He realised that his former life would be as false and artificial, an entirely foreign concept, to these people as their world was to him before his immersion in it. Jackson could feel the coolness in that short reply, so he ventured a different comment.

'Why would you be putting yourself to so much trouble for my daughter, Graham?'

Jackson still harboured a very mild sense that Graham's interest in this affair might be generated from something much deeper than compassionate, altruistic concern for Sophia. He still carried anxiety that he must be at least twice her age. Graham took some time to answer, thinking how to respond to that question.

Finally, he looked at them both in their unease and said, 'When I met her on the road that day, she hit me as so elegant and charming. Then she saw me at the shed on her own doing and that led me to having all the benefits of the new shearers. When she came to me a few weeks ago in some sort of trouble, I was struck by the fact that why would she come to me? She must have dozens of much more suitable people she could ask. If she came to me, there must be a very good reason. She did not know then anything about where we are going. That is just a complete stroke of luck for us all, I hope.'

'What do you know of her trouble?' asked Jackson.

'Not much. But she was awfully distressed and beaten up when she came to me. I understand this bloke is a complete crook.'

At that comment, Edith wiped a tear from her cheeks.

Then Jackson replied, 'Yes, apparently. It is all coming out now.'

'He was on parole, I understand,' said Graham.

'Yes.'

'That figures!' snarled Graham. 'Well, my understanding of the set-up, mate, is that this will not end until he is shot dead by the police. The court system certainly will not protect your family. The police might, but not the courts,' said a bitter Graham.

Edith began to sob gently. Jackson sat in silence, contemplating all he had just heard.

Next morning, keen to arrive, they left as early as possible. Graham drove into Cobar and pulled up in the main street. He told the couple to remain there and he would be as quick as possible. He came back shortly after loaded up with groceries. He headed out of town and on into the stark, arid, outback on a rough, gravel track that produced a long plume of khaki dust that hung in the air and drifted slowly off to the left. After some time, he came to a ragged, laughable attempt to display a name with the barely discernible 'Wilingubra' roughly painted on an inadequate, slowly rotting piece of ancient hardwood. He slowed right down and turned to enter the shuddering large metal grid. The Butler boys' old vehicle that they used to travel from the house to the gate was just inside the fence.

It took some time to traverse the track that was the driveway into Sid's place, but finally they pulled up to the homestead. Sophia ran out enthusiastically to greet her parents. There was a tearful reunion, with much chatter. The Butlers and Graham unloaded the ute and left them to it.

When ready, they were invited inside. Mr and Mrs Faulkner were so grateful for all this kindness so far that they were unable to convey it entirely. During their first encounter, Jackson expressed concern that he was separated from his daughter by such a distance. He also intimated that he could not aid his daughter way out here if her threat ever discovered her whereabouts.

To this comment Graham simply replied, 'Sid is an excellent shot.'

There was a long earnest discussion. Both the Faulkners were mystified why the Butlers were so accommodating in their troubled times. When they tried to offer recompense, the Butlers simply said they could all sort that out later. Besides, Sophia was an accomplished horsewoman and was proving to be of considerable usefulness about the place. It was all left at that for the present until something happened to cause its ending.

That happy event occurred, as predicted by Graham, with the fatal shooting by the police of the obviously deranged person who had caused all the violence. In a final shootout in some wild country not all that far from their properties in the Tablelands, he was fatally shot after declaring he was not going to be captured.

The police were still mystified as to the whereabouts of Sophia. She was not with the perpetrator at the time of his demise. They never were informed exactly of her location, only that she had been safe for the duration. The episode had a traumatic effect on all the Faulkners, especially Sophia. Her parents realised that without the assistance of an obliging Graham, not to mention the Butlers, things might have turned out much worse. They were very appreciative.

Jackson, through his many contacts, arranged for a friend to fly him out to Cobar in a small private aeroplane to get his daughter as quickly as he could. He said on departing that he would contact the Butlers shortly to finalise compensation which, he pointed out, they abundantly deserved.

On her final return to the Faulkner home after the ordeal and hibernation in far western New South Wales, a duration that extended to just over four months, there was to be a gathering. This was not so much a celebration or even a party, more a recognition of a rebirth and salvation, or a recovery of a potentially fatally lost daughter. It was to be only family and a small collection of the extensive Faulkner property employees, who numbered many. One of the first to be invited was, of course, Graham Longley.

When Graham questioned whether he would fit in with the Faulkner throng, he was severely admonished by both Jackson and Edith and assured he was rather admirably suitable for that gathering. Jackson had eased his qualms concerning any amorous directions from Graham towards his daughter from comments and asides from both of them alleviating any concerns he had there. At the gathering, Graham rather unashamedly made as many enquiries as he considered polite into a multitude of Faulkner property running matters. He learnt much. Many there did not really know why he was invited or his involvement, and Graham did little to enlighten them.

Graham learnt a few more things about the Faulkners at this little gathering. Firstly, he was slightly intrigued to discover that the Faulkners had a maid, something he thought was no longer possible. Secondly, he was introduced to yet another surprisingly elegant, charming and stylish woman whose name was Ophelia.

She was a rather accomplished and expert exponent of all matters relating to things equine. In fact, she was an Olympic silver medallist from the Australian Equestrian team. She was Sophia's maiden aunt, Edith's unmarried sister. Graham had the impression that Edith and she had possibly been discussing Graham in light of his also being single.

Graham was particularly struck by the sheer irony of this

encounter. He was amazed at the gravitas of his new circle. This new woman oozed class and breeding, much as Edith and Sophia did. She had attained accomplishments way beyond his meagre abilities. He simply would not encounter such elegance or capabilities in others in his former life. These people did not move in his lowly circle in the crowded city where these sorts of encounters could be easily avoided and often with little disguised attempt at politeness. Yet here in the rarefied confines of the sparse rural atmosphere, he was treated as an acknowledged equal, sought after and appreciated for some service that he regarded as of little import. He found himself comparing this woman to his Jenny. He was not impressed with himself for so doing. Anyway, what could they ever find in him to make him appealing to their sort of character, or to fitting into their rarefied lifestyles?

Ophelia had intimated that she was unaware of the full story relating to his involvement regarding Sophia's recent event but was aware that he had a central part in her possible survival. Graham found her particularly amiable. His defences were alerted.

A short time after all this, Jackson pulled up at the huge conglomeration that was Graham's shed complex. He hunted around looking for him. He discovered him in one of the shed yards attending to rails. Graham stood up and acknowledged him. Jackson said hello, then chatted for a short time.

'Sophie says you don't live around here. That must be a nuisance.'

'No, not really, at the moment.'

'How come?'

'My aunt and uncle bought this place about thirty-five years ago, Jackson. It used to be one huge property but, as you can see, it's been split into six smaller blocks. The original homestead is that one over there,' he said, pointing to the Wheatleys'. 'This block only had the shearing shed on it and then the Davidsons next door built their house about thirty years ago on their block and so did the Johnsons further down. The Johnsons is the place with all the cattle.'

'You mean those Brahmans?' said Jackson, slightly derisorily.

'Yes,' smiled Graham, 'but they're Santas.'

'Yeah, well, they all look like yaks to me,' said Jackson.

'Yaks!' laughed Graham. 'No, they are Santa Gertrudis, cross-bred *Bos taurus* with about three-eighths *Bos indicus* in 'em. I've spent a lot of time with Bert Johnson and his cattle, learnt a lot from him about them. Not sure I want that stress. They are a bit big for me.'

'Wouldn't they be better at Cobar?'

'Not really. It's too dry, and the feed is too sparse for them there. They are really suited to Queensland and the Territory; they thrive in the tropics.'

'Well, Sophia said that the country out there is no good for anything much.'

'Yeah, it's hard all right. Speaking of Sophie, how's she going now?'

'She's fine but still jangled over it all.'

'Well, you must worry about her.'

'Yes, we do. She's quite a concern for us both.'

'I suppose, Jackson, if I may be so rude as to say, that you must be worried about any blokes that she takes up with, I mean in a long-term situation. You know, things like inheriting the place, that sort of thing.'

'It's always in our minds, Graham. You don't have any family?'

'No, Jackson, nothin' to speak of.'

His tone was decidedly cool. Jackson picked up on that note.

'Anyway, your folks did not build here then?' said Jackson.

'No,' answered Graham, still smarting from his inner grief at that question. 'My uncle was going to build a place here but, of course, he got quite ill straight away and it never happened. Ain't that life' he said with a mild bitterness not missed by Jackson. 'They bought the place in Captains Flat as an interim. Paid nothin' for it at the time. It's still not worth that much. Why my aunt stayed there for so long I still haven't figured out.'

Jackson could see some rather large looking sheep in a nearby paddock and asked if they could wander over to inspect them. Graham agreed, but asked Jackson to wait a second while he retrieved a bag of feed from a shed. He then walked to the near fence.

Graham yelled out, 'Come an' get it, boys!'

The animals raised their heads and began to saunter and trot up to him. He placed some of the feed in a long metal trough and the sheep, some of his few rams, devoured the treat and allowed themselves to be handled while they so partook. Jackson observed the animals and noted their characteristics. They were rather magnificent for such an open state.

'So, what's your plans now?' asked Jackson.

'Well, I'm slowly getting out of agisting the neighbour's sheep and moving into my own. I'm looking at lowering my micron count to make my crimp finer and raise the curvature. The aim is to get to longer staple and higher fleece weight. I'm also trying to get longer hauteur, and less noil and card waste. I'm looking at bare breech merinos as well, anything to reduce labour and stress.'

'Well,' said Jackson, 'you've certainly done your homework.'

'I'm also looking into SAMMs and Dohnes for Cobar, though the goats are doin' pretty well out there.'

'The DSE must be horrendous in that country,' said Jackson.

'Yes.' replied Graham, 'but it does carry some stock, mostly ferals. The main problem out there is government interference with management.'

'What do you mean?' asked Jackson.

'Government policy on issues keeps changing all the time. Things like native vegetation, water reforms, timber resources management, wilderness legislation, threatened species protection, heritage protection, land rights – it goes on and on. There are so many different kinds of leases out that way.'

'Crikey, that's a handful, mate!'

'Tell me about it,' said an annoyed Graham. 'You met Sid. A nicer more placid bloke you'll never meet. How he copes with all that is beyond me. You think it's hard coping here? Try goin' out there and coping with all that, plus the terrible climate and the isolation. You need to be a special type of person to survive.'

'You're right there, mate,' said Jackson. 'How on earth did you come by that place?'

'Well, my uncle inherited it from his father and somehow never bothered to unload it. I just inherited it by default.'

'Going to keep it on?' asked Jackson.

'Probably, mate. Sid an' Fiona are such a nice couple. I can contribute in a small way to their survival out there, plus I find it sobering to have that reminder in the background. Besides, surprisingly, it's quite a novel concept to be involved in.'

'Yeah, that it is.' replied Jackson.

Jackson carefully surveyed the whole scene while talking to Graham, taking in all he could of the enterprise. He departed deep in thought.

A few days later, he contacted Graham and asked him if he could spare a few hours to visit him and Sophia at their property. Graham gratefully obliged. He arrived on time and was enthusiastically met by a beaming Sophia who ran up to him and hugged him profusely. Graham could but hesitantly reciprocate and rub her back gently. He was struck deeply by her embrace and the heady essence of her presence and the scented aroma of her delicate perfume. She was a wonder to him. How anyone could hit her was a complete mystery to him.

Mr and Mrs Faulkner greeted him more civilly and with obvious deference and reverence. Edith was a picture of understated elegance; he could see where Sophia got her poise from. Graham wondered why they would call on him. There was some general chit-chat, then Jackson asked Graham if he would like to accompany them to the nearby shed. They departed the open air for the large metal shed that was obviously housing many sheep. He could tell by the incessant bleating emanating from within. They entered through the oversized sliding door.

Jackson said, 'Graham, I do not wish in any way to impinge on your breeding program, but if you considered something in here as fitting in with that scheme, we all would be delighted to offer you a couple of rams by way of thanks and acknowledgement of all you have done for us.'

Edith nodded and Sophia smiled beguilingly at him.

'Truly, Jackson,' said an embarrassed Graham, 'that is not in the slightest necessary. You have repaid me many times over already with your kindness and advice offered so freely.'

'Rubbish,' said Jackson. 'Take a look at these here,' he said cheerily.

They entered the shed and sauntered up to a couple of pens holding two large, magnificent rams and two young ram hoggets. All were docile and in excellent condition. The two older were four-tooth rams and the two younger were about two-tooth. They were outstanding. Graham realised that normally these may be beyond his ability or desire to invest in because of their price and risk of subsequent loss.

Jackson enquired, 'Would these fit in with your program? These have all tested under twenty microns.'

Chapter Six

'Any one of them would be admirable, Jackson, but they'd be out of my league right now.'

'Well, I'm offering all four to you if you'd like them.'

Graham was speechless. He gaped at the three of them. Edith was looking at him quietly. Sophia had a large grin on her face. Jackson continued.

'They have all been constantly handled and would soon come up to you in the paddock. Would you like them?'

'Please take them,' enthused an appealing Sophia.

'I can see you'd like them, Graham,' said Jackson. 'Good. I'll deliver them tomorrow about mid-morning. Can you be there then? I'll arrange for all the official paperwork to be done this end.'

'I don't know what to say,' replied a very nervous and embarrassed Graham.

'Now,' said Jackson, 'I've been thinking about Sid and Fiona. Sophie here has given me a few ideas, and I think I'd like to repay their help in some way and maybe the best would be to send out a couple of boys to do some work on the neglected infrastructure Sophie has mentioned. You know, some fencing, that damned awful grid and a couple of crossings, that sort of stuff. What do you think?'

'Of course, that would be helpful, but truly we can't accept that sort of help.'

'Nonsense,' said Jackson. 'Good. that's sorted. I'll see you tomorrow. You check up with Sid and I'll arrange it all this end.'

Jackson was certainly a man of action and used to being

obeyed. Graham was overwhelmed, and it showed.

That evening, Graham rang Sid. Next day, as arranged, Jackson turned up at Graham's shed paddock towing a tandem wheeled trailer with a stock crate containing the four animals he had seen yesterday. They were unloaded into a small yard near the shed and left for Graham to attend to as he saw fit.

Jackson then said to Graham, 'Did you get onto Sid?'

'Yes,' replied Graham. 'But we really don't want anything from you.'

'Good!' exclaimed Jackson. 'Now look, I've got two young blokes that'd love to go out there for a couple o'weeks. One of 'em is quite experienced with firearms. Might help you with your feral pigs. When would suit?'

'Anytime,' replied Graham.

'Good. They can leave in two days if you like.'

It was agreed. They went out in a small two-tonne truck with a few other practical items and some gear that would be useful in that environment.

CHAPTER SEVEN

It was about six years now since Graham had upped anchor and moved to Captains Flat. He had settled into a rhythm of life with which he was in harmony. He had gradually removed all of the Wheatley's agisted stock, reducing the stocking rate on his pasture to a much more conservative level with his own bought sheep. He had been slowly purchasing expensive, good quality rams and some ewes to improve the value of his clip. This aim had been aided considerably by the overwhelmingly generous donation of the four rams from the ever-grateful Faulkners, with whom he maintained a close liaison.

He had spent a lot of his meagre income on refurbishing the long-neglected infrastructure of the property that his aged aunt had left somewhat derelict, mostly fencing and the shearing complex yards. He managed to replace the recalcitrant and uncooperative Snow with the much more agreeable Billy Sergeant shearing team, again by way of the Faulkners, and this had given him a more pleasant and quicker learning experience in that important field.

Graham was mildly confused as to why the Faulkners had maintained so close a personal relationship with him. He did not entirely believe that his endeavours in that field regarding Sophia were worthy of quite so much gratitude. He regarded it as a particularly significant milestone and a major achievement in his brief sojourn into the world of rural endeavours to have managed to retain that status, which gave him a latent sense of personal pride in attaining this feat. He looked on that relationship as a crowning glory so far, along with semi-mastering his sheep raising caper.

The Faulkners gave Graham much food for thought. They were at the other end of the grazing industry from him. At the welcome home gathering for Sophia's return from Cobar, Graham experienced the refinement of a seriously wealthy and modestly elegant grandiose homestead. Sophia was their only child and, as such, was exceedingly treasured. It dawned on him that she held more for them than just a state of daughterhood.

Graham had read in some rural publications something about succession planning. At the time, it had little impact on him or his thinking. When it came to an enterprise such as the Faulkners, he suddenly could see that the issue of inheritance must be a constant consideration. It occurred to him that, sadly, he thought the Faulkners would probably dearly have loved to have had a son or two. Girls probably would marry and move away.

Mrs Faulkner had hinted to Graham that Sophia was a strong-minded young woman with a will of iron, much like her dad. He thought that would make sense because, to be such a successful show jumper, one would need a strong personality. She never really came across to him that way, at least not in his presence, but it made sense.

The Faulkners must be taking a very keen interest in her male companions, he concluded. It would be a dilemma that he was grateful not to have in his life. His succession planning did not arise. He did not even have a will.

One of Graham's most personally satisfying aspects of this move south was the perceivably enhanced demeanour of both his parents. Both were overjoyed at his vastly improved character and the enormous climb back out of his former total despair to this new air of coping and being more fulfilled. Not only was his manner gaining some meaningful outward display, but he also seemed to be succeeding at his new endeavour rather well.

This gave them a much more contented outlook. Furthermore, they were also now gaining some considerable personal benefit from partaking in what was becoming almost a family affair, and a successful one at that. Seeing this overall improvement in his parent's bearing gave to Graham a marked sense of greater self-worth. His father was in his element, playing with all the equipment and having a say in some of the financial decisions.

Over this time, Graham had taken to his new environment wholeheartedly. He regained all of his former physique, losing his slothfully imposed weight gain and toning up his figure through his constant physical work. He also reduced considerably his former indulgence with alcohol, the reason for its use slowly diminishing with the passage of time, distance and the rigours of his new occupation. His sleep patterns did not improve all that much, as he still slept fitfully and awoke early, but now he had a good reason to be up and about.

That was not to say Graham did not think of his family often. He so wished that he could be sharing all this with his erstwhile seemingly happy family. He wondered often what they were doing and what plans they had for their futures. He selfishly hoped that they had no other man in their lives. It still pained him to think of it all, especially the disturbing manner and spiteful people involved with the torrid affair, but the pain now did not automatically lead to the bottle and deep depression. He maintained a firm friendship with the ever sympathetic and knowledgeable Peter Knuckey, to whom he often turned as his fluid circumstances rose and fell over time.

Graham had scrutinised the backyard from the earliest. It was evident to him that the whole scene was in a state of animated suspension. It appeared that Tom Butler had been operating all this area in a dynamic manner but, on his death, it seemed that nothing had been touched from that day. There was a tortuous pathway through this organised mess that led indirectly to the deep inside that was the operating workshop right at the back where Tom obviously carried out all manner of repairs and maintenance. It was tricky to get to, but it was navigable. Tom Butler had amassed a huge collection of every type of tool and many instruction manuals. It turned out that the vehicle workshop manuals themselves were in a large wooden box with a sliding wooden lid. That at least kept them in a reasonable state after all these years.

Graham had often come into this accumulation and tried to sort out exactly what was there, but it was a low priority for him. He had not proceeded very far into this process and quickly lost enthusiasm when confronted with the sheer magnitude of the endeavour. However, what intrigued him was that Tom had spent a lot of time in here and had plenty of paper and notebooks in one of the rough, home-made drawers under the bench. On one of these rummaging episodes, he came across a small, ancient, battered and dog-eared, black covered notebook into which Tom had placed a few neatly categorised notes. The reason he had not discovered it earlier was that the floor of the drawer was a black painted piece of masonite, thus disguising the black notebook that was secreted on the base of the shelf. He might never had discovered it if it were not for the fact that the drawer contained a large collection of heavy metal files, one of which got caught on the side, so he had to empty it entirely in order to remove the drawer and the offending stuck file. The notes appeared at first only to relate to some inventories and cataloguing, but deep inside were a few pages with altogether different scribblings. He would investigate this find inside later. He placed it on the top shelf of the kitchen cupboards when he entered the house.

Richard had taken great delight in being assigned the not so onerous task of attempting to sort out the conglomeration of assorted equipment that was contained within the backyard shed complex. It took some time, as Graham was not overly interested in its contents. He diligently sorted, catalogued and separated into suitable heaps the esoteric collection of farming equipment, fishing gear, car parts, small implements, shearing paraphernalia, veterinary apparatus, irrigation gear, tools of every imaginable type, fencing wires and building materials. Among the stash were several workshop manuals and mechanical publications on old Holdens, Land Rovers and several tractors. The cars were still there, but there were no tractors.

Richard managed to extract the two vehicles from within and attend to their mechanical requirements with much input from an accommodating Tony next door, such that they could finally be fully registered again, using the ancient number plates and making them usable about the farm. He was no mechanic either, but much more proficient than Graham ever would be. This was the result of his belonging to an older generation of often insufficient and meagre means where some home mechanical knowledge and being more self-reliant was advantageous in reducing expenses.

One disturbing event that rocked Graham's world a little was a long conversation he had with his devoted mother one cool, dark weekend at the cottage. It began innocently enough with chit-chat about how they were all going, now that Graham had seemed to settle down admirably. Graham mentioned something about his wondering about his lost family and their state, when his mother responded with a strange comment.

'Well, Louisa once told me that she thought her family was cursed.'

'What do you mean?' asked a very interested Graham. 'And who is Louisa?'

'You know, that rather attractive older cousin of Jenny's. She came from Laurieton, up north. She was at that weird naming ceremony we went to for Julia's child, Jenny's sister's kid.'

'Oh, yes, I briefly remember speaking with her. What do you know, though, about this family curse?' he asked keenly.

'She said to me that she had a bad feeling about this child and that it was not going to live very long. Remember, it was killed in that horrible accident on the south coast years ago. She told me she thought Jenny had a bad aura about her too.'

Graham shuddered.

'Did she say anything about the curse, though?'

'No, no more, not to me,' said Dora. 'Why do you ask?'

'Because Jenny had the same theory. It is weird.'

'Tell me more,' said an intrigued Dora.

Graham was familiar with most of the details, as Jenny had many times promulgated her theory to him over their time together whenever some family trauma or other arose. Graham explained that Jenny had a sensitive side and could be easily directed into the esoteric or divine by events that seemed to her not to make sense.

Jenny's mother's maiden name was Mainwaring, pronounced 'Mannering', though she and her parents insisted on pronouncing it as it was spelt; that is, Main-waring. That was beside the point.

Jenny had a mildly obsessive sense that the family was cursed. She would introduce the subject with her cousins at regular and appropriate moments, but mostly they dismissed it as fanciful and improper. This particular curse on the family had its origins in the first decade of the nineteen hundreds, though its genesis had much deeper roots – a strange and black family history involving some nasty events in the deep past. Jenny's ancestor – she thought his name was Alfred Mitchinton, though she was unsure of his first name – was well connected in the early days of the prospering colony of New South Wales. He held a prestigious government position in a centrally located important and pivotal arm of administration. By all accounts, he was not a particularly robust character. He had come from a long line of minor though well-connected genteel families of British stock who, as many other families had done, migrated to Australia to escape the tuberculosis attacks that killed many people in the then unhealthy, cramped, cold conditions of the times, the British climate being especially detrimental to those of less vigorous make-up. He had married, unusually, a refined lady with French Huguenot roots stretching back centuries, who had drifted to the colony of New South Wales from

England after escaping the centuries-long persecutions of that particular sect in Europe. It instilled in that family a mild persecution complex and a reserve and guardedness that was transferred to their offspring.

Alfred and his wife had four children: two girls, followed by a boy and finally a third girl. The problems all began when his wife gave birth to a fifth child, a son who died within weeks of being born, sadly closely followed by his mother, who did not recover from the ordeal and the trauma of the events. Alfred dearly loved his wife and needed her in his life to be a success. Poor Alfred was so distressed by this twin occurrence, and being of doubtful fibre himself, he quickly deteriorated.

To compound this unfortunate alignment of events, his caring government employer made, what Graham continually reminded Jenny, was a fundamentally fatal decision in giving their traumatised officer an entire year off work on compassionate grounds. Now Alfred had nothing to do but miss his departed wife enormously and neglect his unfortunate children. He was already weak of mind and unable to cope, so he took to the bottle.

The upshot was that he would lie about at his wife's grave and drink himself into oblivion, finally taking his own life on her plot. Suicide in the strict era of the early nineteen hundreds was a mortal sin. He was buried in an unmarked grave in an isolated and remote, bushy, suburban cemetery. In Graham's mind, this was a suitable fate for such an evil act that impacted far more on the living than it did on the departed. Alfred's generous government pension was immediately revoked and his four surviving children were literally thrown out onto the street to be cared for by whomever they could rustle up themselves. Jenny followed their fate closely through contact with her aunts and many cousins and this was where she formulated her theory of the curse on the family.

The eldest daughter was about eighteen when Alfred died. She promptly married an Irish ne'er-do-well whom her father had, up till then, forbidden her to see. He was well educated and came from some background, having a small stipend from a family estate back in Ireland that gave him the sense that he need never work again. This he promptly did, forcing this child to make ends meet by her ability as a seamstress.

This woman went on to have two children, both girls, more contemporaneous in age with Jenny, cousins who only added to her belief about a curse by their own rather messed-up lives.

Alfred's second daughter was only about sixteen or so when her father died and was sent to live with a maiden aunt in Sydney for a few years. Strangely, she also married an unsuitable Irishman, who eventually deserted her and their only child, another daughter, at the age of five. This younger cousin of Jenny's married a ruffian country bloke and lived in isolation in the bush somewhere – most unusual for her family, and quite a come-down. They seemed to have lost contact with her over the years. Her difficult struggles in surviving such a hard life only added more fuel to Jenny's growing sensation of foreboding.

The third child, the son, was about fourteen when Alfred died, and as acknowledgement for the existence of the now departed father, was apprenticed to a workshop associated with the things that Alfred had involvement in. This poor son somehow got entangled with the daughter of the foreman of the factory and married her quite young. This could have turned out satisfactorily but for the fact that the woman was a member of a rather strict and reclusive religious sect that effectively cut him off from the rest of the world, and especially his family. He eventually had only one child, a boy, Jenny's grandfather. When his weirdo wife finally died, he made contact with his estranged family again and Jenny met up with most of her lost cousins.

The fourth child was the last girl. She was about twelve at the time. She was also packed off to the same maiden aunt with child number two. However, she had deformed legs, rendering her with mobility issues. She did not marry and died at an old age.

This was a brief outline of complex family failings that reinforced in Jenny's mind that her family was cursed because of the deeds of the grandfather. It did not go unnoticed to Jenny that almost all the progeny seemed to be female and that the name was to die out. It haunted her mildly throughout her existence, such that she intimated to Graham that she felt the curse descending onto her too.

Jenny could not explain the sense of dissatisfaction with her lot, which to most observers, was a most agreeable one. However, after Graham left, she fell into a brooding and meaningless existence of single motherhood, an occupation she could not fully explain why she so desired, other than it was offered to her as an option at a time that she was susceptible to suggestions.

Graham never really adhered to this theory, but its raising its head at this point concerned him. He told his mother so. He had little concern for such meaningless diversions but, mindful of his own misfortune within her association, he hoped the so-called curse did not devolve further on to his own offspring. Graham's mother tried to assure him that she doubted such a thing applied, but he was now more mindful of it. It troubled him. He pondered that conundrum. Other unsavoury aspects of the complex family history were raising their latent traits, things Jenny had told him of the family's historic misfortunes. His children rose in his thoughts. Graham had a weird sensation; a cold shiver crossed his spine. He little knew that this topic would arise again in the dim future, and in a most unusual way.

The other major concern during this period was his association with the strange connection to Cobar. He found it, for some reason, quite a puzzling affair that this seemingly disconnected, distant, bizarre involvement was somehow rather attractive and exciting to him. He never decided whether this was the insanely peculiar nature of the totally foreign atmosphere or whether he just found it so novel and interesting.

It was an arduous trip out to the property, though he did traverse most interesting country. He tried to travel out there about two or three times a year, especially at a time that may be more beneficial to the struggling, though ever benign and sanguine Sid and his young family. He adored the accommodating, friendly Fiona, who possessed such an agreeable personality.

His father, Richard, could not believe the wonderful experience of so alien a prospect. He also adored the lovely Fiona and engaged her in animated discourse at great length. Richard and Tom, apart from being keen fishermen, were also, in their day, avid hunters in the cold climate area of Tom's domain, being rather expert at procuring supplies of the once abundant rabbits that used to plague the Tablelands. Richard was enthralled at the prospect of re-engaging his neglected shooting prowess, though on a much wilier and larger prey, the abundant wild pigs in the outback.

Graham clearly remembered as a very small child visiting with his family various outback gem fields. Richard had been a keen amateur fossicker on several gem fields of the Northern Tablelands and the Lightning Ridge opal fields, where he recalled fossicking in the ubiquitous mullock heaps that abounded in the semi-arid countryside looking for discarded potch or other forms of 'colour'. Richard found Cobar to be a rich source of employment in that field of endeavour as well.

The boys could travel out that way in complete camaraderie, thoroughly enraptured in their new experience. Richard was captivated by the clarity and spectacle of the crystal clear, dark, outback skies, revealing in unequalled splendour the contents of the huge rivers of sparkling, shimmering stars. He could sit outside and gaze for hours. Dora did not wish to partake in this adventure, finding the comforts of the cottage quite to her satisfaction. She managed to make some nice friends with the other ladies of the close-knit village so far from the big smoke.

During these sojourns to the wilds of the far west, Graham contributed considerably to the improvement of much of the sparse infrastructure of the enormous property. The focus of the enterprise was shifting from conventional grazing to the utilisation of the free and prospering feral goat herds that thrived in this arid semi-desert country.

Things were moving along comfortably for the Longleys, and apart from the creeping advances of old age, all appeared to have turned a very advantageous corner for them and their prospects. This was all down to the benevolence of their Aunt Alice, nothing that they themselves had really arranged. On the horizon was to be a big shock that would alter this illusion, but before that eventuated, there was to be more drama for Graham.

CHAPTER EIGHT

Sophia Faulkner was a serious and responsible young woman, mindful of the potential and hoped-for outcome of her generally planned out future within the hierarchy of the Faulkner dynasty. She dutifully began her tertiary education with this prospect in mind, concentrating on, in her case, veterinary studies. She had studiously avoided any romantic attachments from the beginning, concentrating on her learning. The episode with the possessive chauvinistic monster that Milton B Thwaites turned out to be was unrelated to her academic circles. She was only extracted from that bungle by the timely intervention of the accommodating Graham Longley.

That disturbing episode caused her even more to avoid any kind of extraneous contact with other than female students. Counted among her few genuine friends in the field of academia were two or three similar young women who were destined to impact hugely on her young life. These women themselves could not have been more contrasting.

The Faulkners had, with some anxious reservations involving matters of separation, decided to send their only child to the best boarding school in Sydney in her younger days. There she enmeshed herself with a few like-minded, talented and refined girls, and together a small cadre of them navigated the lengthy route that eventually saw some of them graduate into various streams at the University of Sydney, including the veterinary course of Sophia's.

This normally would be of no real interest, except, their lives became interwoven in some strange patterns that impacted on Graham again, and for a familiar reason. This episode occurred towards the latter part of Sophia's study.

The Federal Police had contacted the Faulkners as it was thought that Sophia was the last to see the missing Renufa Shamasus. Sophia had denied any knowledge of her whereabouts but, as she seemed to be the last known contact, the police were interested in talking to her, often. It was becoming an issue for her and her family. She had travelled down to the home property to gain some relief from the constant harassment and seek comfort within the family. When the embassy of the missing woman engaged the services of the notorious Mr O'Brien and then requested a meeting at their home, they contacted Graham to discuss matters.

Graham detested solicitors for good reason. He found Mr Deane in Queanbeyan supercilious and slightly pompous, though he basically conducted his affairs satisfactorily. He found his own divorce lawyer, Peter Knuckey, one of the few genuine and sympathetic people he had had to deal with over the whole sordid affair of his demeaning divorce. It was to him to whom he now always turned when matters required any clarification or counsel, and there ensued a growing friendship. He had sought copiously over this emerging matter, and received very good advice, guidance and directions.

Graham was somewhat in awe of the Faulkners. In their presence, he felt a slight inferiority because of their exceptional standing in this otherwise insular society, their knowledge compared to his and their gravitas in this social order. In his previous employment, the disparity would not have had any of the scale it did out here in this community; it would have been diluted by the sheer magnitude of humanity in his previous world. He tended to be taciturn and introverted in their presence, and that was how they perceived him – it was one of the factors that strengthened his endearment to them.

When Jackson Faulkner contacted him out of the blue, he was a little surprised. He asked if Graham could manage another visit to their home soon. Graham was decidedly unsure about all this constant and seemingly uncalled-for attention from such a noble family. He was in for another shock.

When Graham arrived at the Faulkners, they were gathered in a small and bright room off the main building. He was surprised to see not only Sophia and her parents, but also another young woman sitting there too. She was introduced to Graham as Renufa Shamasus. He was taken by her appearance. It reminded him of his initial impression on first seeing Sophia emerge from behind the stricken horse float on the lonely, deserted bush track.

She was rather striking, with smooth, bronze coloured skin, as if it were over-tanned, long, coal-black hair, piercingly deep, dark pupils and irises that gently moved about snake-like in her slightly almond shaped eyes, their darkness enhanced by the milky white of her eyes. She was obviously foreign.

His attention was quickly drawn away from his appraising of her by Jackson's urgent manner. Jackson had introduced her simply by name, not elaborating in any way. He was rather solemn and, Graham thought, uncharacteristically a little nervous and tentative.

'Graham, I'm afraid we may have a big favour to ask you. It is rather urgent and also very disturbing. It may also involve a little danger.'

Graham was all attention. 'Yes,' was all he said.

'Renu here is in a spot of trouble, and we were wondering if you could manage to repeat for her what you managed to do for Sophie.'

All he was prepared to say at this point was, 'Renu is a visitor in our country and has run into, shall we say, cultural difficulties associated with her background. She is now being hunted similarly to the way Sophie experienced.'

Graham listened intently and made no comment. His suspicions were rising and his doubts also. He was not happy. His immediate thoughts leapt to the Butlers.

'You mean, you want me to ask Sid again?'

'Yes, possibly,' said Jackson.

'I don't know. That's an awful imposition,' responded Graham. 'Tell me more about … Renu, is it?'

Jackson looked at Sophia. She wriggled forward in her chair and explained that Renu was a twenty-five-year-old woman from a kingdom in the Middle East. She was a princess in her own country, the daughter of a minor princeling. Her father had been the ambassador in Australia for many years. All his seven children had grown up and gone to school here. Some of the boys were at university, usually at ANU, but the girls were normally sent back to their own country at sixteen or eighteen.

Renu circumvented that fate by studying pharmacy at the University of Sydney with a view to working in a family facility back home, on the condition she returned home when she had finished her studies here. However, she had since subsequently been promised to a distant cousin in marriage and he wanted her now. He was more than twice her age and had at least two other young wives. Renu had never even met him. The embassy sent out a courier to return with her, but she escaped his clutches and Sophia brought her here.

Her escape was rather ingenious. Sophia had persuaded a couple of appliance installers who were working on the same floor as their flat to agree to what they thought was a student prank. She convinced them to place Renu in the empty large appliance box and remove her down to their van out in the street. They were to take her just around the corner and Sophia would drive around and pick her up there. This way they could avoid the two men on surveillance watching the unit block, as Renu's building had only one street entrance. She suspected that they had surveillance on her mobile phone through her GPS so she abandoned it in the flat, further delaying their pursuit.

The other girl living with them told them that the police and the two embassy staff came to the flat with a warrant but, of course, she was gone. They were rather annoyed that she had slipped from them, and they took her abandoned phone away. Sophia drove immediately from the flat near the university down the coast road to Batemans Bay to avoid any toll cameras and then up to the property through Braidwood.

Graham did not like the sound of this at all. He asked the group if they minded if he rang someone about it. He assured them it would be in the strictest confidence. He took out his little-used mobile telephone and flipped the top. He hunted through and found a number. He dialled it.

'Hello, Peter. This is Graham Longley in Queanbeyan. Could you ring me back as soon as possible, please? I will need some time to talk to you.'

He closed his top and sat back in the chair.

'Are you asking me to take Renu out to Sid again?' he asked.

'Possibly,' said Jackson.

'I'm not sure about that. He's not there for ...' he stopped. His mobile rang softly. He flipped the lid and said, 'Hello, Peter. Thank you for ringing back. Have you got a few minutes?'

Graham spent some minutes explaining the situation to

Chapter Eight

Peter Knuckey in Sydney.

Then he said, 'Peter, I remembered you had a couple of contacts in the refugee area. What can you tell me about that?'

Peter did indeed have some serious contacts in the refugee and immigration area and would make some enquiries and get back to him as soon as he could. Graham explained that he could do no more until he heard back from Peter Knuckey. In the meantime, he would try to smooth something out with Sid and Fiona if it got that far. He went back home with a disturbed heart.

Peter did get back to him, one day later. He would put Renu's case before the agencies on the quiet. Peter had empathetic views on some refugee and immigration cases. He was not directly involved in that field himself, but had close contacts with some expert practitioners in that sphere. This case seemed to qualify for that kind of consideration. Peter was given a lot of practical and useful advice about her circumstances and duly passed that onto Graham.

Graham passed some of that on to the Faulkners. They dearly wished, more for Sophia's sake, to remove Renu and her problem to a much safer place than theirs, and as far away as possible while it was sorted out to whatever final conclusion. Graham was almost coerced into accommodating their immediate wishes by removing Renu to the relative safety of the Cobar outback. Graham explained that Sid and Fiona were apparently willing to accommodate the idea if Graham thought it appropriate, which he secretly did not.

Before it was finally agreed, however, he returned to the

Faulkners and had a serious chat to them all. They convened to the sunlit small outer room again and sat down. Graham was uneasy. He spent some time staring at Renu.

'Renu, tell me about your childhood.'

There was general confusion. What did that have to do with anything? Graham responded that he simply wished to ascertain how suitable she would be in relocating to the deprived and difficult conditions offered by the outback property. Had she ever had any experience with dry, low-humidity, heat-filled settings? Graham pointed out, without trying to put too much emphasis on the matter, that he thought Renu was rather a cultured and refined, might he say, delicate young woman, not the type to thrive in the hostile outback, no matter how safe it might be, especially with no family fallback, such as Sophia had.

She explained to the gathering some of her relevant upbringing, and while she might be from a family of noble connections in her own country, that was not to imply that she had not experienced hardships conducive with the nature of her natural environment. Graham was not fully convinced. However, the others all agreed that her safety was paramount and out to Cobar she should go. Graham reluctantly agreed. Sid and Fiona were prepared to take her briefly if Graham, and Jackson for that matter, thought it appropriate. The Butlers were nothing if not compliant and accommodating. Graham found that characteristic a little foreign to his own city-bred make-up. Graham suggested that Edith drive her to his place in Captains Flat in an unfamiliar car and he would take her from there.

Jackson thought, *here we go again with all this cloak-and-dagger stuff. Graham seemed to be obsessed with it in these kinds of cases.*

Anyway, if that was what he wanted, they would comply. It was arranged.

Graham had one other request to make that dazzled Jackson. He coolly stated, as he was leaving, 'Whatever you do, do not mention my name to anyone in any way. If they ask, tell them my name is Long. Is that clear to all? We don't want them searching up any records about me to trace her. Is that clear?'

Jackson sighed softly. They all agreed.

Renu was taken by Graham out to the Butlers in his old Land Cruiser. He suspected that she had never roughed it quite like this in her privileged young life. It was an eye-opener for the both of them.

Renu had been safely ensconced out at the property near Cobar only for a matter of days. She and Fiona seemed to get along fine. That would be important. Graham thought that Fiona was so lonely out there that almost any company was welcome.

Graham was again invited over to the Faulkners. This time he sat in the large and elegant 'old world' and ornate lounge room with Sophia and her parents. It was slightly dark and cool, not aided by the enormously high ceiling and heavy curtains generously plaited around each of the tall but narrow windows. They were arranged along one set of heavy lounge chairs.

Opposite them sat the two interlopers who had requested this gathering. One was a federal policeman, Sergeant Triticini. The other was James O'Brien SC, a supposedly reputable Sydney senior counsel renowned for his shrewdness and aggressive approach when defending. They had all been agitatingly awaiting the arrival of Graham. They were unsure at this stage why Mr Long was required to be there, other than he apparently was their confidante in tricky matters.

Graham had no idea what had transpired between them before his arrival. Once he arrived and introductions were made, James O'Brien moved out of the chair and stood by the window with some papers spread on the small table.

He said, 'And what exactly is your involvement in this matter, Mr Long?'

'I'm not entirely sure yet, O'Brien. We will see in good time,' he said rather disrespectfully.

'Well, as I was saying, we are convinced you people are involved with this travesty and know the whereabouts of the absconder. We have a warrant to search this entire place if needs be, so please comply with this lawful request. We are trying to avoid a scandal and a severe diplomatic incident which would prove quite embarrassing for the government. We believe you are involved with the abduction of Ms Shamasus and the subsequent removal of her from her lawful guardians. Her country wishes for her to be returned at once. There are serious consequences for interfering with foreign embassy personnel and withholding information about her.

She is required to return to fulfil her cultural obligation in her home country.'

Jackson was a little overwhelmed by all this bluster and the two ladies were nervous about the ramifications. They tentatively and cautiously turned their gaze onto a so far silent Graham. The two visitors, seeing this occurrence, also expectantly turned their gaze on the reticent Graham. He sat stony-faced and dead still in his seat, peering at the floor in front of him. There was a long awkward pause.

Graham sat deep in thought, still staring at the floor. He was not thinking about the substance of O'Brien's harangue at all. During this rant, the sheer irony of all this had suddenly struck him. Here was a man defending the right of one human being to dictate the life of another. Yet, he had been in the same position only a few years ago. This time, however, the circumstances were reversed. In his case, all the cards were stacked against him in favour of the wishes of the woman. Here, all the cards were stacked in favour of the men, no matter how demeaning they planned to be to her wishes.

Graham was wondering, surely this learned counsel must actually believe in what he was doing, or was his whole demeanour dictated by money alone? His mind was cast back to an early childhood memory where he clearly recalled the old, often misquoted saying, 'money is the root of all evil'. It had stayed with him forever. The correct expression of that homily was 'the *love* of money is the root of all evil' – a totally different meaning. He clearly recalled that all God's favourites in the Old Testament, such as Abraham, Isaac, Job, David,

Solomon, were all filthy rich – anomalous to the teachings of the New Testament, another point of confusion for the weak-minded and easily confused. Furthermore, money was such an artificial man-made concept; it bore no authenticity in the natural world or the spiritual one. It operated outside and independent of the laws of God and nature.

He was deep in these philosophical musings, slipping away from the reality about him. His companions thought he was considering the conversation at hand. He was soon brought back to actuality by a determined and abrasive Mr O'Brien saying rather tersely, 'Well?'

Graham looked at O'Brien. All his dislike for the pomposity and contrariness of legal minds that could seemingly defend any old indefensible stand seethed up in him.

He said slowly and deliberately, 'Let's not muck about here, O'Brien. Do you ever actually listen to yourself, mate? Do you actually believe what you've just been espousing? What a complete load of drivel! Firstly, we are talking about a twenty-five-year-old woman here, not a commodity of some sort that you can just trade as you see fit. While in Australia, she is subject to Australian law and is entitled to our legal protection. Have you any idea who and what sort of travesties you are demeaningly trying to advocate? This woman has been promised, against her will, to another man who already has three wives, as if she were a stray dog needing a home. He is at least twice her age and disposes of those he does not care for in a rather unsavoury manner.'

He paused, then continued in the ensuing stony silence.

'We are certainly under no obligation to reveal anything to you, even if we did know anything, and you well know that.'

'Ah!' pounced a triumphant O'Brien. 'You do know something about it?'

'Nar,' sniggered Graham derisorily, 'you've given me enough info here to start a riot.'

There was another difficult pause. Graham continued.

'In fact, you know that you really have no right to even be here, talking down to us as if we were serfs. As for a diplomatic incident, as you laughingly call it, I'll give you a diplomatic incident, mate. One word from me and this will be all over the papers and the television by tonight. Don't you think the refugee advocates and the human rights people, not to mention the anti-slavers, are dying to reveal this kind of sordid affair to the public? It is only our silence that is keeping this scandal out of the public eye. So, you might like to mind your step, mate.'

James O'Brien did not expect that retort. That was not going to put him off, however. He countered with 'We can bring much pressure to bear here, Mr Long. You've got to return this woman to her embassy.'

'We haven't *got* to do anything, O'Brien. This is not Russia.'

The room fell silent. The Faulkners saw a different side of the apparently reticent and mild-mannered Graham Longley.

'Show me this warrant you supposedly have,' said Graham.

'That will not be necessary, Mr Long. I have already stated that I am in possession of such and that will be the end of it.'

'Oh no, it won't, sport! You show me this so-called warrant you supposedly have in your possession, or I'll arrange for you to be turfed out 'o here by the staff of this place.'

'You can't touch the legal representatives of the federal government in the course of their duty.'

'Oh, can't I, just! Show me this document or you're out 'o here.'

Mr O'Brien reluctantly shuffled through the papers on the small table and retrieved a sheet. He sullenly passed it to Graham as he was exiting the chair and moving nearer the window to read the document. He perused it carefully.

'Just as I thought,' said Graham. 'This is non-compliant with your requests. You don't even have the correct authorisations, mate. This is all a bluff.'

'That is a legally obtained and correct document, young man,' said a savage O'Brien.

'Yeah,' snarled Graham. 'for a different set of circumstances. See here.' he said, a hint of triumph in his voice. 'That is not appropriate for this case, and you know it.'

'That is a legal document, Mr Long.'

'Yeah, it's legal, all right, just like my licence is legal. But it does not apply here, sport, does it?'

Mr O'Brien was momentarily stumped. A pall of deathly silence descended on the room. The policeman shuffled nervously in the corner.

'Well, that'll be an end to that, then, won't it, mate?' said Graham.

'No. The embassy will invoke its diplomatic status and demand her return,' said O'Brien. 'The proof is in the pudding.'

'No, they bloody well won't, mate. You know full well that the human rights forum will take this to the High Court, and then I'll show you a diplomatic incident, mate.'

It appeared to all that a state of stalemate had been reached. At this position of impasse, Mr O'Brien began to collect his papers and gently thumped them on the table to organise them. He then proceeded to place them in his briefcase that had been sitting on the floor beside him.

'You have not heard the end of this, Mr Faulkner,' said an irritated O'Brien.

'I think we have done just that, O'Brien,' interjected Graham. 'And I'll thank you to stop harassing these people here or you might just get yourself entangled in some proceedings too. So why don't you take your portly personage out of here along with "Constable Plod" and reassess your moral compass, you pompous, deranged pursuer of the defenceless and wronged. I don't think you are motivated by anything other than the lure of filthy lucre and who you think you can tread on.'

'There's no need to be offensive, Mr Long.'

'You may be offended, O'Brien; that doesn't mean you are right.'

With that, a defeated O'Brien and the federal policeman sauntered out the doorway escorted by a silent Jackson, followed by his family.

As they exited the door into the yard, Graham said, 'Oh, by the way, O'Brien …'

He stopped and turned to look at Graham.

'The proof is not *in* the pudding – the proof *of* the pudding is in the eating thereof, sport.'

Mr O'Brien gazed at him in confusion. Then he waddled off to his vehicle.

After the two had driven away, Jackson turned to Graham and stated, 'I had no idea you were familiar with the law, Graham. That was quite dramatic!'

'I'm not, Jackson, but I have very good contacts that are, and they advised me thoroughly before I came here this time. Look, I'll be going now. Make sure none of you ever ring her on any of your phones,' he reiterated.

Graham departed the scene with some trepidation. He was not certain his blustering methods would convince anybody to cease any further investigations. Certainly, the embassy staff would brook no defeat on this matter. He had no idea what sort of outcome lay ahead for either the Faulkners or Renufa Shamasus.

As he thought, the embassy staff were not used to being thwarted in these issues on cultural matters. They lobbied the Federal Government and threatened retaliation if there was not a speedy and satisfactory resolution in their favour.

Graham was not involved, nor were the Faulkners, but legal manoeuvrings were conducted behind the scenes and, according to Peter Knuckey, counter threats were made. The refugee lobby threatened to expose the whole matter on the international scene, an outcome that the foreign state wished to avoid. Renufa Shamasus was secreted to some sympathetic activists, and as her life was moderately threatened, her whereabouts were concealed.

Shortly after, the ambassador was recalled along with all his family. Apparently, that foreign state did not appreciate the mishandling of sensitive cultural affairs. That alleviated much of the threat to Renu. In time, she was able to resume a more normal life in her expatriate community and all seemed to work out satisfactorily, for her at least.

Once again, Graham, and indeed the Faulkners, were indebted to the benevolence of an acquiescing Butler family out in the sticks at Cobar. If nothing else, it endeared Graham even more deeply to the Faulkners and earned him deeper respect. He was not overly happy with the burden on the Butlers, though, despite their willingness to accede to these continued impositions.

CHAPTER NINE

The days were long and hot in early December. Graham spent most of them out at his property. The drive was rough and dusty, and the road always needed attention. If he were not staying out at the farm in the shearer's quarters or, more likely nowadays, in the old caravan he had set up there, he would not arrive home in the village until after dark – quite late this time of year. He normally did use the cottage as the facilities were better and most of the gear was stored there. He still had not bothered to get around to thinking about building a proper home on the farm somewhere near the sheds; his priorities lay elsewhere.

This day he was fortunately a little earlier, as he had planned on doing a few jobs in the workshop before dark. He drove into the driveway and set the dogs to their yard prior to feeding them, closing them in there for the night.

Chapter Nine

He wondered why they were so reticent to follow their usual routine. He hastened towards the backyard where he was startled to see three young children at the back door.

Graham peered at them in bewilderment momentarily, but nothing popped into his mind as to whom they were or why they would be so determinedly ensconced in his yard, not moving at all at his appearance there. Suddenly and with hastening alarm, it dawned on him that they were – no, could not be, surely! – his own three children whom he had desperately tried, and mostly succeeded in, blocking from his conscience. *How could this be?* It could not be possible. A quick haze of fear overcame him as he gazed at the apparitions so unexpectedly presented there in front of him.

The light was poor in the deeply hidden village among the degraded hills and the evening was now well advanced. Even so, in this inadequate light, and even in his mild panic, he definitely recognised that the eldest child, a well-presented and rather elegantly imperious little miss probably – no, definitely – was Sally. The other two therefore must be the boys, whom he barely knew as he was turfed out of their lives when they were quite young.

Graham pulled himself together quickly. The dogs were also seriously surveying the unfamiliar scene, tails wagging gently, alternately gazing at him and them, unsure what to do, awaiting his command. He shouted at them to get into their enclosure so he could shut the gate. After that, he walked determinedly to the three children who had not moved at all. He peered at them.

'Sally? Sam? Ben? Is that you?'

Sally stood resolute, gathering the two younger boys to her side and replied, 'Yes, Dad – er, Graham. We have come here to be together.'

Graham was dumbfounded, his mind was racing. *What on earth did she mean by that remark, and what the hell has happened to Jenny? I bet she's had a different idea about that particular suggestion! Not to mention those despicable in-laws, or for that matter, the over-bearing, intrusive and interfering legal system that removed them from me in the first place.*

Finally, he said, 'How did you get here? Where are you staying? I mean, where's your mum? You better come inside. Is that all you have with you?'

He unlocked the door and led them into the compact kitchen which, with the four of them and their meagre gear, was now rather crowded. He told them to sit at the table while he fiddled with a couple of items and then stared at them blankly, trying to take in the spectacle that was imposed, goodness only knows for how long or short a time. He closely surveyed the three of them, the almost emotional sense nearly overwhelming him.

No one spoke.

Sally appeared competently in command of the situation and was obviously the leader. She was shortish, attractive with a lovely figure, even at … she would be fourteen now, he surmised. No, he did not surmise, he knew exactly how old she was. She had some of Jenny's appearance and was rather elegantly dressed for a schoolgirl. She had her mother's light brown hair, piercing, determined eyes and a countenance that reeked of efficiency and capability. The boys were emanating an air of compliance and subservience to their sister. They were well dressed and slender, almost underfed, he deduced. They all peered at him expectantly.

'What are you doing here?' he asked.

'Mum's in a nut house,' enthused Ben, totally uninhibited and with some excitement.

'Shh!', demanded Sally.

'We want to be together with you,' continued Ben with all the exuberance of an excited ten-year-old.

'Quiet!' demanded Sally, trying to take command.

Graham just stared at them in turn as this circus unfolded but was as quickly brought under control again by Sally. He looked at her as much as to say to begin at the beginning. Graham sat at the vacant side of the smallish table, looking at her, waiting for the story.

Sally was every bit the lady he remembered Jenny to be at the beginning of their romance. She spoke in a cultured and educated voice.

Her mother, as best she could recall it, at first revelled in her new-found freedom and social life without Graham, and the three children were initially packed off to a boarding school. That was short-lived, as money became an issue. Sally initially despised her father for abandoning them so callously and never paying maintenance. She made sure he understood that point. Money became a serious concern and then life became a struggle. Eventually, they had to abandon

Dover Heights and move to Liverpool, then Campbelltown. It was horrible.

Sally began to observe that Jenny slowly took to drinking and possibly taking other drugs and eventually became unstable. She mumbled something about a curse. Sally said she never understood that comment. Jenny's parents were not interested in the children, but finally agreed to take on Sally, but the boys could go to foster homes. Sally decided that that was not going to happen. She had done a lot of research into Graham's life and, when she discovered that he was not married and lived a stable life, she planned an escape with the boys. She had long ago realised that not all, if indeed any, fault actually lay with Graham, with the exception of abandoning them financially. Somehow, Jenny's crude and unsavoury asides about him seemed not to ring true with her, at least not her vague memory of events.

Sally had, through her mother's law firm and with the aid of the agencies, surreptitiously arranged for some discreet enquiries to be made on how her father, Graham, was faring in the world, for, deep down, she never forgot him. She never fully understood why he seemed one day just to disappear. She discovered that he had moved from Sydney, then to Queensland and then to rural NSW. From there, it was not so difficult to ascertain his circumstances.

When conditions were right, she acted. The grandparents were in Europe for twelve months on yet another trip, and Jenny was in rehabilitation again for a few months. School holidays were approaching, so now was the best time to act, as it was getting harder for her to maintain the family unit under all the disintegration occurring around her. And act she did. They caught a train from Sydney Central to Queanbeyan, then scrounged a lift to Captains Flat in a bus. Now here they were.

Graham was bitter at how his precious children had been so abandoned by the very system that had originally removed him from their lives. However, the same system would surely not now allow them to simply wander into his deprived little life without a serious fight and probably repercussions. He could see the whole process was fraught with disaster and hurt, no matter how fondly his children wished it so.

The night had well and truly set in by now. Graham realised that they must be hungry and tired. He would rustle up some dinner. Oh, and he had better feed the dogs; they would be wondering what was going on. The struggles would start in the morning.

Sally could have the main room, which his parents would normally use, and the boys could share the other spare room that was larger than the third little room that Graham had been using since moving there. Sally was very proficient at managing all the necessaries for preparing the rooms. Graham felt a little inadequate at the whole scene and a little overwhelmed.

Graham had a bad night, tossing and turning, his stomach in turmoil and his mind racing in all sorts of disastrous directions. He rose very early and saw to the children. He decided his first call should be to his aging parents in

Mooloolaba. Then he rang the ever-reliable Peter Knuckey in Sydney who had advised him throughout the whole torrid affair. Then he reluctantly approached the local police station where he was relatively well-known, being a small-town local, having dealt with them on several issues such as gun licences, driving licences, registrations and the like.

The children had not been reported as missing, so no one knew they were absent; so much for the 'care' of the State. Matters could rest for a brief moment while the police made some discreet enquiries, and no other action was taken at this stage. He put the police in touch with his solicitor in Sydney. Nothing eventuated over many days, so Graham initially decided to incorporate them into his busy life while matters rolled on and his solicitor carried out more investigations.

Sally was a city girl tried and true and the bucolic was not for her. But, for the boys, this was the life for them. They could not believe the freedom, the activity, the structure, the physicality, the endless variety of sheer movement, dealing with dogs, sheep, chooks, wildlife, motorbikes and old cars, and the endless interesting characters that inhabited Graham's world. And Dad ate meat! All you could get!

The only limiting factor for the boys was the issue of hydatids. When they asked why the dogs were not allowed in the house and had to be locked up away from the place, Graham had to explain about the hydatid parasite that could infect sheep and dogs and from there to humans. It was a sobering lesson – one of many to come.

In a mildly euphoric panic, Graham's aging parents decided

then and there to race down immediately to attend to the children whom they had not set eyes on in years. They would normally avoid the hottest part of the year on the Tablelands, preferring the more temperate climes of coastal Sunshine Coast. Graham did not object to this idea and the action was set in motion. The boys by now were so enamoured of the farm activities that they accompanied him every day while Sally remained at home.

The arrival of the children's paternal grandparents was momentous. They had had no contact with them for over eight years and the sobering influence of a much more 'normal' set of elders was to have a profound effect on the impressionable young children. They had hitherto been under the doubtful manipulation of rather eccentric, unbalanced adults who inculcated dubious attitudes in ones so young and malleable. There was a general movement down one room each as the parents arrived, Graham moving into the small lounge room.

The little house suddenly went from almost unoccupied to overflowing with life, with three children and three adults. By default, and a general, passive agreement, Graham's mother, Dora, eagerly assumed the role of mother, taking over the whole affair of cooking and washing. Despite her infirmities and advancing years, she was not going to allow those things to deprive her of her so longed-for and rekindled maternal desires. She grew in confidence and self-pride at the new position of being needed and useful to a brood. Graham's father was unsure how to deal with the three children after so long apart and having been under goodness only knows what sort of strange influences from his weird in-laws. He would have to tread warily initially as he did not want to alienate in any way his already estranged family.

Graham was unsure how to cope with all this. He contacted his divorce solicitor, Peter, in Sydney and explained the position as it stood right now. The solicitor suggested a plan of action and would get back to him very soon. This he did with the following summary of what he thought was happening. Jenny had deteriorated over several years and been in rehabilitation many times. The prognosis was not promising. The children were often, though reluctantly, housed with Jenny's parents, but this was not a satisfactory arrangement, and they were often left alone at the rented property in western Sydney.

This time, someone had advised the authorities that the children would be accompanying their grandparents to Europe for a lengthy visit. That someone was assumed to be Sally. All was well. So far as the State was concerned, the children were in safe keeping. Graham asked that the State not be advised until absolutely necessary that the children were with him and his own parents in the country.

Sally was the problem. She was clearly not interested in the rural pursuits associated with Graham's life. The boys loved it and thrived. Graham had already lost Sally once; he was not going to risk that again. How to incorporate her into this new paradigm? Graham sat down with Sally to try and determine what to do. Sally was now fourteen and could not just be abandoned to the wilds of the isolated bush habitat that was Graham's life. Sally was cool and reserved and harboured latent resentment towards her father – indeed now, both her parents – for her deprived childhood, interspersed with bouts of the high life whenever her mother was in a position to indulge. It was clear to all that Sally had no desire to relinquish city life and entertained notions of pursuing tertiary studies. It turned out that Sally was quite academic and very studious; that was her desired path in life.

Captains Flat had adequate primary schools but no high school. They were located in Queanbeyan or Canberra, the 'Bush Capital'. Queanbeyan had no tertiary establishments but its huge neighbour had at least three.

Graham had a modest income, more than adequate for himself and even his parents. His income, however, might have difficulty stretching to the needs of possibly now previously underfunded offspring. While his income was spasmodic and sufficient, his outgoings were considerable. He had indulged himself in the Land Cruiser, tractors and much new fencing to address decades of neglected maintenance of the block. He had deliberately kept his income small to avoid paying anything to what he thought and assumed, incorrectly it now appeared, was an already generously remunerated wife.

On enquiry, Graham was staggered to discover that Jenny had indeed not gone back to work as he had surmised, but rather survived on less than generous government pensions, a fact that rankled with him severely. His modest income would not have been enough to maintain her in a high lifestyle. He somehow doubted she would ever have acquiesced to a life in this isolated backwater of a situation. He was very bitter that his poor children had suffered so, especially as he had thought them well maintained.

Graham's solicitor finally had to contact the authorities over the entire matter. By this time, the children had been with Graham and his parents for several weeks and their life and education were now in the position of needing concrete direction. The State authorities were severely embarrassed by the whole saga and Graham's solicitor, at Graham's angry bidding and to the extent that he safely could, admonished the people supposedly administering this affair. He threatened to reveal all to the press in very unfavourable terms if Graham was now not going to be finally given some control over the events as originally desired by both himself and his long-suffering children.

The State contacted the local police and their own local office and discovered that the children would be best treated as remaining where they were, pending further investigation. This allowed Graham to set in motion the required needs of his brood. The two boys could attend the local primary school where they had already made many friends with the local children. Sally would have to travel into either Queanbeyan or the Bush Capital to attend high school. It was so arranged for the interim.

Graham finally sat down quietly and alone with Sally. Sally always came across to Graham as aloof, cool and reserved, almost distant or bordering on contemptuous or disapproving of him. She had obviously borne the brunt of maintaining family unity. This had instilled in her a maturity and poise of a much older child. Graham inwardly admired her and realised that the so far lucky state of his children was doubtless entirely down to her. He fully understood her attitude and realised that probably no amount of attention on his part would undo the hurt and deprivation she endured at the hands of the State, and to some extent, himself. He had contributed in no small way to this condition in resigning his position, but the entirety of the dilemma was not in his hands.

He asked her what she thought she would wish for into the future. She clearly indicated that she aspired to academia, not rural pursuits. The boys were in paradise here, not so Sally. She would accept that, for the present, she must remain domiciled in Captains Flat but, eventually she wished to move to the city. She planned to pursue an academic career. Graham secretly hoped it was not a legal one.

Sally's reserve was not conducive to socialising, and in this small society, she had much difficulty making friendly contacts. She, as much as Graham had initially done to his eternal shame, now regarded the locals as slightly beneath her standards. She did not openly say as much, but Graham could read the wind. He could not think how to counter that perception. The two boys, on the other hand, found copious friendships with many local lads, playing boisterous physical pastimes in the conveniently placed generous ovals and parks located almost opposite his cottage along the banks of the river that ran through the village. The main street of this village ran beside the headwaters of the Molonglo River and, with the enormous passage of infinite time, had produced many productive riverine floodplain flats where the terrain was particularly fertile and easy to maintain. In the earliest days, these were used to run and fatten stock on them – hence, the name, Captains Flat. Captain was rumoured to be an old bull that regularly wandered away from home to graze on the lush flats beside the river.

Graham's parents had hinted obtusely that they could contemplate moving themselves from Queensland to be nearer the family, say, in Queanbeyan, or even Canberra. Graham had dismissed this suggestion as inappropriate. Richard and Dora had responded that they could, in their latter years, live in the warmth of sunny Queensland and be lonely and alone, or adapt to the cold and be near the family and useful. Sally could even live with them to achieve her aims. It was really not a difficult decision – they preferred the latter. It gave Graham much to think on. He was now always conscious and fearful that at any moment, some officious interfering bureaucrat could simply apply their own interpretation of how Graham should be dealing with his own family and remake his life again. He did not want that happening a second time, especially if his parents had arranged to move at great inconvenience.

In the meantime, the government moved slowly, and the attitudes within were slowly vacillating and becoming more realistic, less agenda driven. In their new eagerness and enthusiasm for veracity, and more potential ability now to right some perceived age-old wrongs, government employees were softening their attitudes. They might have been remiss in some of their early rulings in their haste to comply with what was now thought to be possibly unsuitable or even unjust decisions. Opinions were moderating as to the severity and alacrity with which they had been dealing out judgements in such matters in the earlier days. Graham's new set-up might now more closely match their revised desired outcomes. The law firm that initially ingratiated themselves into Graham's life was also a strong advocate for the more even-handed approach to family matters than in years past. Things were finally looking up for the once divided family.

The newly reunited, enlarged family unit did not have a lot of time to embrace their new conception when a seriously dramatic event occurred, unforeseen by any of them, and certainly not on their horizon. That was the early death of Jenny, the children's ailing mother.

The news came as a total shock for Graham. He felt slightly woozy and light-headed as it sank in. His solicitor relayed the tidings as soon as he had heard it from the facility. It was still shrouded in some mystery as to whether it was entirely natural or self-inflicted. Well, 'natural' would be a misnomer, as her health had deteriorated severely following incessant bouts of depression and drug usage, both medicinal and recreational. Had the curse struck her down?

Graham surveyed his short life with his wife. He still loved her. He was not sure why; he just knew deep down he did. He would have taken her back if things had turned out differently. She still was his legal wife because he had refused her many requests for a divorce. He hoped that had not contributed to her faltering. He was still her legal guardian, at least in law if not in reality. Her weirdo eccentric parents were yet again still in Italy. It seemed they were contemplating moving there; hence, the many trips overseas.

He had never grown to hate Jenny; in fact, he hankered for a return to their earliest days, when she was a different person. The woman he had married he still loved and revered. It was the advent of the children that was the catalyst for her metamorphosis into the stranger she became to him.

He sat the three children down in the still dingy little kitchen and prepared to impart the news. He was slightly haggard and quite distraught about it all. They sat expectantly, awaiting his comments. He finally announced in a slightly quivering voice that their mother had been pronounced dead from organ failure this morning. He awaited their response.

Sally sat in stony silence, contemplating the possible conclusions from such news. The two boys said nothing initially.

Finally, Sam said in a matter-of-fact manner, 'Well, I'm not surprised, and maybe good riddance.'

Graham was mortified and stunned. He replied, 'That's a horrible thing to say!'

'Yes,' agreed Sally.

'Now you listen to me, all of you,' said Graham firmly, looking mostly at the boys. 'Jenny, your mother, was, still is, and always will be your mother. And you always remember that. She was not always responsible for all her actions, and no one can ever really know another person. I want you to always remember that she was in many ways a lovely woman, and a good mother. She got you this far, and without my help.'

There was a stony silence in the room. Graham could easily have crumpled into an emotional mess any minute and he desperately wished to avoid that in front of his children, whom he really still did not fully know, despite their time together.

'Now, there will be a funeral service in the coming weeks, and we will all be attending that together,' he stated.

'I won't be going,' stated a defiant Sam.

'Me either,' agreed Ben.

'Oh yes, you will,' insisted Graham. 'And you will be respectful to your mother and her memory.'

Graham was disappointed in his children's response to the news. He had hoped for a little better. Surely, she can't have been that bad to them such that they would react as they had. How much of all this sadness was attributable to him, he often wondered. He wracked his brain many times to discover exactly where he failed as a husband. What better could he have done, what changes would have carried them through together?

On hearing the news, both his own parents were mildly glad. He chastised them kindly, leaving no doubt that disparaging remarks about his dead wife would not be welcomed in his hearing. They were puzzled at his demeanour but certainly rejoiced in the removal from their lives of this possible threat to the new-found happiness that had transpired from recent events.

The funeral was delayed for some time in order that her parents could be contacted in Europe. There was also an autopsy to be performed. It revealed little that was unknown and confirmed more or less the previous diagnosis. Graham wondered if part of the problem was not a broken heart at the way she had appeared to be deprived of the ideal life that she had sought, apparently in vain. Graham really did not know what his wife required in the way of the disposal of her body, but he assumed she wished for a cremation.

Jenny's parents were aware that Graham had not acquiesced to a divorce, a subject rather touchy with them. He reminded them very tersely that it was none of their business. This fact gave to Graham the lawful position of next-of-kin to Jenny.

The funeral service was arranged as a small affair with only the immediate family and a few pertinent relatives present. It was a cold, brief and sombre service devoid of any spiritual connotations as he assumed she would wish. Jenny's parents attended in rather gawdy attire, inappropriate, he thought, and ambivalent to the solemnness of the occasion.

Jenny's father was a weedy little morsel of humanity, thin, gaunt and covered in a grey mass of untidy hair over his head and face. He looked as if he could do with a damned good feed. He was rather insignificant and demure. He had been, before an early retirement, originally a shire engineer in several rural regions in more remote locations before landing a position in a more significant city shire. He finally ended up as the chief engineer on a major development project located on the coast of New South Wales. He was thorough in his trade and, by all accounts, quite a good engineer. He was not Graham's cup of tea but one trait he possessed, one that Graham believed he genuinely exhibited, and that was a severe case of industrial honesty. He would not acquiesce to the rorting systems exhibited by some of the shire council employees of over-ordering items and pocketing the difference. When he refused to condone or participate in such activities, he quickly fell into disfavour with his fellows. This caused him much angst and led to his moving often from shire to shire. He was a stickler for the rules and honesty. Graham admired that in him.

Jenny's mother was a strange person, at least to Graham. She had met her husband when they were both at university together, she studying arty-farty degrees of little real use. She had accompanied her husband on their employment wanderings through the wilderness of rural shires, delivering to him three daughters in the process. She was a strong-minded, feisty woman of particularly determined views, brooking little accord with opinions that did not coincide with hers. It was obvious to Graham who wore the trousers, so to speak, in that relationship.

Jenny's two sisters were older than she. Both were quite attractive and intelligent girls, married to or cohabiting with quite nice men. Graham might have got along with them better had things not turned out as they had.

There were also a few cousins and more distant relatives, including Louisa, the prophesier of the family doom, at the sombre little affair that was Jenny's earthly farewell.

Graham ensured his three children fully understood the significance of this event and tried to instil some respect in them for their departed mother. Graham's parents attended in ambivalence, rather grateful for the removal of this potential difficulty in their now more fully restored family life.

Little passed between Graham and his two main in-laws, except when Jenny's mother made a sarcastic comment about his deserting his family responsibilities and that she might still have been here if he had done his duty.

At that comment, Graham turned to face the old pair. He gazed at them in silence. They stared back at him in defiance. He peered down at them for some moments. Then he responded, severely and with a lot of pent-up dislike for the nasty couple that he held primarily responsible for the demise and disintegration of his family life. He moved a little closer to them and stood over them threateningly. A false calm descended upon the sombre group in the confines of the darkened, cool atmosphere of the morbid little chapel, as the expectant crowd peered at the protagonists. Then he let fly, in the hearing of all attending.

'You obnoxious little pair of total degenerates. Just look at you. Take a good hard look at yourselves.'

Jenny's mother tried to react. He cut her short with a threatening raised arm and a withering spray.

'Don't you even try to say one word, mate!'

A short silence ensured, while he menacingly peered at them.

'If you both had been half-decent adults, half-decent instead of filling her head with your senseless and irrational stupidity, Jenny would never have thrown away our lovely life for some meaningless utopia that does not exist. My children would have had a decent upbringing and Jenny would still be alive. I know you were behind her silly ideas of single motherhood. You wanted her married to the state, not to a man. You were so engrossed and mired in your own existence and idiocy that you didn't even have the wit to know the children were missing. You should be investigated for criminal parenting. Unfortunately, there is no law against stupidity. You,' he said, waving his arm in the general direction of the other family members, 'all of you, interfered with my life, my children's lives and my marriage. You all knew exactly how I should be living. Well, this is the end result of your interference. Your daughter is dead. You don't even seem to understand that fact. You keep right away from me, my family and never, never, try to contact any of us again. Is that clear?'

The old couple cowered slightly in their embarrassment. Jenny's mother had probably never been spoken to like that before, certainly not by a mere male or a member of her family. Graham presented a dominating and fearsome spectre on this occasion, and she could but absurdly cringe before him. He was rather annoyed, and it showed in his manner. He sincerely meant every word. The others looked on in stunned silence, realising he meant what he said and that it probably applied to them also. He made it clear that they were never to contact them again – none of them!

The children and Graham's parents looked on in mild

disbelief at their father's and son's explosion. None of them had ever witnessed such a performance from the usually mild and docile Graham R Longley. It showed a side of him that was latent and unknown.

The air was sombre at the cottage on their arrival home after the funeral. It was a new reality for them all. Graham was solemn and pensive for some time after the event. He felt he had failed Jenny somehow in their time together. His brittle soul would take some time to recover.

CHAPTER TEN

Queanbeyan is a genuine town, built where it is for a reason. It is on the railway line to the south that once travelled all the way through to Cooma and Bombala. It is still in use today from Queanbeyan to Sydney. It was there decades before Canberra was even thought of. Canberra had an artificial feel about it. Graham had heard it referred to as the 'Bush Capital' and a good sheep paddock ruined. It genuinely does have kangaroos hopping down the main street.

Queanbeyan is an attractive city. It is on the river; in fact, it is the Molonglo River, the very one used to fill Lake Burley Griffin, the centre piece of Canberra itself. It possesses some lovely buildings and much industry. It once even had its very own abattoir.

Graham's parents were now seriously contemplating

moving back down south to be near the family. They had been exploring Queanbeyan and much of Canberra for a suitable place. Queanbeyan was closer, cheaper and still in familiar New South Wales, not the foreign ACT. They considered units and a house, but as Sally might come to live with them, they preferred a larger house.

Sally was a mature and advanced young woman, quiet and reserved. The two boys were boisterous and energetic. They loved to accompany Graham to either the farm or to Cobar. As the Toyota only carried three passengers, one of the four males had to miss out. It was lately more common now for Richard to be the unlucky one. Graham contemplated buying a bigger four-wheel drive that would seat four, but he began to realise that creeping old age was bringing out the accumulating infirmities with which Richard was increasingly being afflicted. This dilemma might have its own inevitable solution.

It was deathly quiet in the cool little house when nobody else was there. It happened one Sunday of a long weekend when the two boys were away with their grandfather out at Cobar. Dora was outside in the front talking to a neighbour and Graham was working in the workshop in the back shed. When the telephone rang in the hallway, Sally arose from the small desk in her room to answer it.

'Hello,' she said.

There was a small delay.

A woman responded, saying, 'Hello. Is Graham there, please?'

The voice was soft and tentative. Sally was not sure of the

Chapter Ten

age of the caller. She sounded more refined than normal. Sally was puzzled.

She said, 'Yes. He's outside. I'll get him for you. May I ask who's calling?'

'It's Sophia here,' she simply replied.

Sally placed the receiver onto the small table and proceeded to find Graham out back. She disturbed his tinkering in the vice and said to him, 'Dad, there's a call for you from someone called Sophia.'

'Oh, thanks, Sal. I'll be right in.'

Graham wiped his hands on some rags and rushed inside. He picked up the receiver and said, 'Hello, Sophie. What can I do for you?'

'Hi, Graham. I hope I'm not interrupting you.'

Sally was more than a little intrigued. Graham appeared to have very few friends, let alone women friends. She tried to listen to the call. She could not, however, make much sense of the call so retreated to her room, where his conversation became a mumble.

Sophia had rung to advise him that Renu and her boyfriend and her flatmate had come down for the long weekend and they were having a get-together tomorrow, Sunday, for a few people. They all would dearly love for Graham to be there if he were free. Could he attend for a barbecue lunch? He initially agreed. Then he had a thought. It suddenly occurred to him that the shy and lonely Sally might get some benefit out of meeting a few more refined people.

'Sophie,' he said tentatively, 'I wonder. Could I possibly

bring my daughter with me?'

'Yes, sure,' said a puzzled Sophia. 'I didn't know you had a daughter,' she said, showing her surprise.

'Are you sure she can come?' asked Graham.

'Yes,' she enthused.

'She may not wish to come, but I'd like her to meet you.'

Sophia agreed readily, though confused.

Graham put the phone down, deep in thought. He went to Sally's room and knocked gently on the door. She turned to look at him in silence.

He said, 'Sal, I've been invited to a barbecue lunch tomorrow with some friends. I'd like you to come with me. You would meet some very interesting people, plus some of the young people are at uni. I thought you might like to talk to them about that sort of thing. Would you be interested?'

She hesitated for a moment. She did not particularly like the kinds of people that seemed to populate Graham's new world. Would she fit in there as a stranger? She reticently agreed, thinking that if they were at university, she might get some pointers. Graham smiled nervously.

Next day, about eleven, Graham and Sally climbed into the uncomfortable and jerky Land Cruiser that Graham seemed to love and departed for the bush. Dora had another neighbour she wished to visit, so no one was alone. Sally had many misgivings about this adventure. She hoped there would be things to talk about other than sheep. She did not accompany Graham much outside of the village, so most of this would be unfamiliar to her.

Chapter Ten

Graham drove over the rough and dusty road out of the village towards the east, passing his own place and on for quite a few kilometres. He arrived at the Faulkner's turnoff and drove into their place. He arrived at the homestead where there were not many cars about. Sophia had said it would be low-key. He looked at Sally, smiled a reassuring smile and touched her arm gently. Two or three people emerged from the rather ornate and impressively large portico affair, that disguised the front door somewhere within its magnificence, and jauntily trotted over to the Cruiser. There was only one car next to his, a small modern sedan covered in dust.

Graham hopped out of the car and closed the door, waiting for Sally to alight. This she did with some degree of inelegance. He headed for the front of the car, and she joined him.

Sophia sidled up to Graham and, Sally thought, rather demonstratively greeted him. Renu was more circumspect and reserved, she having a young man on her arm. Graham concentrated on Sophia and introduced her to Sally. Then he turned to Renu who proffered a delicate hand which he gently clasped. She in turn introduced her boyfriend, Tobias Matthews, a fellow student from Sydney. Graham perused him closely. He was tall, well-built and polite, sporting a neat, dark, short beard and matching dark hair. He was casually but neatly dressed in what Graham determined was probably designer gear. There followed some small talk and they then progressed inside.

Once Sally was introduced to the senior Faulkners, she was more or less alone with them for some time. They were just as surprised as Sophia to learn that Graham had a family. They tried to learn as much as she was prepared to divulge. Sally was ashamed of her family failure so was reticent to reveal much at all, other than her mother was dead and they had moved back in with Graham.

Sally was astonished to learn that Graham was regarded as rather a hero among the crowd here, at least those who knew the stories. She intimated that no one of her family had any idea or knew a thing about his antics involving both Sophia or Renufa. She could not understand how that could be. Sally was finally able to spend some time with the younger women and made many enquiries about their studying and life at university.

On the drive home, Sally was very quiet. She was deep in thought.

Finally, Graham asked, 'What did you think of all that, then?'

'Why didn't you tell us about what you did for those girls?'

'Never mind all that,' said Graham. 'What did you think of the Faulkners?'

'They're all right, I suppose. Very nice people.'

'I wanted you to see that there are people around here who are, shall we say, a little more upmarket than some of our contacts. They are not all below your type. I was just like you are, Sal, when I first came here. I was, I'm sorry to say, very judgemental and belittling of our neighbours. It took me some time to realise that that attitude is wrong. I'd like you to see that all people here are worthy of our acquaintance. They just live on a different level from what you are used to.'

Sally was quiet and reflective. She had a lot to digest from this encounter.

*

One evening, Sally went to put a little-used item up onto the top of the kitchen cupboard. In so doing, she inadvertently knocked off a small black notebook that was not obvious from the floor. She placed it on the bench after flicking through it and deciding it was nothing. She alerted Graham to its existence, and he acknowledged that he had forgotten about it some time ago. In the evening, Graham remembered the old notebook, retrieved it from the kitchen bench and sat at the table to peruse its contents. It was so old that it was probably of no interest at all. He opened it and half-heartedly perused its contents. It consisted mostly of lists of tools and equipment, but Graham was not sure whether these were to be acquired or were already in hand. Anyway, it was of little consequence now. However, nearer the middle of the book, Graham found some notes and he at first did not know what to make of them. Were they genuine or a fiction of some depth of imaginative creativity?

He read and reread them, not knowing what to make of them at all. There were some names mentioned that were familiar and local, but there were other, much more disturbing entries that meant nothing to him at this stage.

The most familiar name was of the old man who was

his neighbour two doors up from him, who lived in a much more derelict and crumbling old house that was awaiting the old man's demise in order to be reinvigorated or possibly demolished. This was Jacob Cranchovic, a former Czech immigrant, who in his thirties emigrated with his industrial chemistry qualifications to work in this once thriving mining town. He was now alone, but Graham thought he might have a daughter somewhere who rarely visited. He was a rather unpleasant and cranky old sod who was not particularly liked by most of the locals; they just let him be in his isolation, which he appeared to desire.

Much more disturbing, however, were the notes that followed his entry. They meant absolutely nothing to Graham at this stage, but were troubling as their content, if of any veracity, were either fictitious or startling.

Tom had written that he had disturbed Jacob out at the farm one Sunday afternoon as he was trying to leave the premises. Jacob apparently occasionally worked out there with Tom on casual farmhand jobs as required in the early days of his owning this property. Jacob dismissed the encounter as his effort, unsuccessfully, to find a lost penknife somewhere in the paddocks. This would have passed muster normally as, according to Tom, Jacob did possess a large World War Two army-issue penknife that he got from an old digger in the village that he was rather proud of. But Tom had written that he was suspicious of his being there on account of two things. One, he seemed to have a lot of digging gear, crowbars and chains in his old ute, the back of which showed evidence of soil being there, and, apparently unbeknownst to Jacob, there was a long colourful sock caught on the inside of the ute wall. It was very distinct, nearly new, and belonged to a young girl, Tom surmised. Jacob was very nervous and fidgety. He was also rather filthy. Tom was uneasy. He thought little of it, however, at that moment, just feeling uneasy suspicion.

Worse was to come for Tom. That evening there came upon the radio and other news services that a ten-year-old girl was missing from the Captains Flat area. Her name was listed as Linda Planter from Queanbeyan. Her mother had been visiting friends at Captains Flat that morning and the child had gone missing around midday. A large search was organised; there were many used and disused mining shafts all around the whole area and it was feared she may have fallen into one. The length of the river was searched and the riparian verges up the steep banks and some of the adjoining backyards.

The name meant nothing to Graham as it was over twenty-five years ago now. He was not sure whether this was just a fanciful scribbling of an imaginative mind or something much more sinister. He could at least investigate the incident. More disturbing to Graham were the following notes which Tom must have added as the events unfolded, as they were in different inks. They hinted at Tom fearing for his life as he determined that Jacob, in his dealings with him, could be unpredictable and volatile on occasions.

Graham was thinking. He would firstly ascertain any information about any missing child from this area twenty-five years ago and might look into the death of Tom Butler. Then he had a sudden thought. He recalled that, among the workshop manuals in the heavy wooden box with the sliding lid that his father had shown to him, there was a large foolscap-sized manila folder with newspaper clippings inside which, at the time, on flicking it open in the confined space of the box, they assumed held articles on motors or such. He would go out and retrieve it immediately.

He grabbed a large torch and proceeded out to the messy sheds. In the dim light of the inadequate shed lights, he rummaged through the large wooden box and retrieved the folder. Richard had removed all the relevant manuals to use on the cars. He checked more thoroughly this time to ensure there were no other extraneous containers in the little-explored box. He returned inside hurriedly.

Graham quickly sat back at the kitchen table and opened the folder. To his horror, what he feared most, there were indeed clippings from a newspaper about that very subject. The folder contained several clippings from the *Queanbeyan Age*, and some from the *Sydney Morning Herald*. Graham read them all with rising concern. The main points he gleaned from these ancient clippings were that the child was never found, there was really no suspicion of foul play and there were no suspects as such. That was the state at the time of these clippings. He would have to check if that were still the case. How could he ascertain the cause of death of Tom after all this time? There must be a death certificate somewhere here. His Aunt Alice was very thorough with her paperwork; she surely must have had one. He racked his brain for somewhere that he had so far not looked. He could ask a couple of the old neighbours who knew the Butlers as well.

Tom had a second-last entry in his notes. He claimed that he had driven out to the farm the next day after the news was out and tried to discover any disturbed area around the paddock near the creek, as that was the direction that Jacob had come from when he disturbed him. He followed his tracks through the long grass but could find little. The only clue he found was around a fairly large boulder that appeared to have been moved, but he himself could not budge it alone. It was conspicuous by its distinct, half-domed shape and location almost alone in the paddock.

The last entry in the notebook by Tom was rather cryptic. He said he was feeling quite ill for a few days now and had been unable to return to the farm to investigate any further. He had finally discovered that Alice had accepted a bowl of mushrooms from Jacob a few days ago and left them cooked in a heavy stew for Tom in a casserole dish while she went to a card night with the girls. He could not connect the two but suspected that a gift from the usually taciturn Jacob would be suspect after their interaction out at the farm and the following developments.

Graham sat back in the hard kitchen chair. His immediate thoughts leapt to the devastating conclusion that Jacob, being a European and a chemist, would have been much more familiar with the death cap mushroom that is now more widely spread in Australia, but back then was little-known to most Australians. The death from its poisoning is almost certain and debilitating and can take several days, usually from liver and/or kidney failure. A country doctor back then might have been totally unfamiliar with its existence and symptoms and have diagnosed something different from that cause.

Where is that death certificate? Graham had another thought. He got up from the kitchen table and headed for the telephone table where Alice still had several old Yellow and White Pages telephone books. He gathered the White Pages and hunted for the name of Planter. Sure enough, there were still several entries under that name in Queanbeyan. He contemplated the difficulty in reawakening for them what must still be a traumatic loss those many years ago.

After much thought, Graham decided to ring his friend and solicitor, Peter Knuckey, in Sydney. He explained his ideas and asked Peter if he could make some enquiries about the case. This he did. He contacted Graham several days later and advised him that the old detective who was originally in charge of the short investigation was still alive and now living up on the North Coast. He could try to contact him for any advice.

Next day, Graham decided to go out to the farm much as usual but this time he would try to explore the paddock that Tom was talking about to try and find this rock. He wandered around for many hours but there were several isolated boulders in various parts of the paddocks, and at first, he could not find the one described. On his third attempt,

Graham came across a large semi-circular shaped boulder about the size of a small table. It was in a position where it was not visible from the road or from the Wheatley's place. All this time, he was thinking of the poor Planter family who never had the whereabouts of their long-lost child verified. He was also thinking of poor Tom and a lonely Alice. Was it possible after all this time to solve a mystery that maybe no one even knew was there? He sat on the rock deep in thought.

Graham decided to try to remove the boulder, but he would need his tractor with the carry-all on the tree-point linkage. He walked back to the sheds. He retrieved the smaller tractor and headed back to the boulder. He shovelled away some soil from one side and tried to insert the protruding end of the carry-all. The rock protested, but it finally began to move away from its position. He pushed it just enough to reveal its entire resting ground as exposed bare earth. He got off the tractor and stared at it momentarily.

Then he retrieved his post-hole shovel and gently began to remove the top layers of soil. Almost immediately, he struck material. His heart sank. He rummaged gently about the exposed material and decided that there was a lot of it. He slowly removed some of the material and exposed bones. Alarmingly, Graham hit a solid metal object near the surface. After carefully examining the rusted-up slab, he concluded that it was clearly distinguishable as a large solid penknife, similar to the one Tom described as Jacob possessing. He put that in his pocket. He would go no further. He replaced the soil and slid the rock back into place.

Graham was in a complete quandary. He stood by his ute back at the shed, deep in thought. He would not rush. He was thinking that he would dearly love to confront Jacob and appraise his response, but he could not think how to go about it to get his confession, if indeed he were even involved. He was certainly no Sherlock Holmes. Then there were the aspersions about the death of his Uncle Tom. Then there were the Planters to consider, especially if this turned out to be a false lead. He did not really know what the bones were from, though even he thought he could recognise a human skull when he saw one. Should he involve the police and, if so when, now or later? Should he tell his parents? What about his own children who still did not know about this development? Then there could be interminable disruptions to his farming program out here on his property and to his stock. What would his neighbours think when they saw endless police cars swarming all over his place? All in all, it was a bloody nuisance.

Graham sat thinking deeply back at the sheds. He would spend the day doing what he had intended to do about the property while he thought about it all. He would try to keep his children away from any kind of drama surrounding this issue. He might ring his parents. Then he had a thought. Maybe his mother had found some documents relating to family matters such as births and deaths that Aunty Alice had stored somewhere else that he had not found. In the meantime, he would try to clean up the old knife.

He went back to the village a little earlier that day. When

he got home, he rang his mother. She had indeed found all of Alice's personal documents in a hidden drawer in her bedroom wardrobe. They were still there and, yes, there was a death certificate for Tom Butler. Graham spent some considerable time on the telephone talking to his parents. They offered to return to the village immediately if he so desired.

When he hung up, Graham whisked himself into the main bedroom, that he actually rarely entered, to retrieve all of Alice's documents that were still placed in her original storage drawer. He rummaged through the half dozen or so documents, mostly certificates and some banking papers, and found Tom's death certificate. He read that with some interest.

This death certificate contained all of Tom's family details, all about the immediate Butler connections, his age, date of birth and death, and, significantly, his cause of death – at least the one that was ascribed to him at the time. Graham read that entry with much interest. It was listed in a short entry that read simply 'organ failure – kidney disease'.

Graham was still unsure whether to go to the police or not. His parents had advised him to do so immediately. He was on good terms with the local squad, having dealt with them on several issues, including the unexpected arrival of his own children. It would still be tricky, though, not at least the impact on him and on Jacob Cranchovic, not to mention what might transpire with the other neighbours. Graham did not need any further disruptions in his complicated little life right now.

Finally, Graham succumbed to the desire to do the right thing – he would go to the police. Most fortunately, Captains Flat was exceedingly blessed with its own rather magnificent old police station, a fact most small communities would never be able to justify. He was motivated by three main factors. He wished to, hopefully, bring possibly some closure for the Planters. He would like to see Jacob brought to justice if he were the culprit, and he would like to set the record straight about the unexpected death of his uncle and the unintended distress and circumventing of their plans brought about by this event.

He photocopied the relevant pages of the notebook, making several copies and then took them and the book around to the police station. He asked if he could see the senior officer about a tricky matter.

*

Richard and Dora Longley were giving this stage in their lives a great deal of searching thought. They knew that they possibly had only a few short years left on this earth. They had let the dust settle after the death of Jenny and established that the State was not going to interfere any further in the lives of the Longley children. They then made the momentous decision to move completely from the warm sunshine of Queensland to the doubtful and challenging climes of the Southern Tablelands of New South Wales.

They spent a great deal of time and effort on researching

the potential domestic establishments in both Queanbeyan and the ACT. In the end, they decided to buy an established house in an older suburb of Queanbeyan. The reasons were many, but essentially, they preferred the familiarity of NSW and prices were cheaper in Queanbeyan. Besides, in Queanbeyan, you actually owned the freehold on your property, unlike the case in the ACT.

The house they bought was rather large, with four bedrooms, a study and a reasonable backyard to boot. It also possessed a reverse-cycle air-conditioner, not a luxury as far as the aging Longleys were concerned, as well as a functioning open fireplace. That was really just an ornament as far as the Longleys considered it as, despite access to unlimited free firewood from the farm, they were not interested in all the hard labour involved with its use.

Sally continued to attend school in town while domiciled at Captains Flat, at least initially. However, the overwhelming convenience and ease of living in her preferred habitat of an urban setting soon convinced her that she could move in with her grandparents. After all, that was one of the main motivating factors in their move south, and Sally had grown to be fond of them both, and a mutual accepting of each party had established an affection that hopefully would only grow. The grandparents felt useful, and Sally felt more accepting of her entire new family paradigm. The two boys were so enamoured of their new lifestyle that they were delighted to be resident in the bush.

Graham was disappointed slightly that Sally moved house

but was delighted that she was so set up as to be nearby and in very safe and capable hands. He settled into a rhythm of constant farm work, learning the seemingly endless teachings of the sheep industry, property maintenance and his other occupation of enthusiastic involvement in the continuous education the property at Cobar afforded to him and his boys.

Interspersed in the hectic occupation that rural property offered was the continued maintenance of a steady relationship with the Faulkners, much to his covert pleasure. Another major distraction was the continuing saga of the developing Planter case which impinged on his limited time.

Initially, the police were tentative about the evidence presented by Graham, but the tangible offering of the mystery body convinced them that there was indeed a case to at least investigate. The body of an adolescent was retrieved from the site and a crime scene was established at the location. Just as Graham feared, there was of course much banter and gossip among the immediate farming neighbours at the sight of all this clandestine police activity. Graham was completely tight-lipped about it all, so they were unable to ascertain at this stage what was actually happening.

The police had to make the unenviable act of approaching the Planter family and reawakening all their trauma. They asked for some DNA from the two surviving sisters and then attempted to make any matches that the limited DNA might yield from such a mediocre sample that the long-buried body might reveal. Their other unenviable task was to approach an aging and uncooperative Jacob Cranchovic. Graham was wary of that aspect of the operation as it would have the effect of revealing his involvement in the whole affair, a position he was not in the least enamoured of at all, especially in such a close-knit community as existed out there.

*

Graham attended every episode of shearing that occurred at his shed. He assisted John Wheatley at every opportunity with his mustering and the myriad other activities that were involved with owning sheep, as well as his now own growing flock that was expanding slowly over time.

He had been noticing that John Wheatley was beginning to show his age and he was finding the sheep work was becoming more arduous and difficult. It was obvious that it was only a matter of time now until he would have to depart this difficult lifestyle. Sadly, John's two boys were not interested in continuing on with the business, so he reluctantly became aware of the fact that he would probably have to sell the enterprise altogether and leave the district. Graham had known the Wheatleys now for about nine or ten years, and John had been a sincere and useful friend to Graham from the very beginning. Graham had given passing thought to purchasing the Wheatley property himself but, deep down, he knew that to buy that valuable property would entail going into considerable debt, something his banking background cautioned against.

Graham's life had dramatically altered from his slow

descent into slothfulness on the Sunshine Coast. After his ambivalent and initially hesitant relocation to bucolic Captains Flat, he had grown in confidence and happiness with the new life bestowed on him by a little known aunt. He now had his grateful parents relocated to nearby Queanbeyan, his reconnected daughter living with them there and attending to her own desires to everyone's satisfaction, and his two boys were growing in physique and confidence with their total immersion into the rural existence that had come with their return to his fold.

He was a little staggered at the turn of events and the subsequent unrolling of an incongruous collection of disparate actions that populated his altered life. He glanced back in amazement at the way his learning ability to conquer the totally unfamiliar grazing industry had progressed. Then there followed a seemingly improbable series of unconnected incidents associated with his new existence, beginning with the unlikely involvement with Cobar and all that flowed from that.

In his short time here, he was already facing undreamt-of circumstances, all needing attention in a profusion of weird occurrences that abounded in his now hectic life. There still flowed from the Sophia affair many consequences for him, not to mention the similar Renu incident. His growing friendship with the Faulkners he regarded as a crowning glory.

Now there were other matters away from the farming property requiring attention. He was mindful that he could lose his invaluable neighbour in John Wheatley at any moment, due to his aging status. He was in the middle of a traumatic incident with the elderly Jacob Cranchovic. The police had finally identified the body as that of the missing child; the Planters were grateful for that revelation. There were no suspects and Graham realised that unless Jacob confessed, there was no way of implicating him in the deed. That had not so far developed beyond suspicion and the police were unable to connect him to the body, a fact that worried Graham because of the cryptic note from Tom about his own demise. Maybe Alice had bequeathed to him her worldly possessions so he could unravel the mystery of the real cause of her happy life being so abruptly cut short. All these disparate events arose out of his new tenure and lifestyle in otherwise sedate little Captains Flat.

Now there was another complex and intriguing event about to occur about him that would lead to considerable disruption and angst as he would have to deal with it alone.

CHAPTER ELEVEN

Over the years, Graham had become very friendly with his immediate neighbours with the exception of the aging and alone Mr Jacob Cranchovic, who remained aloof and distant – and suspect, though no one else knew just how suspect. His immediate neighbour, Tony, also now aging and alone, became a particular friend, especially to Graham's parents who both found him congenial. However, this relationship was about to finally explode into shattering revelations that would reverberate for some time and distance.

It took many years for the details to slowly evolve from the depths of the hidden secrets that Tony possessed. The pieces, separately, did not overly mean much at first but Graham began to become involved with a devastating event that occurred many years earlier as it slowly emerged. Scattered, disparate facts began to gel, particularly as Tony aged into infirmity.

Firstly, Graham learned a few years after arriving there that Tony had had a girlfriend whose name was Micheline. She had been a teacher's assistant in town but had been killed many years ago in a tragic skiing accident at Thredbo. She and Tony were both avid skiers, it appeared. Graham thought that Tony was Italian but commented that Micheline was rather a pretty name and seemed to him to be French. Tony just nodded his head in silent agreement. Tony had been alone since the demise of the charming Micheline.

One day, while Graham was in Tony's house having a cup of tea with him, he noticed a letter on the sideboard cupboard addressed to a Mr Antoine Missel. To Graham, that sounded decidedly German and not French. He was intrigued. He thought little more about it over the next few years. As Tony aged and became more infirm and unsteady, Graham began to become more involved with his neighbour's life by way of more assistance.

Tony spent a week in hospital in Queanbeyan late one winter. On his return, Graham and his parents, especially Dora, offered more assistance to his ailing neighbour while he recovered. Tony was definitely going downhill. In one of his sojourns into a separate room to get some papers on the desk for Tony, Graham noticed some other papers and a book, possibly in Hebrew, with a Star of David on it. He was rather disturbed; firstly, that he had not known his neighbour could possibly be Jewish and secondly, if so, why would he not tell his friends.

Graham was disturbed by this revelation but was unsure

how to ask him. He had worked with several Jewish bankers and always found them to be most amiable. Finally, he decided to ask his friend the question, but how to go about it? He left it in abeyance for the moment.

The next piece of the puzzle was the inadvertent revelation by Graham that he had a particularly agreeable solicitor friend in Sydney by the name of Peter Knuckey. Graham had intimated occasionally how much he detested the legal system, but Peter was a rare exception. At the mention of the name, Tony's demeanour noticeably changed; even Graham could see the alteration. He let it pass for the moment.

It all finally came together one coolish, quiet Sunday afternoon while Tony and Graham sat alone together in Tony's sparse little kitchen, though much grander than Graham's. Tony asked Graham if he knew whether his solicitor friend, Peter Knuckey, was in any way related to the once disgraced Inspector Ian Knuckey. Firstly, Graham was amazed that he would recall so lucidly the mention of his solicitor's name so casually cast into a conversation some time ago; and secondly, it finally hit Graham why the name Knuckey always rang a bell with him, but he could never decide why. Graham asked Tony why he would ask such a question. There was a long silent pause in the conversation. Both men sat in deep contemplation. Tony's reply, when it came, sent shivers down Graham's spine and a cold flush struck his face.

'Graham, you and your folks have been good neighbours to me these last few years, much as Tom and especially Alice were before you. I am an old man now, Graham, and I know that I have not got all that long to live.'

Graham looked at his friend with compassion.

He continued, 'Graham, I have no one here in Australia to leave things to and no one will miss me. But I would like to tell someone a few things that I know about that may be of interest to others.'

Graham looked at his companion. 'Don't you have folks in Italy, Tony? I could contact them for you, you know.'

There was another long pause. Tony looked at his neighbour and finally stated, 'Graham, I am not Italian. I am French. My real name is Antoine, but for reasons I'd now like to tell you, I always used Tony to disguise myself. Also, Graham,' he paused, 'I am Jewish.'

Tony stared into Graham's face to gauge his reaction. There was none, so he continued.

'I wish to be buried in the Queanbeyan cemetery in the Jewish section, if at all possible. Do you think that can be arranged?'

Graham replied, 'I'm sure it can be. Are you asking me to do it?'

'Well, possibly, as there would be no one else.'

Graham assured him he would try and ensure it was done, again asking was he sure there was no one he should inform.

'What about the house, Tony?'

'I only rent this place, Graham. Have done so from the beginning.'

Graham was surprised. For some reason, he had assumed Tony owned the place.

Tony continued, 'Also, Graham, I live mainly on the small remittance that Chellie's trust sends to her. I have never told them she is dead. She came from a well-known French industrial family and was well off herself. They send euros to her account. I still operate it.'

He looked sheepishly at Graham. Graham was thinking that that little detail might have to be attended to as well on Tony's demise.

'My family is in the aeronautical industry in France in a big way, but it never appealed to me,' Tony said.

Tony stared again at Graham, then continued. 'Graham, I have secrets that no one knows about. But I also have some knowledge that others may find of note.' He paused, long and steely. 'Graham, if I tell you some things, would you try to pass them on to those that need the info?'

Graham nodded in agreement.

'I came to Australia in the early sixties with my girlfriend, Micheline. We met up with several others, but one in particular became our special travelling companion. His name was Werner. He was German. He was a mechanical engineer, and I was a panel beater and spray painter. We were all here on travel documents. We met a man in Sydney who offered us a job in his workshop in Newtown in Sydney. We ended up staying for several years, illegally. Newtown was very central, near to the city, had a bus stop just around the corner, and the train station was just across the road – very convenient.'

He suddenly stopped talking. Then he said, 'Do you think your solicitor is related to Inspector Ian Knuckey?'

Graham was dumbfounded. What a weird question!

'Why do you ask?' he said.

'If that were the case, I would like to tell you something that he would like to know.'

Graham responded, 'I don't know if he is, but I can find out if you like.'

'Do you remember the MacIntyre case of many years ago?'

'No, not particularly. Though I do recall the name, now you mention it.'

'Well, you see, the man we worked for was Donald MacIntyre.'

He looked at Graham to gauge his reaction. There was little, so he continued.

'One night in about 1980, there was a shooting at his workshop. Two people were killed. I saw what happened afterwards. I never told anyone.'

'Why?' asked Graham.

'Well, you see, we were really illegals, but more importantly, I saw what they did to Donald MacIntyre and poor Werner from our rear balcony. You see, we had no idea what was going on in Don's place. Chellie and I lived next door in the upstairs part of the grocery shop next to Don's workshop. No one knew about us. The place was destroyed in a blast during the trial years later. It is no longer there. Anyway, when they came in and arrested everybody they wanted, we were left alone. Our back balcony was right next to Don's, and we could just step across, but they wouldn't know that. We could hear everything they said in the back lane. We wondered why they took Knuckey over to the police station right opposite our workshop that night but put Werner and Donald into a van at the back of the workshop next morning when Don returned from wherever he had been. As it turned out, I gather he had been to the airport, but no one knew that at the time. Then this bloke came out and began to speak. We were horrified.'

'What did he say?' asked Graham.

'It was horrible. He said to the man with him, "Now you get rid of those two. I got rid of the two inside last night. Hindie has set up Knuckey."'

'Why didn't you just kill Knuckey too?' asked the other man.

'No, we need a scapegoat and he's our man. You leave all that to me. Now go and get rid of those two. And Morangill, make sure you lot find that woman – I want her dead too. Oh, and make sure you knock off Hindie as soon as possible. Now, get going! I'll never forget the way he emphasised that weird name – Morangill.'

'That name sounds familiar. Anyway, what happened next?'

'When we realised what was going on, Chellie and I packed our stuff into our campervan and left immediately. See, we left owing rent as well, very bad. We headed for Queanbeyan as we had a friend who was teaching at one of the primary schools. That's how Chellie got this job here as a teacher's aide in this village, through our friend. It was nice and safe for us and very remote. We were very happy here.'

'What happened with all the others?' asked Graham.

'There was a trial and Ian Knuckey was accused of being a crook and was dismissed. I did not follow it very much until, years later, Jessie was arrested. She obviously escaped and survived for years. Her trial was a sensation and Knuckey was cleared and so was she of any involvement. But I was too scared to come forward. But, Graham, Jessie is probably still alive and would like to know what little I know about it. She lives in Sydney, I think.'

Graham had let Tony tell his tale uninterrupted as he had become enthralled with the details. But he was a little confused, so asked, 'Sorry, Tony, who was Jessie?'

Tony replied, 'Jessie MacIntyre, you know the famous author, who lived for years in the Kimberley. May still do, I don't know. She was picked up by Don at the markets. You remember, it all came out at the trial.'

'No, not really, Tony. It was a little before my time, I think, and obviously not that interesting to me or I would've remembered.'

'Well, she was a child at the beginning and Chellie spent a lot of time with her, playing in the small park opposite Don's place and looking after her in our place when Don was busy. We got to know her very well.'

'And you think this Jessie would like to know something?'

'Yes. There's something else, Graham. Micheline kept a small diary and she wrote down most of this in it at the time. Jessie might like the evidence. I'd like her to get it when I'm gone. See, no one knows what happened to Donald MacIntyre or to Werner. Their families would like to know.'

Graham was in confused silence, staring at his strange neighbour.

Then Tony said, 'Graham, I have some items that I'd like to give you if I may. Would you take them from me now in case anything happens?'

'Sure,' responded Graham.

Tony got up from the table with some difficulty and asked Graham to follow him into the back room. There he retrieved a box containing all the details. He pointed out that there were many clippings, the small diary and some of the novels that Jessie MacIntyre wrote under different names. It included her own large diary that was published years later. Would Graham relieve him of this burden? Graham accepted the box and they departed the room. He would go through it later.

Graham was totally stunned by this barrage of incredible information. He sat in his shed contemplating the story, staring at the box. He did not know where to start. His family was inside, but he needed to be alone for a minute or two. Then he had a thought. Even though it was a Sunday afternoon, he decided he would try to contact Peter in Sydney as a starting point. He went in and picked up the landline; he preferred that system to his outdated mobile. The phone rang.

'Hello, Peter? Graham Longley here. Could you please ring me back asap? It is not urgent, but I need to ask you something.'

He hung up the phone and sauntered back to the kitchen where some of the family was gathered. Shortly after, the landline rang; he hoped it would be Peter. He rushed in to pick it up.

'Hello ... Yes, thank you so much, Peter. Sorry to disturb you on a Sunday ... Well, thank you anyway. Look, Peter, I've just had a most amazing conversation with a friend here. Do you by any chance know an Ian Knuckey? ... Yes, that's him! Amazing. Listen, Peter ...'

Graham repeated some of the story Tony had told him. Peter agreed to contact his uncle in Woy Woy and get back to him.

Sometime later, Peter got back in touch with Graham in Captains Flat. They had a long talk. He told Graham that he had discussed the whole affair with his uncle. He was very interested indeed about any further information, as they had not been able to definitively pin the murders on a now suspect and retired Inspector Stolt. They were unable to persuade Jessie MacIntyre to ever go anywhere near a courtroom to testify. Ian had asked one point that he wished cleared up, however, and that was the passing mention of the name Morangill. Could Graham please clarify that name for him? He agreed to make further inquiries of Tony. Peter was unsure why Ian wished this information.

During the course of the conversation, Peter revealed that his uncle had suffered badly over the whole sordid affair and that most of the family disowned him at the time. Peter, though, rather liked his uncle and Aunt Beryl. Peter had been quite young when most of this had occurred so had never really fully understood the implications. He had maintained a modicum of contact with his uncle and found his restitution rather inspirational. It had influenced him considerably towards choosing a career in the law to facilitate the defending of those at the mercy of a suspect system riddled with flaws and inconsistencies.

*

Peter revealed the entire story as told to him by Graham to his elderly uncle in Woy Woy. Ian Knuckey sat back in his tatty old armchair after getting off the phone. He still pondered that infamous MacIntyre case often. The heartache it had caused to him and his long-suffering and now frail wife, the years of isolation, the being ostracised by all and sundry, including his family, was followed by a totally unexpected and long-abandoned hoped-for reprieve – the final rising, phoenix-like, from the ashes of a desolate wretched existence in the turbid backwaters of a dingy little unit on the Central Coast. He had always been grateful for the somewhat tenuous but nevertheless actual contact his successful nephew Peter had made with them both. He knew that the bulk of his amnesty was due to that redoubtable defence lawyer and friend, Caxton Tennex, and the dreamy angel-like personage he still knew as Jessie MacIntyre. He knew that she was now married and used her married name, and where she lived, but he told no one. Ian Knuckey was one of the very few people in the world who had a direct contact to Jessie MacIntyre, or Jessie Summers as she now was. He understood the gravity of that rare privilege.

During the conversation with Peter, Ian Knuckey was struck by the mention of the name Morangill. That was a particularly unusual name and a name that rang a bell with Ian. That was because that name belonged to a disreputable family of long-standing in the annals of crime in Sydney. It had cropped up many times over the course of his investigation resulting from the Jessie MacIntyre case, involving crimes dating back decades. It was the name of the offender in the motor accident that killed Senior Constable Josef Hindler. At the time, it had borne no known connection to the MacIntyre trial. Weirdly though, it had also cropped up in connection with his coming across the Summers name. The offender in the motor accident that caused the deaths of John Summers' parents way back in 1939 was one Dominic Morangill, now long dead. Ian wondered if those deaths were really an accident. He would reinvestigate the old police evidence, what little there was of it left.

Ian Knuckey waited until the next Sunday afternoon as he knew that that was often a free time for Jessie because of other family commitments that did not involve her. Jessie Summers was disturbed to have more information being raked up so long after the devastating episode in her tortured life. She did not need any more disruptions. She was, however, very interested in any information regarding the demise of her first mentor, Donald MacIntyre in Newtown.

Ian Knuckey passed on to Jess all the details he had been given. He advised her that there were quite some papers available plus a small diary of the now deceased Micheline. These were in the hands of a Graham Longley who, Ian assured her, was of a reputable character. Surprisingly, he lived in close proximity to her abode, though he did not know that fact. What would she wish to do about this development?

Jessie Summers would dearly like to get hold of this information but was desperate not to reveal herself to anybody. She had succeeded, so far admirably, to achieve this aim but challenges were always arising. However, fate might intervene and assist her in both these endeavours. In a long and convoluted process, this was achieved.

Jessie and Thomas always attended the Cooma Show. It was usually held towards the end of summer and was quite a small show. It had the usual sheep and wool judging, a small cattle ring, sheepdog trials, woodchopping, but it had an unusually large and competitive showjumping competition.

Thomas, Jessie and particularly a now elderly widower, John Summers, always attended the show, not only for the camaraderie of their industry cohorts, but also for the general social interchange that was often missing in their day-to-day lives. Thomas and John would spend considerable time watching and talking to the sheep and wool exhibitors and discussing their industry. One of the chief and very successful exhibitors was one Jackson Faulkner. Jackson and Edith would attend every year also, along with Sophia. Sophia was an ardent and successful showjumping exponent and competed regularly far and wide. As a kind of mentor, her aunt, Ophelia, would also often attend, though rarely competing in these small-town events.

The Summers family, for some reason, had never submitted entries into any of the rural competitions. The Summers men were, however, keen observers of the progressions being made in the wool industry. This was not a field that was of any real interest to Jessie, she much preferring to check out the very small cattle pavilion and particularly the rather extensive horse and showjumping arenas.

Jessie found the sheep pavilion rather dull, having no real affinity with this side of farming. She would accompany her husband briefly to the sheds, then usually depart. On arrival this particular Saturday, they sauntered up to the exhibitors and those standing about the well-used boards and chatted to the men there. John seemed to know everybody and would renew acquaintances with them all. He and Thomas would chat together at some length. Jess knew very few of them and found their conversation of little interest. John was conversing to a man to one side of the judging when she decided to depart. She went up to Thomas to say as much when Thomas turned and acknowledged her. He took the opportunity to introduce her to the current company.

He introduced her to the man as Jackson Faulkner. He was rather an elegant and sophisticated sort of man whom Jess seldom ran across in her daily dealings. Next to him was his also rather superior consort, his wife Edith, and their daughter, Sophia, who was dressed obviously to participate in the showjumping events. Beside Sophia was another rather refined woman, introduced as Ophelia, Edith's sister.

Jess found them rather pleasant company and thought she might advance their relationships under normal circumstances, but that was not her desire. She was about to depart when a strange event occurred. She had barely turned to go when a man approached the remaining group, taking her departure as a cue to interrupt. The effusive and demonstrable greeting that attended the new arrival by the otherwise sedate Faulkner clan, especially Sophia, struck her as odd.

The new arrival was dressed more for the city than the country and did not really exude to Jess that feeling of being a real country person. However, his name gave Jess a shuddering jolt. He was introduced as Graham Longley. She was totally frozen for a second. She wheeled around and stared at him. She did not know what to do. She did not really want to meet this man this way right now, if he were the right Graham Longley. She kept walking for a few paces.

Jessie watched him while he chatted with the group, but he did not stay long. Ian Knuckey had told her that Graham Longley lived in Captains Flat, a small village out of Queanbeyan and did not mention any rural connections. How would he know the well-known Faulkner family that the Summers knew well?

Jess wanted to find out more about Graham Longley from Ian Knuckey before she would reveal herself to him. Things already were not adding up. Why was he here for a start? She would follow him for a while. He spent a lot of time in the arts and crafts pavilion and watching the sheep dog trials.

She wandered down to the extensive horse paddocks under the ancient trees that lined the far surrounds of the large arena of the Cooma showground. Jess was interested in the horse side of the show. There were a lot of horse floats and horse people and horses scattered in profusion all about the shady side areas of the grounds. She spied Sophia. Sophia was attending to her horse and idly chatting to Ophelia when Jess sidled up. Sophia saw her and said hello. They chatted momentarily, Jess patting the compliant animal caringly on its nose, Ophelia gazing in turn at the newcomer and then at the events still proceeding out on the oval.

Then Jess said to her, 'Sophia, how do you know Graham Longley?'

'Oh, he's a dear friend of the family. We owe a lot to him.'

'You do?'

'Oh, yes. He has been very kind to us. We value his acquaintance dearly.'

'But I thought he lived in Captains Flat,' she heard herself saying, rather alarmed at her own brashness. Sophia was taken aback slightly at that presumption. She replied defensively, 'Well, he does, but he owns a big place out on the Shoalhaven River.'

Jess could detect the change of demeanour in Sophia. Ophelia stared at her disconcertingly. Jess hoped she had not offended her.

'I'm sorry, Sophia. It's just that he reminds me of someone I once knew, that's all. I was surprised to see him here, of all places.'

'Well, he's a very nice man, a real gentleman,' she said still a little defensively. 'Do you ride, Mrs Summers?' she asked a little coolly.

'Yes, Sophia, but of course not at your standard,' she said demurely.

Just then, Graham appeared from among the throng of horses and people, nervously dodging about among the throng of large and powerful animals that he was still rather wary of.

He approached Sophia, saying as he got close, 'Hello again, Soph. How's it going?'

He acknowledged Ophelia with a sedate nod, wary of her presence. She was an extremely accomplished and decorated horsewoman of some note, who travelled extensively throughout Europe and America with the horses. He was still a little surprised to see her here at this relatively minor show.

There was a cool quietness. Sophia said, 'Fine, Graham, thanks. Graham, may I introduce Mrs Jessie Summers? They have extensive property down this way. She is the wife of Thomas whom you met in the sheds. Mrs Summers, this is Graham Longley.'

Graham propped noticeably, with a sudden alarm on his countenance, staring at the new person before him.

Jess was standing by the railing of the large oval that was the showground, but still under the extensive cover afforded by the huge array of mature trees that surrounded most of this part of the grounds. Jessie rarely removed her hat in public or her sunglasses. She realised that her eyes were a giveaway to her potential identity. She had stunning eyes, and they often attracted the gaze of the unwanted. Jessie thought that Sophia was so young and preoccupied that she would not be aware of her story of many years ago now, similarly with Ophelia. However, now she had no hat on, it being in her right hand. She had also removed her sunglasses earlier because of the extensive shade and placed them in the top of her high-buttoned shirt.

Graham knew instantly who she was. He stared almost opened-mouthed at the apparition before him. His mind was racing. He suddenly recalled the several comments that Tony had made about her stunning appearance, even as a child. She possessed mesmerising, penetrating glassy eyes that distracted interlocutors. He instantly recalled her own rare comments about herself in her long-ago released diary in which she had described the Aboriginal women referring to her as *Yarnimindin Tagai Gan* – sky eyes – her cobalt blue eyes apparently reminding them of the gentle blue of the mellow dry season cloudless skies. Just for the briefest moment, he was transfixed by her withering stare of a pent-up hunting animal about to pounce. It was slightly alarming to him. It lasted micro-seconds, but he saw it. Tony had remarked about it to him several times as well.

Jess said softly, 'Hello, Mr Longley.'

He pulled himself together and replied, 'Hello, Mrs Summers, is it?'

'Yes,' replied Jess softly.

'Nice to meet you, Mrs Summers,' he said, staring at her deeply, ignoring Sophia completely, who saw this drama unfolding before her and was confused by the stark change in Graham's usually composed demeanour. There followed an embarrassing silence. Sophia wished to remove herself from this awkwardness, so intimated that she must prepare for the events. Ophelia followed her into the arena, glancing sideways at the minor unfolding drama before her.

Graham, still staring at Jess, initially said nothing. Then he realised his place and mumbled, 'Oh, yes, yes, Soph. And good luck, sweetie.'

'Thank you, Graham,' she replied.

Jess watched as she departed, leading the magnificent animal towards the stewards' tables, chatting to a bemused Ophelia.

'How did you find me, Jessie?'

Jess was not prepared for that request. 'What do you mean?' she asked.

She spoke in a refined and softly spoken tone. He recalled Tony had mentioned that she was always 'different', even as a child; she had always had a quietly demure façade.

'Come off it, Jess. I know exactly who you are. Do you think I could mistake those looks?' he said to her, looking her straight in those big blue eyes. 'Your appearance is too well known to me after all of Tony's files.'

'Who's Tony?' she said, putting her hat back on her head.

'Tony. I'm sorry. You probably know him …' he paused, '… knew him as Antoine. I'm still at a loss as to how you found me.'

Jess realised that Graham probably was the Graham Longley that she sought, but knew not how to arrange it safely for herself. In her silence and shame at the events unfolding about her, she resumed her usual code of long pauses and intermittent silence. She had already replaced her hat. She fumbled for her sunglasses. Graham just stared at her, drinking in her elegance, her aura, her enormous gravitas that was way beyond his undeserving insignificance. He thought the Faulkners were superior beings; this was a whole other level of unattainable style and grace, not to mention infamy at a notorious level – way out of his experience.

Finally, she said in her soft way, 'Graham. I am so sorry. I did not mean for us to meet in this fashion. I truly had no idea you were here. I thought you lived in Captains Flat and would never come this far down as a city boy. Ian Knuckey led me to believe you had no rural background.'

He said to her, 'I have information that I feel you would wish to know, and through a strange ring of circumstances, I discovered that you exist. I have no interest in furthering your torment over this whole horrid affair. It was really Tony – sorry, Antoine – who wished you to know this information. He was so despondent at not being in a position to tell you himself. Things I can tell you about if you wish. The main items he thought were the things about Donald, oh, and somebody called "Werner".'

She looked at him. He found her countenance rather beguiling; she had weathered the ravages of time admirably. She still possessed enormous presence. They departed the hectic horse grounds in silence towards the calmer pavilion side where they could converse more quietly.

Jessie headed for the bar area which was raised up above

the sloping ground one end and level with the road at the other. There they found a long table and bench seats located away from the bar and secluded enough to be private. They sat looking at each other momentarily, not quite knowing where to start.

'I believe you have some documents for me,' Jess began.

'Yes, Tony – sorry, Antoine – kept Micheline's small, ragged travel diary with some notes about that day. He had some other papers and several copies of your novels plus a copy of your own diary. I am sorry, but I have read the novels and your famous diary. I hope you don't mind?'

'No,' she replied sedately. It aggravated her that people had access to her innermost feelings that she did not have of others. She found it embarrassing.

'I'd rather like to keep them, if I may,' he stated.

'By all means,' she said. 'I have copies of everything myself.'

'How am I going to get the other stuff to you?'

She said nothing. Jess did not particularly want anybody knowing her address and was reluctant to visit him to retrieve them. She was thinking.

'Why do you keep calling him Tony?' she asked.

Graham explained how he knew Tony and why he used that name. She was saddened.

Then she said, 'Can you tell me anything about Donald?'

'Sorry, not really. Nothing more than Tony already told me. The diary's all in French. Ian Knuckey would be very interested, though.'

'How do you know him?'

'It's rather strange,' he said, 'but the solicitor I had for another matter is actually his nephew who became a friend of mine. I don't normally like lawyers, but he is different.'

Jess could identify with that.

Then Graham stated, 'By the way, it is very uncanny, but would you believe, there is a weird connection with the Summers name as well. One of the crooks who was involved with the death of one of the cops had a most distinct name, "Morangill". That name was also connected with the death of John Summers' father, a connection Peter told me about when his uncle raised the weird connection. It seems this bunch of crooks uses this form of murder basically to eliminate undesirables. When I heard your name as Summers and met John, I was totally staggered by the whole thing. Ian is now reinvestigating a whole pile of cases where these people may have been involved. It really is just weird.'

Jess was suddenly rather startled. 'You mean, John Summers' father was murdered?'

'Ian is now investigating. Nothing yet.'

Jess was stunned. Surely, John's parents were not murdered too! That was supposed to be an accident. She was deep in thought.

Just then, Thomas came along the roadside entrance to the bar area and spied Jessie. He hastened over and sidled up beside her.

'I've been looking everywhere for you, dear. I would never look for you in the beer garden.'

She reintroduced him to Graham. They sat in silence for

a moment, Thomas conscious that he may have interrupted something.

Then he said, 'Pop is getting tired, we may have to leave when you're ready.'

She just flickered a wisp of a smile in acknowledgement. As they sat in awkward silence, Sophia and Ophelia came up the stairs and spied them. She hesitated, then ventured over to the table and asked if she could join them. There was no indication that she could not, so she and her aunt sat on the bench seat next to Graham.

'How'd you go?' asked Graham, his tone appeared to Jess to be genuinely concerning.

'Fine. A couple of good rounds. The competition is quite strong here. Still awaiting some events. Ophie here thinks Starlight may have an aggravated off-side cannon bone or splint bone or bruised tendons. He seems a little jerky to me today, but I think he will be all right.'

'You remember my husband, Thomas?' asked Jess.

She nodded her agreement. Graham and Sophia had an amicable little interlude, apparently oblivious of the others, then Sophia said, 'I hope I did not interrupt anything.'

'No' was the general agreement.

Thomas saw his grandfather wandering out of the arts pavilion and went to get him. He returned and John sat next to Jess. John was a big man, well-built and well presented. Graham was impressed with his aura despite his advanced years. John did not say much. Then Jackson and Edith saw their daughter at the table and headed over to join them.

Chapter Eleven

Jackson sat at one end and noticing that there were no drinks on the table, asked if he could supply any rounds, his shout. There were a few takers, and Thomas, Sophia, Ophelia and Graham agreed. Jackson wandered off to the bar.

On his return with a tray loaded with drinks, he sat down and all sipped who had one. Graham was suddenly struck with the weirdest sensation. What was he doing here in this incongruous gathering with this esoteric assortment of characters? He surmised that no one else there apparently had a clue who Jessie Summers really was, though he deduced Thomas and probably John did. He felt so out of place with this world-famous author, the wonderfully talented Sophia, the world-travelling Olympic equestrian, the well-known Jacksons and the apparently equally well-known Summers clan. Yet, if they only knew what he knew about some of them …

There was a noticeable lull in the conversation; it was decidedly stilted as no one seemed to be able to engage in a meaningful dialogue. In the awkward silence, invaded only by the slowly increasing numbers of chattering patrons entering the beer garden to socialise, Ophelia proffered, 'It seems we are all rurally oriented to some degree. What is your connection to the world of horses, Jess?'

Graham and Sophia thought they detected a slight degree of belittlement in that somewhat pointed reference.

Sophia promptly inserted, 'Oh, Mrs Summers lives on an extensive property owned by the Summers family.'

Graham hurriedly added, 'Yes, she has an extensive

background. I say, Soph, that Starlight is a remarkable animal,' trying to steer the conversation away from Jess.

'Yes, he is indeed a most courageous competitor,' she answered tentatively.

In the silence that followed, with all looking slightly awkward, Jess proffered, 'He is indeed a wonderful animal, more wonderful than I think you may realise.'

'What do you mean?' asked an intrigued Sophia. All faces turning to peer at the stern countenance of the serious Jessie.

'I think that animal is right-handed. You may have trained him differently. You see, you can usually pick which is the horse's preferred side by observation. You can tell by the way they stand, the way they lead off and the configuration of their leg muscles, also from the way he jumps, the preferred leading front leg, the method of landing and the tilt of the head. If you observe horses in the paddock, they tend to stand head-to-tail on their left side, a prey–species survival ploy. It may be one reason that we mount them from the left.'

She looked at Graham and said, 'I learned all this from Norm and Peter.'

She knew that only Graham, and maybe Thomas and John, would have a clue what she meant. Then she continued.

'Most horses seem to prefer the left by nature, though that is not always the case. Also, you can quickly pick up which way they trot and plunge in a circular yard as to their preferred side. A well-balanced horse that can work in both directions carries himself – and his rider – better. The result is smoother turns, balanced circles, more effortless and graceful lateral movements, more even stride length in both directions, more rhythmic canter and transitions, and better flying lead changes. Starlight appears to be decidedly right-sided. But then you would know all this, I guess,' she said pointedly.

She was not sure how much of this information was new and to whom. Silence reigned supreme. Graham smiled inwardly. He touched Sophie lovingly on her arm, out of sight.

Jess was used to snide remarks being aimed in her direction. She had detected early on in her life that women seemed to dislike her. She much preferred the company of men. Normally, she would ignore barbs, real or imagined, and take solace in her inner strength and the sure knowledge of her own worth, plus her achievements. She was touched by the offering proffered by the delightful and petite Sophia. She looked at Graham.

The next short while passed in mild pleasantries of no real note. Then Graham suggested he might make tracks back to Captains Flat. That seemed to be a catalyst for a general breaking up of the amazing, though brief, interlude in Graham's more humdrum existence. He wandered around to the other side of the table and put his hand on Jessie's shoulder and said that he would like to get her the items as soon as possible. He suggested tomorrow being a Sunday might suit, to which Jess agreed immediately as Sunday would be very suitable. He suggested that he could meet her at ten o'clock at the information bureau at the park in town. She agreed. The others all watched in mild bewilderment. He bade a sincere heartfelt farewell to the Faulkners and Sophia in particular, then acknowledged the Summers.

Graham drove home in a state of mild euphoria at the unexpected turn of events at the normally sedate and uneventful little Cooma Show. He was rather looking forward to renewing his acquaintances with the delightful Jessie Summers.

With the family except for the two boys now domiciled in Queanbeyan, the next morning allowed Graham to have some business that would require his absence. He gathered up the box of items the late Tony had given him plus another little box that contained the original novels and her diary. He left early to be there in plenty of time. He waited on a park bench near the information office at the end of the park.

Just before ten o'clock, he saw Jess walking towards the building. She greeted him sedately. He asked her to follow him to his vehicle around the back of the park under the trees. This she did. He opened the passenger-side door and revealed two boxes on the seat.

Then he said, 'Jessie, I brought these two boxes as one contains the novels and your diary from Tony, just in case. I have read them all. There are no notes in any of them. I hope you don't mind, but I would like to keep them.'

She looked at him, saying coolly, 'No, that's fine.'

She was again conscious that everybody had access to her innermost thoughts through her ancient diary. It shamed her so to know this was always the case for those who knew her and had read her thoughts as a child.

She rummaged through the papers and retrieved the small, tan, dog-eared book that was about the size of a thick notebook. She quickly began to thumb through it, becoming unconscious of her company. She paused here and there to read but was searching for the notes on the night in question. It was near the end. She became totally engrossed. He watched her in fascinated silence. He was unaware of her proficiency in French.

Finally, she closed the small tome and glanced at him with a countenance reflecting mild contentment. She would delve into its depths at her leisure. She thanked him most profusely. He accompanied her to her vehicle, carrying the small box for her. He gave her one last overly exaggerated stare, then bade her farewell. He did note that she drove a rather large vehicle for such a modest woman, reflecting her outback persona. He normally would not note such things, but it was very similar to the vehicle that Sophia drove.

CHAPTER TWELVE

Graham's days slowly settled back into more mundane activities associated with running the farm. He always considered living this form of life would entail mostly a commonplace routine with little excitement. He regarded Cobar as rather a bizarre and bewildering adjunct to his otherwise ordinary life.

The twin excitements of the Faulkners and now the incredible collision of his existence with the exotic Jessie MacIntyre were, he surmised, aberrations that could not possibly be duplicated. He secretly hoped for that to be the case. He was more than happy to lead a very ordinary life. He had somehow regained the tenure of the family that he had reluctantly written off as a lost cause. He had restored to his long-suffering and exceedingly supportive parents a modicum of happiness that went some way to alleviating their suffering and loss associated with his traumatic separation from his children. They had even moved down to be near him and his new family.

His elderly strange neighbour that he knew as Tony had died within a few weeks of revealing to him his incredible story. That had delayed his efforts to contact Jessie but had activated a flurry of renewed investigations into old criminal cases wherever the Morangills were thought to be remotely involved.

This had resulted in two facets. One involved the MacIntyre case, the other one concerned, disturbingly, the redoubtable John Wesley Summers through the agency of Graham's revelations and Jessie's connection to his family. It set Ian Knuckey deep into old territory and occupied vast amounts of his dwindling ability to carry on with this type of work. He became intrigued as to whether the Summers' fortune had been purloined by a relative showing profound initiative or had been pilfered by criminals. There was a hint that crooked bookmakers and underworld criminals associated with the racing industry might just have had enough of the exceedingly lucky or disreputable punter who was John Summers' father continually fleecing them, legitimately or not. That might now not ever be fully revealed. It was a bitter revelation to the aged John Summers when Jessie finally exposed it to him.

Graham had a couple of complications associated with Tony's death to attend to for his departed friend. He travelled into Canberra and found the French embassy located in the legation area of the capital. Here he attended to the twin concerns of Tony's demise and the issue of the continuing forwarding to him of Micheline's family remittance from Europe. They were very grateful for the information.

The only other unresolved issue arising in his new existence was the Planter case and, in tandem, the now suspicious death of his Uncle Tom that had left Alice alone for so long. The old man, Jacob Cranchovic, had suffered a stroke and was taken to the Queanbeyan hospital not long after the revelations came to light. This event may have had the result of depriving the police and Graham of being able to definitively ascertain the truth about the child's disappearance. It all depended on the severity of the stroke. The suspicions remained but no proof. At least the Planters were finally assuaged.

The other potential concern arising in the near future was the possibly imminent removal from Graham's world of his most fondly thought-of neighbour out on the property along the Shoalhaven River. John Wheatley had aged in the years that Graham had known him, and his departure was looking decidedly more certain. Graham had momentarily considered, for the briefest of moments, buying his neighbour out. The place had excellent pasture, was well developed and maintained and, above all, possessed a rather pleasant homestead, something Graham had up to date avoided investing in on his own property. There would be a considerable saving there to put towards the purchase price if he did rethink the idea. This was highly unlikely, however. He quickly realised that the debt involved would probably be too great for him to service with all his other financial commitments now about him.

Chapter Twelve

In his declining years, John Wheatley had become most friendly with the Longleys, especially Richard and lately Graham's two boys, whom Graham sent over to assist and work for free with John at every opportunity. Sam and Ben learnt all the tricks of the trade from John's vast experience and knowledge. They would in time surpass considerably Graham's own level of knowledge and abilities. The Longleys also spent some time out at Cobar. Here again, Graham's boys became far more advanced than Graham at outback skills and abilities. They would often go out there for longer school holidays to assist and to learn.

Sally was the odd one out. Graham felt there was an air of mild antipathy towards him, she never really forgiving him for deserting them and ceasing financial support for them from the start. Living lately with saner adults had slowly begun to unwind this sense of abandonment within her as she was exposed to a pair of willing exponents expressing their one-sided and prejudiced opinion of the whole sordid affair. As Sally's relationship grew and developed more deeply into the more normal rapport associated with that of grandparent and child, her admiration and love for them grew accordingly. Graham tried to fight any obvious prejudicial opinions he became aware of but realised he was not in a position to defend everything about his departed wife.

Sally was aware of Graham's opinions of the law and understood this fact. She did realise, however, that he was particularly friendly with Peter Knuckey, something she found bewildering. As her understanding of the facts about his case developed, hastened along by her grandparent's version, realistic or embellished, she began to be attracted to that field of the law. She had raised the issue of her tertiary studies several times with Graham, but he was very cool about her studying law. He tried to direct her to other fields, such as veterinary science or engineering, but she made it clear that she had no affinity with animals and engineering appeared to her to be rather a masculine area.

The issue came to a head one Sunday when all the family gathered at his parent's place in Queanbeyan for lunch, while they were all still available to do such things. Sally and Graham sat on the veranda in the warm afternoon sun with Richard. Sally raised the issue again. Graham could see that she was serious about this topic. He sat in silence, thinking.

Then he said, 'Sally, I would never stand in your way to do anything you wish to do. If you really would like to try in that field, I will encourage you all the way.'

She just smiled and looked at Richard. They had obviously discussed this issue at length.

Then Graham said to her, 'Sal, I have been thinking about this since you first raised it. As you know, I am very good mates with Peter Knuckey. If you really want to think about this seriously, I may be able to take you up to talk to him. You probably know,' he continued, peering at Richard, 'that he and his firm tend to deal especially in that aspect of the law. What do you think?'

She sat in silence, then said, 'I'll think about it, Dad.'

Sally was encouraged by her father's comments and

gave that suggestion much thought. She was unsure about the circumstances surrounding a large legal office and the interpersonal relationships such a new concept would entail for herself. She was inclined to accept his offer to attend such a place on the ground floor, so to speak, before she became too committed and then found that she did not like the set-up, or the course for that matter. She hinted that she may be interested. What did he have in mind?

Graham rang his friend, Peter Knuckey, in Sydney and broached the topic. Peter was more than happy to accommodate his friend after all they had endured together. He offered to receive them at his office in the city if that was acceptable. It was all finally arranged.

Graham and Sally caught the bus that operated between Canberra, the Sydney airport and Central Railway Station, and arrived in the city mid-morning. They had an eleven-thirty appointment. Peter ushered them in shortly after their arrival. Sally had never met Peter before, but she knew a little about him from both Graham and her grandparents, both of whom spoke highly of him, his firm and his work for them in the past. She knew nothing of his later involvement in the MacIntyre case.

They were in there for thirty minutes. Sally was unsure exactly what to ask but tried to get a feeling for the atmosphere of the place, the sort of work the firm did and Peter's part in it. Sally ensured that Peter understood that the traumas associated with her father's affairs were the guiding factors that had inspired her to think about pursuing this kind of life, and that his involvement had also been an influence. He was mildly touched. They departed shortly after and returned home by bus with a lot of information for Sally to contemplate.

Sally completed her high school year twelve and achieved exceptional results. There was no doubt she was a talented student, almost topping her year. She enrolled into Law at the University of Sydney and moved into student accommodation in a nearby suburb.

The next interaction with Peter was a little more serious. Graham had asked if, towards the end of the first year at the course, she could again speak to him to ascertain her direction and any specialities she should consider. He agreed again readily.

They arrived this time about mid-morning and were again ushered into Peter's office. They had a brief chat about general matters, then Peter said, 'I have arranged for you to meet the main partner and founder of the firm.'

Graham was a little surprised at this turn of events. He was more than impressed at the attention his daughter was receiving. Peter led the two of them to the large office at the end of the floor where he had first met the manager of the practice years ago now. He remembered her well. They were ushered in, and Peter bade a polite farewell and left them.

Dr Leslie Charmers sat in her large leather chair and watched as her former client and his daughter sat in the chairs opposite her. She was silent for a moment, then began.

'Good morning, Mr Longley, Ms Longley.'

Graham nodded in polite acknowledgement. Sally just smiled a muffled hello. After some preliminary comments and enquiries about the course and her progress through it, she said, 'Ms Longley, after you expressed your interest in this field to our practice, I have been following your advancement through the course to date. I still have some contacts at the Law School and you have been progressing very well. Are you still interested in this form of legal practice?'

'Yes, I think so. I have not found anything else to attract me away from it.'

'Ms Longley, you show considerable promise.'

'Thank you, Dr Charmers. I try to achieve the best I can do.'

'Ms Longley, we do not normally offer cadetships at this firm quite so early in a student's progress through the course. But we have been observing you and have some favourable reports about your application to your studies. If you still consider this form of work as your desired choice, I am prepared to offer you a formal preliminary cadetship here. It would entail some attendance at this office where you would receive experience in law work and even some attendance at court. An early introduction to the sort of things we do here. Are you interested?'

Sally looked at Graham. He was speechless. She turned back to Leslie.

'I think that would be very kind of you and most acceptable for me to be gaining an early insight into this field. I think I would be very interested. Thank you.'

'You would also receive a small remuneration for your time here and be able to contribute to the cases as required.'

'You're very kind to do this, Doctor,' said an overwhelmed Graham.

'It's not a favour, Graham. We surmise Sally here has great potential. She seems to know what she wants in this area. That is uncommon in young students, often besotted with a false view of the glamour they think arises in this line of work. Your daughter's life experience for one so young is also in her favour.'

'Well, it is very kind of you to offer this to her,' he said.

'We have had some dealings with your family now, Graham. Always the interactions have been most cordial, despite any ructions that resulted from proceedings. I surmise Sally here will fit in admirably. If this all seems satisfactory, I will get Peter to organise it for you.'

'Thank you very much,' was all an overwhelmed Graham could say.

Sally likewise thanked Dr Charmers sedately.

Graham was slightly embarrassed at the rather generous turn of events. He was very pleased for Sally to be given this unexpected benevolence. He was thinking about the twisted trail of circumstances that had led to this opportunity for his deserving daughter.

Over the next few years, as Sally graduated through the law system and her studies, she gleaned a better insight into her father's case and circumstances. She did not pry, but issues arose between her and Peter that shed light on her father's messy, though rather typical for the times, case that went some way to lessen her sense of abandonment and dispossession on her father's part.

It rather alarmed her, the little that she learnt from both Peter and Dr Charmers about how Graham's original case had panned out and the ignominy imposed on Graham by an uncaring system, at that time more predicated on agenda outcomes. The restoration of his children and the way he had gone about it when they turned up at his property in Captains Flat gave way to a sense that he had a real desire to regain his lost children and was prepared to fight for them this time. They stressed that they, at Graham's bidding, caused a considerable stir in legal circles over the whole sordid affair. It had gone some way towards a softening of legal rulings and a more conciliatory approach to family matters, especially if the desires of the proponent's motives were other than incompatibility, as was the case in Graham's issue. It was simply just a matter of 'I want it' on Jenny's part.

She became more than just a colleague of the Knuckeys, visiting him and his family at their Inner West apartment often. Graham became more involved with the Knuckey family as well, as he visited his studious daughter in Sydney as often as he could.

Ian Knuckey sometimes stayed with his nephew in Sydney on the rare occasions that his wife Beryl needed to spend time in the hospital there, or he desired some interactions with Jessie Summers. It was on one of these occasions that Sally managed to meet him at Peter's. Ian Knuckey told her nothing of her father's contributions towards any of the instances when he had shed light on matters, only insinuating that Graham was a most advantageous friend and acquaintance, providing much valuable information. Sally was again confused as to the extent of her father's exchanges with these people.

It was through Sally's association with Peter that she crossed paths with the famous Jessie Summers. Jessie often stayed in Sydney at her Rushcutters Bay apartment with Thomas. Ian Knuckey was staying with Peter to contact Jessie over continuing matters related to the MacIntyre saga. Peter and Sally were in court together when Ian asked him to meet up nearby at lunch time. He agreed. Ian had been talking at length to Jessie in town and they also agreed to meet.

Ian had arranged a corner table in a well-known restaurant convenient to all. Sally was still quite shy and reticent. She knew Ian was highly thought of by Peter and to some extent by her father, Graham, though she had no idea why this was so. She always listened intently to any conversations she was privy to as she was always mindful of learning more. She was surprised to see a stranger there with the aging Ian, a rather elegant and superior sort of woman. She appeared to Sally to be out of place there.

Jessie was normally quite at ease with the Knuckeys. She was, however, suspicious of strangers, though slightly less so if they were associated with the Knuckeys. She was anxious and concerned at the revelation of the name Longley. Jess gave her new introduction a glaring and penetrating stare that uneased poor Sally, she not being used to quite such a piercing and withering countenance. Ian realised that this was unsettling for both of them, but tried to ease her concern by intimating that Sally was a most reliable and trustworthy associate. He pointed out to Jessie that Sally knew nothing of any matters pertaining to herself. That comment rather bewildered Sally but seemed to ease the tension slightly for Jessie.

It took some time for Jessie to be in any manner of ease with the young and reticent Sally. There was limited conversation, except between Peter and Ian, and the room was mildly noisy for Jess.

Finally, she asked, 'And how's your father going, Sally?'

Sally was staggered that that would be asked by this person of all people.

'He's fine at the moment,' she responded, rather confused and looking at Jessie through knitted brows. 'How do you come to know him?'

'Let's just say our paths have crossed with some considerable advantage to myself, and, may I say, to the Knuckeys as well,' said a mysterious Jessie.

On learning of these encounters, Graham was delighted that his once deprived daughter was now moving in such exalted circles. He hoped some of this adventure was going some way to compensate her for his neglectful approach to her parents separating. After Sally's enquiring how he knew Jessie Summers, Graham simply dismissed her probing by insinuating she was another weird encounter that he was unable to define as normal. Sally was totally bewildered yet again about her enigmatic father.

CHAPTER THIRTEEN

It appeared that life was not quite yet finished with Graham and his interactions with Jessie Summers.

Graham was working alone out at his farming property on a quiet Sunday afternoon. The boys had returned early to their grandparent's place in Queanbeyan as they both had sporting commitments that weekend. Graham had driven out to the farm early Sunday morning as he had the whole day free to work in the sheep yards and pens adjacent to the shed.

He had parked his ute around the back of the shed as it carried much gear and tools that he needed access to close at hand, so it was not visible from the road. About midday, he noticed a large white vehicle pull up in the expansive gravel area that abounded outside his entrance grid, an area large enough for semis and sheep trucks to manoeuvre. It was a well-used area that many travellers used for checking on any aspect of vehicular problems.

Towards the far south-eastern end, the gravel melded into the more familiar roadside verges of tangled weedy scrub and long grasses. Here it plunged away from the edge of the road and into the boundary fence with a dip that terminated the suitable gravel parking area and commenced the roadside vegetation. He wondered why anyone would attempt to park in this more difficult and out-of-the-way spot, unless they were up to no good, as this position would render the vehicle slightly less visible to any passing traffic.

Graham always carried a good pair of binoculars in his ute, so he retrieved it from the toolbox in the rear of the tray. He was a little surprised to see that the vehicle was a large, familiar-looking white Land Rover Discovery, similar to the one in which he had seen Jessie Summers drive to Cooma to meet him when he returned to her the papers that Tony had. Graham would not normally particularly take note of people's cars except that the two exotic women he had encountered both drove these striking vehicles.

Ordinarily, Jessie's would not have registered with him except for a couple of factors. For one thing, Jessie had a bull bar on her Rover, not a common accessory on this particular vehicle. Secondly, she had two large aerials, one at each corner of the bull bar. She apparently used the community-based radio channels that the truckies used when she travelled about, listening in mostly on road conditions and any hold-ups. Thirdly, Jess also had a roof rack on her car, not that common on these vehicles. Hers, however, was a wire basket arrangement of only moderate size and contained a spare tyre chained to the affair – quite distinct. Graham initially wondered, if this were her car, whether she was paying him a visit, though he then realised that she really did not know this address.

He watched for some minutes through the binoculars and finally saw a scene that horrified him. A man got out of the driver's side and moved around to the passenger's side. He opened the door and manhandled the passenger, whom Graham could not identify at this distance, rather roughly and pushed that person with indelicate actions. Graham was suspicious. He watched as the man trundled the captive unceremoniously and roughly into the opened rear doors and pulled out the cargo cover attached to the rear of the seating area. Then he slammed the two doors closed. He determined that it could possibly be Jessie as the person was short and slim; he noticed her blonde hair even at this distance. It was perhaps a female. He decided to investigate.

Graham gathered up the three dogs he had with him and ordered them to climb into the tray of the ute. He retrieved the semi-automatic .22 rifle he had with him, plus his smallish, sheathed hunting knife. If this were indeed Jessie, he knew enough about her to realise that she still feared for her life and could expect retribution at any moment. Also, if this were her car, why was she not driving it?

He started up the truck and headed slowly out towards the front grid. At the grid, Graham turned deliberately left onto

Chapter Thirteen

the large, gravelled area and manoeuvred slowly up to the other car and parked closely behind it, more or less blocking it in. The man approached and asked what he wanted. He was a big man, solid, well-built and of a particularly sour demeanour. He looked vicious. He was wearing a set of clothing, hinting at hunting or rural work, though well presented.

Graham hesitated for some time, watching him carefully. Finally, he got out of the truck and stood by the door.

'You okay?' asked Graham.

'Yes, thank you,' replied the other man rather gruffly.

'Who's that with you?' asked Graham.

'There's no one else here,' he replied.

Graham reached in and retrieved the rifle. Then he took a couple of steps back towards the tray and looked in at the dogs and said, 'You boys ready?' The dogs were usually docile and timid, except for Rusty. He had a temper and could show veiled traits of deep dingo breeding if he were crossed by recalcitrant sheep. Could be very handy right now.

Graham's heart was beating furiously and he felt a little queasy. He turned towards the man and began to walk towards him, exposing the rifle for the first time.

The other man was suddenly all alertness. He began also to move towards Graham. Graham yelled out at him to stand still. He refused. He was reaching inside his work coat. Graham summoned the dogs.

He yelled out, 'Okay, boys, Rusty, Toby, Clair, here. Get out!'

The three dogs leapt out of the tray with such enthusiasm

and vigour that they startled the other man. Graham again yelled at them, 'Walk up!'

The dogs were momentarily confused. There were no sheep in sight. They stared at the man and then at Graham.

He again yelled, 'Walk up!'

They headed towards the man.

Then he yelled, 'Rusty, away to me!'

Rusty immediately departed the other two and circled away to the right of the now nervous man. Rusty now began to growl. The man, surprisingly, appeared to be petrified at the unfolding scene. He began to retreat, an excellent manoeuvre as far as Graham was concerned, as that indicated to the dogs that action was afoot. They scurried towards him, now very animated as this was a new experience, gathering in and rounding up humans never before seen by them.

Then Graham yelled, 'Get back!'

The dogs stopped in their tracks, eyeing their quarry with steely determined glares.

The man stumbled and tripped in his now induced panic and began to scream for help.

Graham yelled out again, 'Get back! Stay!'

The three dogs stood rigidly still, eyeing the man as they would a recalcitrant sheep, Rusty desperately wishing to advance.

Graham wandered over to the now prostrate man attempting to shield himself from the non-existent dog attack. He was on his side, both arms loose about his head in case.

Graham stared at him. Then he said, 'Have you got a gun?'

'No,' said the man.

'I don't believe you,' said Graham. 'Remove your coat.'

The other man began to remove his coat, still staring wide-eyed at the dogs stealthily creeping forward.

'Lie down, face on the ground,' demanded Graham.

The man did so. He revealed his under-arm holster with a weapon. Graham indicated that he was to gently remove it and toss it to the side. This he did. Graham kicked the gun further away and then patted each of the dogs in turn and whispered comfortingly at them. He gave Rusty a particularly generous handling.

Then he commanded, 'Hold!'

They set themselves to guard their prey. Then he sauntered over to the passenger's side of the Rover, all the time keeping his eyes on the prostrate man. He opened the door. He had hoped that there was no one in there. Then he walked back to the rear doors, still glaring intently at the prostrate man. When the man denied there was anyone with him, that was the second clue that something might be amiss. There'd better be someone in the rear here or he was in real trouble. He lifted the outer door, then dropped the lower. Then he tugged back on the cargo cover and it sprang forward to its closed position. There in front of him on the messy floor was a bedraggled and drowsy-looking Jessie Summers. Her arms were tethered at the wrists and doubly secured about her ankles. She was going nowhere. She appeared for all the world as one who had been mistreated. It reminded him momentarily of Sophia Faulkner.

He asked her, 'You all right?'

She did not answer. She was a little drowsy. He cut the wrist ropes with his hunting knife that he had grabbed from the trunk and then the ankle ropes. He helped her gingerly to sit up and wriggle forward to get out of the back. All the time, he kept glancing back at the nervous prostrate figure on the ground still eyeing off the glaring dogs.

He asked again. 'Are you all right?'

She nodded slightly and cupped her face in trembling hands covered with grime and dust.

'What's going on?' he asked.

She could not reply. He began to assist her to alight the car. She was unsteady and shaking slightly. She stood momentarily holding his hand and steadying herself against him. She was becoming weepy.

'Who's this bloke?' asked Graham.

Jessie steadied herself some more, then finally replied in a soft and trembling voice, 'He was going to kill me, Graham. What are you doing here, anyway?'

'This is my place here, Jess. But why on earth would he stop here, of all places?'

'He is waiting for the others. Three more men coming behind in a stolen Mercedes. They can't be far behind.'

'Well, let's get you out of here.'

'No.' she said. 'They won't be expecting me to be free. I'd like to catch them here now and find out more from them.'

'Let me call the police. There is a station in Captains Flat. They can be here in half an hour.'

Chapter Thirteen

'No. I don't want to involve the police,' she said, gaining in strength as she contemplated things, becoming a little steadier.

'No. We can't handle these kinds of crooks on our own. I'll call them now. Besides, they'll be armed like this one is.'

'Where's his gun?' she asked. 'And can we tie this guy up with something?'

'I have a dog chain in the tray.'

'That'll do nicely. Get it for me.'

Graham left her. She began to walk over to the man. Graham grabbed the chain and returned to Jess. She picked up the discarded weapon and checked it for its usability.

'Who sent you?' she demanded.

He was silent. She kicked him viciously.

'Who sent you?' she demanded again.

He was writhing in surprised pain at the stabbing boot. She stamped hard down on his exposed hand, severely damaging his bones.

'I won't ask you again,' she said. 'Who sent you?'

He peered up at her defiantly. She stamped again on his injured hand. He grimaced in pain and let out a muffled yelp. She then grabbed his free arm and wrenched it back behind him and pressed down on it, twisting it severely and demanding again, 'Who sent you!'

'All right, all right, I'll tell you what I know.'

He told her what he knew, but it was not much more than he had already bragged to her in the car about who organised this, who knew where she lived and who knew that she would be alone on a Sunday while all the other family members were at Bridgehead.

He was in some discomfort. Graham gave her the chain and she secured it about him in an uncomfortable condition and frog-marched him over to the Rover. She shoved him into the rear compartment and slammed the two doors. The other three men would be close to here by now. She suggested that they hide behind the front of the Rover and accost them with the rifle and his handgun and maybe those wonderful dogs. Graham was not at all convinced that this was the right course to pursue. He again argued for the police to be informed before it was too late. She did not wish it. Finally, he said to her that that was not the right thing to do, and he would ring the police. This he did on his dodgy mobile but it did work out here, surprisingly. They would be here as quickly as possible, and in at least two vehicles.

Jess was not happy at involving the police and revealing herself to strangers, especially the police. The second car arrived about ten minutes later. Graham had secured the dogs back into the tray of the ute, there to await further orders. Their eagerness was greatly aroused. Jessie had given them a thorough patting in appreciation of their efforts and to ensure they realised she was a good guy.

The second vehicle contained three men. They were a little surprised to see the Rover out of the way and no sign of their man. And what was this other vehicle doing here? The three of them got out of the car and headed for the Rover. Jess had purloined Graham's rifle and she and Graham were hiding behind the Land Cruiser.

Suddenly there was pandemonium. Jess revealed herself from behind the tray, as did Graham, and the three dogs were sent hurtling out of the tray to assault the three new arrivals as before. Amid much shouting, barking and various other noises, including a rifle shot or two, the three men ended up on the ground face down and being exceedingly roughly handled by Jess. Graham was surprised at her total lack of restraint and her readiness to employ what he thought of as excessive violence.

Jess tried to interrogate the new arrivals, but they were not a lot of use to her beyond what she had been told by her lone assailant on their trip to this point so far. Graham was very keen for the police to arrive, the sooner the better, as he feared Jess might deal out her own justice. He realised that, from her background, she was more than capable and prepared to mete out her own idea of retribution.

While awaiting the arrival of the police, Jess had rung Thomas on Graham's mobile at Bridgehead and informed him that there had been an incident.

'What's happened?' asked a nervous Thomas.

'It's all all right now, Thomas. It's a bit complicated. I may be late home.'

'Where are you?' he asked.

'I'm out in the——'

Graham grabbed the phone from Jess before she could complete her words and said in a surprisingly authoritative voice, 'Thomas, it's Graham Longley here. We met at the

Cooma Show some time back, you may remember. Look, there's been a serious incident involving Jessie … No, incident, not accident. She really has no idea of the seriousness of this situation … Yes she's fine, now, but Thomas, she is going to be tied up here for some time … We're near Captains Flat, Thomas, but listen, mate, she's in no fit state to be driving anywhere. Can you arrange for a couple of blokes to come up and attend to her and retrieve her car? I live in Captains Flat, mate, right opposite the hotel. Just wait outside that and we'll contact you. I think she will be tied up for some time at the cop shop … No, there's one in Captains Flat. Just wait at the pub and we'll find you … No, all is now fine. Just a lot of tidying up to do. She can explain it all later … Captains Flat is near Queanbeyan … Yes, up the highway or directly via Numeralla, though that's a bit rough. Just wait outside the pub.'

Graham closed the call and stared at Jess. She was coolly staring at him. Jessie Summers was not used to not being in control of her situation. But deep down she knew he was right. He had saved her life and rescued her somehow. She was shaking still.

The police arrived shortly after in two vehicles and with flashing lights. They quickly took control of the situation and began to interrogate people. The four perpetrators were gathered in and placed into the paddy wagon.

Jess did not want any police driving her car, so Graham arranged for one of the young constables to drive his Toyota back to the station with the three dogs on board and he would drive Jessie's car himself. He would not allow her to drive in her present state.

They were sometime at the police station. Jessie was not a cooperative subject. Assisting them with their enquiries was not how they would have described it. Finally, Graham had to reveal more to them than she wished, but the story so far was forthcoming enough for investigations to begin. She wished for her contacts in the various integrity commissions to be alerted.

It was nearing dark when they finally departed the police station. Graham drove the patient dogs in his ute back to his house and Jessie followed him for the short distance there driving her own Rover. He pulled into his driveway and Jess followed him. Thomas, in his old Falcon ute, moved over to the house when he finally saw Jessie's car arrive there.

Jessie was very keen to be under way and return home. Graham looked at her and Thomas and at Damien whom he brought up with him to return both vehicles without Jess having to drive one of them. Graham had suggested that that would not be a good idea as they must have at least a two-hour drive back to Cooma. Thomas agreed. Graham said that they should have a cup of tea or something as Jess would have had nothing all day and was still showing signs of distress. It was agreed, reluctantly.

They sat in Graham's small and cluttered little kitchen, mostly in silence, initially. Thomas and Damien finally learnt more of the gruesome details and the trauma to which Jess had been subjected. Graham then suggested that they all go over to the hotel opposite and have dinner, then they could all stay the night at his place. Jess was horrified.

Jess knew that Graham had access to her diaries and much newspaper reporting, plus whatever Antoine had revealed, so she was reluctant to be in his presence, despite his potentially life-saving actions. She realised, however, that she had been affected severely by this event, way beyond anything she had previously experienced, even Thomas being shot at the Cooma saleyards. This current episode had been of the longest duration and her fate had been clearly laid out for her by the obliging and immodest assailant. He was so confident in its finality that he had detailed her demise and the thorough planning that had gone into it by certain parties. He did not name them directly but hinted regularly at their conspiratorial brilliance and knowledge about her private life that indicated to her that she would possibly never now be secure or safe in her domestic arrangements.

Jess was deep in black thoughts about the culprits. She was seriously contemplating how she could eliminate them herself. She was thinking maybe she should depart her present life, including Thomas, and abscond away somewhere safe and alone. When Graham finally suggested they stay the night at his cottage, she began to see the merit in this idea, however much she detested forced socialising. It might go some way towards easing her turbulent mind.

Thomas rang Warren Costello, the biological technician, who lived at their other property, 'Auvergne', and advised him that there had been a development and they would not be returning until about midday tomorrow. During the evening, Jess, who sat mostly quietly listening to the others, began to unwind her fevered thinking and learnt a lot more about the man who had undoubtedly saved her life this time. She was conscious of the weird circumstances surrounding this event and how strange it was that their paths should cross in this fashion. His connection to Ian Knuckey, through his own bitter experience, which she discovered had cut him deeply, the improbable relationship with the now departed Antoine, whom she had not seen in decades, the uncanny way they had met at the Cooma Show – she was contemplating that she could never come up with a plot this unlikely in one of her novels.

Graham had a rather pleasant evening with his imposed acquaintances. He was always very enamoured of the rarely encountered and erstwhile most mysterious Jessie MacIntyre, the veil of esoteric and impenetrable anonymity and vague exotic existence that normally would not penetrate his sedate little routine life. She was suddenly there and in a most uncharacteristic vulnerability. She was suddenly more human.

Thomas was a pleasant and charming young man, exhibiting unbounded love for his threatened and distressed wife. Graham was touched by the depth of his caring. His mind wandered momentarily to his departed Jenny. He still, after all this time, fondly recalled his early times with her. Damien was an unusual character: verbose, enigmatic and espousing with non-stop chattering on all and every topic. He was obviously well-versed on many issues. He and Jessie seemed to be most amiable with each other. Graham found himself bathing in the surreal atmosphere in the incongruous drab little kitchen and contemplated his departed aunt.

CHAPTER FOURTEEN

The evening passed in some bewilderment for Graham, mixing as it were with such distinguished sheep people and other exalted company. He was still mindful of his own perceived inadequacies in this domain. Thomas kept enquiring of Jess if she were all right. Jessie appeared to Graham to be exceedingly preoccupied. He put that down to her traumatic incident. He was not yet fully cognisant of her normally reserved and detached nature. He did wonder if she had been drugged in any way. She denied that, but he was not entirely convinced.

She seemed to rouse more noticeably when they all departed the cottage for the magnificent hotel almost opposite. She was still very quiet, but her calmness seemed to be returning.

It was much later in the evening, however, that matters

began to emerge that would lead to developments that would impact on Graham considerably. Jess did not talk much, but, when they were back at the house, in a quiet break in the diminishing amount of conversation, Jess was emboldened to pose a question.

'May I ask, Graham, why you live in Captains Flat and not out at the farm?'

Graham divulged that he surmised his accommodating aunt, who was herself childless, had bequeathed to him this estate out of compassion for his own family disintegration, a circumstance he was at pains to emphasise had cut him most deeply. He had intimated to Jessie just how much contempt he held the judicial system. This was something with which Jessie could totally concur and empathise. Graham did not seem to detest the police force with quite the same degree of animosity, not a stance Jess could harmonise with. He hinted at the now suspicious demise of his long-dead uncle and the foiling of their plans to build out at the property. He pointed out the subdivision history of his place and why he had the shearing shed. He had not entirely forsaken the thought of one day completing his aunt's wish to live out there.

'But don't you find it awfully inconvenient with all the travel?'

'No, not really. It is all I have known. It suits me fine at the moment. I won't say I haven't given it some thought, though.'

Jess was most intrigued. She had noticed the for-sale sign on the adjoining property that was once the original homestead. Graham seemed at ease with the questioning, so

Jess ventured another one on a topic she would normally not venture into.

'How do you come to know the Faulkners so well?'

There was a slight pause from Graham. Then he replied, 'It's a long, complicated story. Suffice it to say, I have had several dealings with them over the last few years in most peculiar circumstances. They are lovely people.' He deliberately refrained from even mentioning the existence of Cobar. 'Why do you ask?'

'Oh, I was just wondering how come they seemed to be so familiar with you, considering the disparity in your locations and level of activity. I thought there might have been a family connection or something, that's all.'

'Jackson has been kind enough to accommodate some of my enquiries regarding rams and I have obtained a few from him.'

Thomas now became more interested, as he had had dealings with the Faulkners in relation to their acquisition of some of Thomas's prime rams too. At that hint, which surprised Graham, he asked, 'I thought the Faulkners were breeding top quality sheep themselves. Why would they need others?'

Jess looked at Thomas. Thomas began to explain the Auvergne enterprise in some detail to Graham. Graham was suddenly very interested in all he was hearing. He began to ask more penetrating questions. He thought that the Faulkner's enterprise was a level above his own in complexity and achievements, but suddenly Thomas was espousing a whole new level of attainment and intricacy.

At the hint of genuine and knowledgeable queries, Thomas

said, 'Graham, if you are truly interested, I would be only too delighted to show you about the breeding facilities and get Warren to explain it all to you if you wished.'

He looked at Jess. She did not indicate any objections.

Graham was genuinely intrigued. He was indeed most interested in furthering his knowledge about the industry into which he had been thrust by his generous aunt. He thought for a minute.

Then he said, 'Could I bring my father?'

'Yes, of course. If he's interested.'

'He might very well be. He's a bit of a talker. Can talk the legs off a wooden table.'

'That's all right. No problem,' smiled Thomas.

'You are this side of Cooma, aren't you?'

'No, The Summers places are mostly all out past Shannons Flat, but we are quite some distance south of Cooma. I'll give you directions.'

It was now getting late in the evening. Graham offered Jessie and Thomas the main bedroom and Damien could have one of the others.

The Summers wished to leave as early as possible next morning, so when Jess was ready, she reluctantly allowed Thomas to drive her Rover while Damien drove Thomas's ute back to Auvergne. They departed with the advice that they would probably have more interactions about this affair with the authorities. They would decide a suitable date in the near future for Graham to visit them at their place south of Cooma.

Chapter Fourteen

As it turned out, that invitation was, Graham thought, rather speedily forthcoming. He was a little surprised at its prompt arrival, as he had previously found Jessie Summers to be rather reserved and distant when it came to contacts. It was all teed up and Graham asked his father if he wished to accompany him on what he determined could possibly be a slightly arduous day, given the travel involved. Richard leapt at the opportunity to accompany his son on a fact-finding mission, as he had found the rural scene quite to his liking.

Graham had agreed to go out the night before and spend the night at his parent's place so that they could get away very early the next morning. Once past Cooma heading south, it was all new to Graham. They arrived mid-morning to a welcoming Thomas and Jess plus an accommodating and very fascinating Warren Costello. Graham found the whole enterprise of extreme interest. Richard was spellbound by the whole operation and followed every word and action most diligently.

The Summers had prepared a lavish lunch which Graham had not bargained on. It was an unexpected event he somehow had not envisioned. In the early afternoon, Thomas and Richard went back out to the sheds to follow Warren around again. This left Jessie and Graham alone momentarily, which he thought had almost been contrived. They sat alone for some minutes, Jessie notorious for her reticence and reserve.

Graham was about to depart when she said in her soft mellifluous tone, 'Graham, I owe you a lot, probably my life.'

'It's nothing, Jess. Truly. That I may have been of assistance to you is contentment enough. It has been a marvel to me to have had the opportunity to meet with such a significant person.'

She blushed a little. 'Nevertheless, Graham, I feel entirely indebted to you and, of course, so does Thomas. I am still rattled by the whole thing and the miracle of your being there at that strange encounter.' He said nothing. She continued, after a pause, 'Graham, I would like to repay your courageous service to me and my family in some tangible way.'

'That's not necessary at all,' he replied.

'Graham, I have been thinking about this since it happened. I'd like to compensate you for the danger you encountered and the actions you endured in saving me. Would you be offended if I were to offer to buy the place next door to you out along the river there?'

'No, of course not! You'd be wonderful neighbours.'

'No, Graham, not buy it for me. I'd buy it for you.'

'What do you mean?'

'I'd like to buy the place next door to you and give it to you as a token of genuine gratitude.'

'I couldn't accept that!' he almost exclaimed. 'It must be worth close to a million, perhaps much more.'

'Graham, you know a lot about me, more than most of my personal acquaintances. I am a very wealthy woman. I am quite content in my life now. That was almost taken from me the other day. You saved me from that fate. I have no one to leave my fortune to, other than the already well-off Summers. They do not need my money. This small act would be a wonderful way for me to repay your intervention. Besides, this way you will be able to have the house out at the property, as you said you would like, and it will not interfere with your own finances. I have spent most of my life in hiding, removed from people. I don't do much for others, Graham. This would be a rare case of that for me and to a worthy cause.'

'I don't know what to say,' he blurted. 'Could we go halves?'

'No. I'd like to do this for you. I have discussed it with Thomas. He's in full agreement with me. He's just as grateful to you as I am.'

'You know Jess, I did something similar for the Faulkners some years ago now and their generosity to me has been overwhelming. But this is gratitude at another level. I could never recompense you for this sort of kindness. Can I think about it?'

'There's nothing to think about, Graham. I have already reserved the property in the name of Jane Ransom. All they need now is the go-ahead from me and it will be done in your name. I will arrange everything from here. Do you know the Wheatleys?'

'Yes, rather well. For some reason, I'd rather they didn't know that I was buying their place.'

'I'll buy it in my name and then transfer it over later.'

Graham could only scratch his face in embarrassment at the offer.

'I'll contact the agent tomorrow, if you agree.'

'Jess, what can I say? Of course, I'd love to have the place, but I mean …'

'Good. I'll arrange it all tomorrow. What do you mean, you did something similar for the Faulkners?'

'I shouldn't have mentioned that, but Sophia ran into a similar attack years ago and she came to me as a complete outsider for assistance. I was able to whisk her away, that's all.'

'How did you meet?'

'That was another strange turn of fate. Weird. A bit like you and me. Very strange.' He wished to say no more. She left it at that. They both got up from the table and headed out to the sheds.

About two-thirty in the afternoon, just as Graham was contemplating returning on the long trip back home, being mindful of his aging father, a strange vehicle meandered down the long driveway into the homestead. Graham was about to arrange to leave when Jessie announced to him that, if he did not mind, John Summers indicated that he would like to renew acquaintances with the man who saved his granddaughter-in-law and who apparently had some information pertaining to his own father's demise, something he did not know at their first meeting.

Graham remembered John Summers as a big man, old and taciturn, a quiet, inoffensive man who, as he recalled, contributed little to the gathering at the Cooma Show. He did subsequently learn that he was a significant personality in local circles and a very wealthy man. He wondered what he could possibly want with him here now. Graham was also mindful that his own father knew nothing of all these intricacies and machinations. He wanted to keep it that way.

John had been driven out by Damien who, Graham learnt, lived opposite John on another of their properties, growing extensive fields of lucerne for their own places as well as for sale. Graham rather liked Damien. It was also obvious to him that that was also the case with Jessie.

John was now restricted slightly in his movements, so Jess asked if he would mind meeting him down at the car to avoid his having to negotiate the stairs into the sheds. Graham and John spent a little time chatting. John was also keen to acknowledge Graham's noble gesture in preventing the possible demise of Jessie. He was also keen to ascertain whether Graham had any more information pertaining to the demise of his own parents so many years ago now.

Graham repeated the details, as told to him by Tony and subsequently Ian Knuckey, of the revelations about the name Morangill. Ian had said something about criminals removing any threats to their then lucrative illegal gambling activities involving the horseracing industry. John's father had been either a threat to them through his financial acumen or knowledge he may have come across. Ian had intimated that it was now too far back in time to probably attain any outcome. Graham had learnt most of this through his contact with Peter Knuckey. John was staggered to learn that the police were contemplating the new possibility that John's parents could have been murdered. They were still investigating. He had hinted at race-fixing, betting irregularities and huge sums of money being exchanged by all and sundry. John was indeed downcast. Graham offered to try to gain anything else Ian

Knuckey might happen to know for him as well. John was most thankful.

Graham was exceedingly quiet on the long trip back to Queanbeyan. Richard tried to be chatty, remarking on the wonderful day, the people, the sheep, the set-up, the lunch, the amazing homestead, the wealth that must be associated with that arrangement, but he could detect the distraction in his son. He was unsure why that was so. He provoked little comment. The only remark that induced any response was the rather indelicate comment directed at Jessie,

'Where on earth did you meet that delightful Jessie woman? How does someone like us come to meet up with that sort of person?'

Graham did not respond immediately, just looked at his father strangely. He was deep in thought.

Then he said, 'Dad, you would not believe me if I told you half the details of her weird life. Just suffice it to say, we met under the most amazing circumstances and I am very grateful to have encountered such a wonder in my life.'

Graham wished to make no more comment at the moment on the affair raised by Jessie. If it came through to full fruition, he was contemplating how on earth he was going to explain that to the unbelieving family. They already knew little if anything about the Sophia affair, apart from whatever the Faulkners had revealed to Sally. He was hoping to keep the Jessie affair concealed as well.

It took three months for the title deeds to be registered, firstly in Jessie's name as Jane Ransom, then transferred over to Graham. He had tried to spend as much time as possible with the departing Wheatleys. They basically sold the place on a walk-in, walk-out basis, except for a bit of their furniture. Graham was already familiar with most of the property, though not so much the house. He inherited all their animals, although he was tempted to remove most and replace them with his now decidedly better quality stock. Telling his bewildered family was going to be the challenge, then what to do with the Captains Flat cottage?

During the time between the Wheatleys finally departing and Graham's sole and final acquisition of their place, some of the reality of the manoeuvre began to dawn on him. The Wheatley's property was slightly smaller than Graham's, but it had originally come with the old homestead. His block was bigger but it had the shearing shed. He slowly began to realise that he had inadvertently about doubled the size of his pastoral holdings. This more than doubled his responsibility and care of the pastured domain, not to mention the flock size. The infrastructure was basically sound, but there was always something that needed attention. He also realised that he had lost his most valued mentor and source of vast amounts of knowledge that was once readily available. He was now really on his own. He would be solely responsible for organising all the activities that involved his shearing shed. He was now doubly grateful for the Sophia-inspired change to the shearing contractors that were a lot more amenable than the original grumpy Snow.

Graham was now thinking deeply about his Cobar

connection, something he began to feel that he was neglecting, certainly not giving it the attention it rightfully deserved. He undoubtedly was remiss in his tardy attention to the more deserving Butlers that lived on the place. He briefly contemplated the thought of selling his interest in the property, but then reconsidered that option on reflection. He realised that his uncle had kept the asset as a tax off-set if the Captains Flat place began to return excessive income. Besides, it was a novel attraction, despite its enormous travel difficulties. It had also contributed enormously to his interactions with the ever-grateful Faulkners. He did venture out there as often as he could, but, with the acquisition of the Wheatley's place, his time was becoming over-occupied.

The other item taking large chunks of his diminishing available time was keeping in touch with his daughter Sally. She was progressing admirably through her hectic study program. Then there were the increasing amounts of court and practice time as the law firm to which she had basically now been indentured was very pleased with their investment in her as an understudy and contributor to their cases. She was willing and talented; they were agreeable to increasing her workload as a result. She was gaining rapidly in knowledge and experience.

It was on one of the now more frequent visitations to Sydney to see her that there occurred an incident involving the aging Ian Knuckey.

On a recent time, he went with Sally to Peter's unit for a Sunday lunch when Ian happened to be there. Sally and Ian got along very well as she found him a source of extensive background information about innumerable cases and incidents pertinent to her interest.

Graham knew that Ian had some knowledge of his own affairs but was not sure how much. However, they did have a lot more in common regarding the seemingly ever-developing MacIntyre case. On this latest visit, while the two of them were alone, Ian asked Graham about the last traumatic incident involving Jessie. She had informed him of most of the gruesome details and the incredible part Graham had played in saving her life. It had led to many further inquiries into other people as well, trying to determine the culprits, though deep down they had their prime suspects – probably Bales, the dubious lawyer married to John's daughter, Audrey. He was of known doubtful character and on whom Jessie had a lot of detrimental information – and he knew it.

Ian Knuckey revealed to Graham some more information that he had been able to discover, thanks to Graham's revelation of the Morangill connection. John Summers' parents were killed in 1939. Six months earlier, there was a jockey of doubtful reputation who was also killed in now what appeared to be suspicious circumstances. It was assumed at the time to be a racecourse accident, but once the Morangill connection was raised, Ian began looking further back.

He discovered a satchel of John's parents' belongings set aside with this suspicious jockey's case items; that was how they were inadvertently misplaced for decades. Plus, there was no suspicion at the time of a real connection; though searches were conducted, nothing was found. The material belonging to John's parent's case included some papers, his wallet, her handbag and a considerable stash of cash in pound notes. There were other racecourse-related incidents going further back that all wound up in the same pile of evidence. John's father's things had got inadvertently collected up in that lot of evidence.

Ian said, 'Jessie told me all about your timely intervention. I believe she would have died but for you. She has lived in fear all her life of this sort of thing. Your connection to her has also been most beneficial to me in my continuing endeavours over the MacIntyre case. Thanks to you, I have advanced to another level in my investigations. It is strange that we have also stumbled inadvertently onto issues surrounding John Summers.'

Graham looked at Ian but said nothing, so Ian continued.

'You know, Graham, John Summers is a clean skin, not even a parkin' ticket. He's lived all his life in Hicksville – it's not even a dot on the map. Yet he has accumulated assets worth millions. I don't know how he did it. You know, his unlisted family company owns several city buildings in the heart of Sydney, plus other valuable property scattered about Cooma and Manly. According to the land records, he paid cash for that property Jessie lives on.'

'Why are you telling me this?' asked Graham.

'You gave us a substantial lead with that Morangill name. As you may know, John's father was a very wealthy man too. But we don't know what happened to his dough. I have now discovered that he may have been involved in some elaborate racing scams. The jockey who was killed six months before the Summers family in 1939 was involved and was apparently skimming some off the top for himself. Not a good move when dealing with the people the Morangills were involved with. I'd dearly love to know how John Summers accumulated such wealth, that's all. It doesn't appear to have come from his wife's side either as, according to me, she was penniless. Her name was Livinia.'

'How would you know that?' asked a concerned Graham.

'Well,' said Ian, 'her maiden name was Avery, and she and her mother were deserted by her father when she was about five. Her father had come into a lot of money when he won a lottery prize, I think it was. Her mother's maiden name was Mitchinton, her grandfather was Alfred Mitchinton, and—'

'What did you just say?' demanded a suddenly agitated Graham.

'Pardon?' responded a startled Ian. 'What?'

'What was that name you just mentioned?' asked a now very alert Graham.

'Livinia?' he proffered.

'No, the other name. The surname.'

'What, the Mitchinton one?'

'Yes.' said Graham deliberately and sternly.

'Why? What does that mean to you?'

'That was my late wife's family name going back a few generations. I think it was her grandmother's maiden name. You have no idea of the intricacies associated with that surname.'

'What, criminally?' asked an incredulous Ian.

'No. That family seems to be cursed, according to my wife. Where does this Livinia fit into the scheme of things?'

'Well, as far as we can tell – she's now dead by the way – she came from this family that was once quite important in the early days of the colony, then her early ancestor, committed suicide in about 1910 and the family fell into poverty. Livinia's mother married this Avery bloke, but he deserted them when Livinia was only about five. She struggled ever since until she met John Summers. So, we know she brought nothing to the union. That's all.'

Graham was deep in thought. He recalled the fate of each of the children of the man who had committed suicide, as Jenny had reiterated the story many times to him. Surely this Livinia could not be descended from that line and be related to Jenny and to him, not to mention John Summers. Surely not! And did she somehow avoid the curse?'

He was keenly trying to recall the relevant details of that particular line. Jenny had told him often enough, but he recalled many times listening with much uninterest to her tale. He wished he had now paid a little more attention to her long story.

*

The issue of revealing Graham's acquisition of the Wheatley's place next door could be put off no longer, as he was now doubly occupied with farming matters and trying to decide where to live. He was bamboozled as to how he could disclose this state without revealing anything about Jessie. He needed his parents to know about this and to advise him on living quarters.

The time had come. The boys were out playing sport with other children and Richard and Dora were at last alone in the house this Sunday. Graham had decided this was the moment. After the usual Sunday dinner that Dora was now in the habit of convening while all the family was still together and she could still manage such a feat, they moved out to the small back sunroom that was pleasant in the warmer weather.

When they were all settled, Graham said, 'I have something I want to tell you, but I don't quite know how to do it.'

'What is it dear?' asked Dora. 'I noticed you seem a little quiet lately. Are you all right?'

'Yes, Mum, I'm fine.'

'That's good, then. What is it?'

Graham sighed a long and audible sigh. 'I have some news for you and I'm not sure how to tell you.'

'You sure you're all right, son?' asked Richard.

'Yes, Dad. Look, I've managed to get hold of the Wheatley's place next door to the shearing shed. You know, the block next door to the farm that has the original house on it.'

'What do you mean? How did you do that?'

'Look, it's a very complicated story. But it concerns that woman, Jessie Summers.'

'You're not involved with her, are you?' asked Richard.

'No, Dad, of course not, not in the way you mean, anyway. But it certainly involves her.'

Dora looked at her husband, puzzled. Richard had explained to her the brief encounter he had had with her on the trip to Auvergne some months back now and the impression she had made on him. He reminded her that that was the woman he was talking about.

'I'd like to tell you the whole story, but it's got some rather difficult circumstances. Could I just say that I have now acquired the Wheatley's place with her assistance and leave it at that?'

'I told you at the time, dear, that woman was something else, didn't I?' he said to Dora.

'You don't know the half of it all, Dad. Could I just leave her out of the conversation? You need to know all this. I need to talk to you about what I am going to do with it all and what to do with the cottage.'

A noticeable stillness descended upon the threesome. Graham awaited their acknowledgement of the facts.

CHAPTER FIFTEEN

Graham was in a quandary. He was unsure what to do. He had a thought. He rang Sophia.

After some quick pleasantries, Graham asked, 'Sophia, are you all very busy over there right now?'

'No more than usual. There is always plenty to do.' she replied.

'I guess so. Do you think Jackson could spare a bloke for a week or so?'

'Oh, Graham, I'm sure he could, for you,' she enthused.

'I don't want to ask him if he can't.'

'I'm sure he would. Would you like me to get him?'

'Yes, please, if he's there,' said a tentative Graham.

Sophia went off to find her father; shortly after, he picked up the phone.

'Hello, Graham, what can I do for you?'

'Jackson, I've just had a call from Fiona – you know, Sid's wife at Cobar. Sid has had an accident in one of the outer goat yards. It appears an angry billy charged at him and drove him into the flimsy-wired yard fence and he lost his balance and was injured by the blighter. I'm going out in a day or so to help for about a week or two. I was wondering if you could possibly spare that young bloke Jason that you sent out before. He was so useful out there with his bike ridin' an' being a licenced truck driver and such. Plus, he is very responsible and reliable.'

'I'm sure he'd love to go out there again. He spoke enthusiastically about his time out there the last time. Would you like me to ask him?'

'If you could spare him, yes, please. I'm planning on going in the next couple of days if possible. I could pick him up in my ute on the way.'

Jackson found Jason and explained the position. He was only too delighted to go back out there. Jackson rang Graham back shortly.

'Graham, he'd be pleased to go out there again. Now listen, how about I send a couple of my guys out there in my two-tonner for a while?'

'No, definitely not. Jackson, it's bad enough that I'm asking you this much. Don't double my debts by sending two blokes. It's just that Sid was in the middle of his best mustering period and it's about the only time he gets the biggest benefit.'

'Well, if you're sure. I'm only too happy to be of assistance here, you know.'

'Yes, thanks, Jackson, but Jason would be a big help for a

week or so. Now listen, Jackson, we want to pay you for Jason's time away from you. We insist.'

'Yes, all right, but let's talk about that later. Are you taking your trailer?'

'Well, at this stage, I was thinking of it. I have a few items I might take out there.'

'I might have some more stuff you can take out with you if you have the room.'

'Well, I won't say no to anything if you have it.'

'If you bring your trailer over here, I'll load it up and you can then get away early the next morning.'

Graham agreed. He took the trailer over to the Faulkner's place that day. He spoke to Jason and some items were agreed to be sent out as well, mostly old star pickets and used fencing wires, cast off but ideal for out west. Graham was very grateful for the generosity.

On the way into the property, he had noticed Sophia horse jumping in one of the large yards attached to the extensive horse facilities. He stopped on the way out and strolled over to watch her in action. She was travelling around the complicated jumping arena in what he thought was rather a hurry, negotiating high obstacles. He was most impressed. She acknowledged his presence on one of her passes with a discreet hand wave. She was not on Starlight but another, very large horse. He marvelled at her ability and courage.

As he watched, he was suddenly startled at the presence of someone else there. He turned to see Ophelia almost upon him as she exited the shadows of the small shed attached to that yard. She smiled beguilingly at him and said hello.

He responded in kind, then remarked at Sophia's prowess. He did not expect to be seeing anyone else there, especially Ophelia. Turns out she was here again to tutor Sophia in the finer points of dressage and showjumping. Together they watched as Sophia traversed the compact course. Finally, she drew the horse up to where they were standing and, puffing slightly, dismounted the huge beast and draped his reins over the rails, giving it a loving rub along its sweaty neck.

'What do you think?' asked Sophia.

'Yes, that's better. See how he strides more comfortably if you control the reins that way.'

The conversation continued momentarily as if Graham were not there, then Sophia said to him, 'Hi, Graham, have you made some arrangements for Cobar?'

'Yes, thank you, and thank you to your father. I will be back in two days to pick up Jason.'

'Glad we could help. Please give my regards to Sidney and Fiona.'

'Will do.'

Just then, Edith approached the group with the maid carrying a large tray with cups, teapots and cakes. She acknowledged Graham and offered all some refreshments. Graham hesitated and indicated he should be going. Sophia pleaded with him to remain. He acquiesced reluctantly, though he did find it attractive to be among so much unaccustomed glamour and talent.

They chattered briefly, Graham listening intently to the

horsey conversation. The housemaid was a plumpish woman, middle-aged and rather plain. It transpired she was the wife of one of the farm hands, had been there for years. It worked out well for everybody.

Sophia got up to attend to the horse and prepared to ride again and the maid removed the items from the make-do bench and departed the scene. Edith thanked her politely.

'How do you know that intriguing Summers woman?' he heard Ophelia ask.

He was a bit stunned at the forthright question. He remained silent for a minute, thinking.

'She's an acquaintance through a mutual friend,' he announced.

'She is a striking person, quite an enigma to me. I noticed you were very easy with each other,' commented Ophelia.

Graham was not quite used to such forthright interrogation about his life, especially from someone who was almost a stranger, and a woman to boot. And what did she mean by that comment? He surmised from the little he had seen of her that she portrayed a very strong personality and a commanding presence herself, quite in fitting with her demanding profession.

'Does she ride at all?' asked Ophelia.

'Oh yes,' replied Graham emphatically, 'but she rides for her occupation, not for her amusement. She was brought up in the wilds of the remotest outback tropics – a very proficient horsewoman, and most knowledgeable about horses and cattle, especially very wild cattle.'

His tone was a little condescending. He hoped he had not been too obvious in casting his opinion of the difference between riding for work and riding for entertainment. Graham could not immediately see the benefits to society of indulging in what he considered a sport, and an expensive one at that, when compared to the rigours Jessie must have suffered in attaining her skills, especially as he recalled that she had learned with much pain, according to her childhood diaries.

A noticeable coolness descended upon the small group momentarily as they digested the essence of that comment from Graham. He hoped he had not offended anyone in particular.

'Is that so?' Ophelia then said. 'She did not strike me as such a deeply rural soul, more your refined city dweller.'

Graham was intrigued by that impression instilled by Jess on others but could understand why she would instil that impression.

Edith sat listening with interest. Then she said, 'Graham, Ophelia is travelling to Europe in four weeks, and we are having a small farewell for her here over that weekend. I was wondering, if you were available, if you'd like to come. We'd love to have you join us.'

Graham thought a moment. He was reluctant to attend, feeling slightly out of his depth with these people. Then he thought, *Why not? They've invited me, so I will go.*

He said, 'Yes, if I'm here, I'd love to come. Thank you.'

'Do you travel much, Graham?' asked Ophelia.

'No, very little, only out to Cobar now.'

'So, you don't go overseas much?'

'No, never been. I don't even have a passport,' he said pointedly.

Ophelia raised her eyebrows slightly and pursed her lips.

'Now, I really should be getting back to the farm.'

He turned to Sophia stroking the nose of the patient horse and said, 'It was lovely to see you in action, Soph. Thanks so much. And lovely to see you both again,' he said to the other two ladies. 'And thanks for the cuppa.'

They nodded in acknowledgment, Ophelia giving him a deep stare. He arose and wandered back to his ute and drove off, thinking.

Graham arranged to pick up Jason in two days early in the morning and take him out to Cobar. On arrival, Graham found that Fiona was pleased he had been able to get to Cobar while Sid recuperated. She also appreciated that Jackson had spared Jason. It would be extra company for her as well. They started immediately on continuing the mustering under the guidance of an injured and laid-up Sid, and trucking of the goats from the property. Jason was a real self-starter and enmeshed himself deeply in the new enterprise. He found it rather exhilarating. The country around that part of the outback had received considerable rain in the previous months, so the ground cover had improved, and the land had dried out sufficiently for the mustering to proceed.

Sid had an old Bedford flat top in which he carted around all the metal panels that were used for the temporary catching and holding yards. He also had another old truck with a stock crate on it to cart the animals to the railhead or the trucking yards for further distribution. Graham could drive trucks but he did not have a licence for use on public roads. Sid did, of course, and so did Jason; hence, his desirability to be seconded to Cobar. Sid gave all the directions from the homestead and the boys did all the rest.

Graham seemed to be a magnet for calamities to occur in order for him to provide a remedy. It was ironic that he happened to be out at Cobar when another unusual and rare drama unfolded right before his eyes.

Graham and Jason were mustering the feral goats to a temporary yard about fifteen kilometres from the homestead near to an earth soak Sid had gouged out in the soil. Jason and Sid's elder son, Eddy, were using the trail bikes and Graham and Sid's younger son, Jimmy, were working the yards. They had reversed the larger stock truck up to the flimsy wooden ramp preparatory to loading it. Luckily this day, the bikes were at some distance from the yards, so the scene was relatively quiet, as no goats had yet been mustered to it. Graham thought he heard the sound of an aeroplane, probably a light aircraft, that sounded rather close for this isolated part of the country. It definitely was not the sound of the far distant bikes.

When it came into view, he thought that it was rather low, even for this type of flying. Then he heard the engine misfiring. He paid particular attention to what was unfolding. He called Jimmy over. The two of them watched as the plane coughed and spluttered then disappeared over a low ridge followed by a dull thud and then complete silence. Graham shouted to Jimmy to get on his bike and go and find the other two and bring them back to the accident site. He would race over in that direction in his own ute. Jimmy dashed off as instructed, away from the bearing of the crash.

Graham headed off in the direction of the possibly downed plane. Once he crested the small ridge, he could see the whole thing laid out in front of him close by. He raced over in his ute, dodging trees and bushes, swerving in the soft loose soil.

The aircraft had come to an abrupt stop atop a tiny sand ridge, ploughing and sliding into a small stand of mallee trees and mulga scrub. Its shattered port wing bent precariously upwards, hard against the fuselage of the stricken aeroplane. The heavy limbs of the clumps of mallee and mulga trees were resting against this upright wing. This had rendered the exit door inoperable, and any passengers inside were trapped. The engine weight had forced the aircraft to nose-dive into the soft earth and fuel was dribbling copiously onto the sandy soil, trickling away from the buried nose. Smoke and small flames were emanating from somewhere within the hissing engine which was also sparking wildly from within.

Graham stopped the vehicle some metres away from the plane in case it exploded, and grabbing a large axe and his sheathed hunting knife, raced over to the port side of the fuselage. He was very mindful of the leaking fuel. He clambered up to see if there was any life. He could not determine that exactly. He furiously began trying to remove the obstructing limbs and branches holding the upright wing tightly against the plane. He was chucking wildly all the debris he could manhandle. Quickly, he was able to slide the severed wing sufficiently away from the door to try and open it. It would not budge. He swung the large axe into the handle and the soft aluminium metals bowed to the persuasion of the heavy blows. He ripped open the damaged door and peered in.

There were two occupants on the front seats, one if not both were the pilots who were unconscious. He peered further in and saw four others, all in various states of bleeding and consciousness. Two were able to communicate. He asked how they were. He was furiously chattering to them, more to authenticate the plan of action that was developing in his mind and that he perceived as required.

Graham knew absolutely nothing about flying. He had, however, gleaned from the rare news items he had seen on aeroplane accidents that they often seemed to be on some form of radar before they disappeared and, hopefully, the pilot had been able to communicate his distress prior to ditching on his own airway system. At least he hoped that was the case. In the meantime, he would concentrate on the immediate job at hand.

He shouted that he must remove the two unconscious men in the front so that the others could clamber out the now accessible door before the thing went up in flames. They were still heavily buckled in their harnesses and securely tethered to the damaged seating. The nearer one was a large man and Graham had trouble undoing his seatbelts. This he finally did and dragged the unconscious man out of the cockpit, onto the damaged remaining wing area and then away from the plane onto the ground. He then tried to unbuckle the man on the right-hand side but he was jammed up tightly against the instrument panel and his damaged seat had removed itself from the floor and turned itself and the occupant hard up against the front. Graham decided to forget him momentarily and attend to the others. He was able to remove the first man's damaged seat and hoick it onto the ground. He began clambering over the damaged front seat area to remove the rest.

Just then the others arrived on their bikes amid much noise and dust. They gazed at the scene in stunned bewilderment. Graham yelled at them to get over there. While the others stood still gazing in a state of shocked bafflement, Graham began to bark instructions. His adrenalin was up and he was feverishly contemplating all the possible outcomes. He immediately ordered Jimmy to return to the house and get Sid to alert whomever they could contact on their isolated communication equipment – the Royal Flying Doctor Service or the local hospital and the ambulance. Graham demanded he return in Sid's large four-door Toyota ute. Jimmy departed in haste.

Graham asked Jason and Eddy to move the three previously removed passengers further away from the scene. They were the first pilot, the second-row occupant nearer the door whom he had dragged out and an injured third-row woman who had managed to clamber out with dazed difficulty. That left another pilot still tethered in his seat, another man unconscious against the starboard window in the second row and an unconscious woman in the third row. He and Jason removed the second-row man, then they attended to the third-row woman. He got the boys to remove all the passengers well away from the stricken plane. It was now beginning to burn with more ferocity.

The others were beginning to panic a little at the sight of the flames and fuel leaking everywhere. They moved away some distance. Graham began to run back into the plane to remove the tethered pilot. The others begged him not to do so. He leaped into the front again as the flames grew stronger, and with much haste, cut the seating straps holding in the last man with his hunting knife and tried to remove him. He was a large man and his seat had turned itself away from the door. It was a most difficult exercise. Just then a small explosion occurred in the engine and the whole plane shuddered slightly while thick acrid black smoke began to billow copiously from the engine and along the ground.

Graham finally managed to get the man loose from his bindings and began to drag him out. There was another small explosion, so Graham roughly dragged the man out and almost flung him onto the ground. He then jumped off the wing stub and began to drag the body away. Just then an almighty explosion erupted within the engine and pieces and flames went spiralling in all directions but mostly upwards. Luckily, Graham and the unconscious man were below the height of the stricken plane as it had stopped atop the small ridge. This allowed for most of the debris to miss them, though they both sustained a little damage from flying shrapnel and burning fragments. The plane at this point broke into several large portions, flopping down about the site.

The others stood in deep fear and mild terror as the inevitable explosion occurred. They could see that Graham and the other man might have been injured. Jason finally ran over to assist Graham to his feet and dragged the man further away from the scene. The noise was horrific and large billows of the acrid smoke rose high into the sky.

Graham had been slightly stunned and was leaning on one elbow following the blast, the unconscious pilot beside him. As Jason began to drag Graham roughly away as he struggled to regain his footing, he yelled to Jason to cease that and grab the other man and remove him instead.

The plane was a dead loss now. It was burning furiously and had ignited the surrounding vegetation. Graham shouted that they should all try to put out some of the more easily attended flames before they got out of hand. The three of them darted about trying to achieve that. Then he returned to the six patients. Of the six, four were unconscious and two were awake but dazed. Graham, trying to regain full alertness and maintain control of events as the others seemed to be unable to self-start, rummaged about in his ute for any old tarps or material that he could use as a ground sheet. Blood began dripping from a couple of his wounds, one on his forehead. He was also covered in dirt and black soot, plus a smidgen of the engine oils. He had little first-aid gear in his ute and no bandages, plus he was annoyingly low on water, at least for this type of demand.

He found a small old tarp and grabbed the large plastic jerrycan of water and struggled over to the patients. With those awake, he ascertained their condition and supplied water. He left the two boys to attend to them. They seemed to need a lot of guidance. Graham was slightly surprised at the state of fright they were in as he expected the Butler boy at least to be a little more able to cope with a dramatic emergency, given his exposure to the rigours of outback life. With Jason, he understood a little more that he might have found this episode a trifling traumatic, given his more urban background. Still, they were of some benefit in this drama.

Then he turned his attention to the four unconscious. They were all still alive; for that, he was grateful. He was unsure what to do now. Just then, Jimmy flew back into the scene in a rush of screaming motorbike engine and flying debris. He rushed up to Graham and peered down at him as he worked. His arrival was quickly followed by a welcome Fiona driving the Land Cruiser ute. She rushed out of the vehicle and rummaged in the back seats to retrieve boxes of things. She had collected several boxes of her first aid supplies from the house and piled them into the vehicle and then followed a hurrying Jimmy back out to the scene of the accident.

It transpired that Fiona was quite adept at emergency first aid, having lived all her young life in the wilds of the outback far from medical aid. Graham was rather delighted for her to take command of those in an unconscious state as he really had no experience at all in these matters. Fiona informed Graham that Sid was busily contacting whomever he could on their dodgy communications equipment while he was still laid up in his convalescent state, his leg in plaster.

Fiona attended rather expertly to those on the ground. She quickly ascertained who had broken limbs and there were several. She attended to the many cuts and bleeding wounds and supplied plentiful amounts of her precious tank water to the parched and stressed conscious passengers.

Graham was assisting Fiona as instructed when he heard the far-off familiar sound of an approaching helicopter. Sid must have managed to contact someone and alert them. The sound grew louder, and he hoped it was coming there. He was right. It hastened into the scene, flying around momentarily, obviously reconnoitring the whole site. It finally landed the other side of the stricken aeroplane, preventing raising the gritty soil and debris from further contaminating the patients as they lay about the area.

Three passengers alighted the still noisy aircraft and ran hastily around the downed one over to the patients. Sid had managed to contact the Cobar hospital and police station and they took charge of arranging whatever was available to be sent to the scene. Luckily, there was a fire and rescue chopper there at the time and three paramedics from the ambulance and hospital were sent out.

Graham was relieved to be removed from the immediate care of the injured. The paramedics were well experienced in this kind of incident and calmly attended to the needy. Fiona was still of some use to the paras as she was versed in minor medical attentions. There was much activity with hopping between the various patients. Finally, it was decided to fly each of them to the Cobar hospital initially and things would be developed from there.

By the time all the hands from the Butler property were finally home and the injured dispatched to the Cobar hospital, it was quite late in the afternoon. Graham was rather exhausted from the mental and psychological trauma of being party to such an event. Sid was rather annoyed that he was physically unable to assist with the rescuing of the six passengers and regarded his contribution as miniscule. He was stunned by what Graham described as the rather over-graphic descriptions offered by the others in recounting Graham's rescues and his re-entering the possibly imminently exploding wreckage. Graham regarded it as no more than any other person would have offered.

The family at Cobar incurred no real damage from their efforts out at the scene, with the exception of Graham. He had sustained several shrapnel injuries as well as some flying debris and burning or hot fluids from the exploding engine. The paramedics attended to him in some detail and requested that he accompany them back to Cobar. This he refused to do and, following assurances from Fiona to attend to his injuries properly, they were in no position to insist. He had several small head injuries and several body blows from the flying fragments.

Chapter Fifteen

That evening when finally alone, but still in some minor pain from some of the inflictions, Graham took stock of the day. He realised in retrospect that maybe he had been tempting fate a little to re-enter the burning plane to save that last man left inside. He thought now how lucky he had been that he and the man were below the height of the high-set wreckage as it ignited in an almighty explosion in its final death throes of existence as an intact entity. It made him survey his life and the fragility of his existence and how close he always was to total oblivion on this mortal planet, and all at the whims of circumstances. He thought of Jessie; she lived this thought for her entirety.

Graham sat momentarily in the ancient, ragged, once probably ornate wooden armchair with its sadly sagging diminished cushioned state that was provided by the Butlers in the small back room that was usually allocated to him on any of his visits. The room was stark, dark and with tall ceilings. It did possess an ancient ceiling fan that was quite adequate for its purpose in the late evenings. The walls may have displayed evidence of once being possibly painted white, but really were just plain boards of some considerable age. It was all rather sombre and could evoke feelings of dismal bleakness in the appropriate circumstances. Graham became rather sombre at the thought of how differently things could have ended. He thought of his own family, and his farm. He was not finished doing it yet; he was not ready to leave this life right now.

This introspection reawakened within Graham a sensation

that he had not encountered now for some years – that of reviewing his existence and the ramifications of his now diminishing feelings of traumatic personal experiences. In this alone time in his normally hectic life, now becoming rarer, he was suddenly struck by the weird awareness of how strange it all became. He began to catalogue in his mind the series of phenomenal experiences that seemed to spring in some sort of order as if ordained by an overall guiding hand since his arrival at his deceased aunt's cottage in the bizarre location called Captains Flat.

Why did he take so admirably to the field of sheep grazing when he came from a background of total ignorance? Why did he meet that delectable being, Sophia, at that particular time, so early in this new endeavour? Why was he so instrumental in whisking her away from that form of danger? Why did his children re-enter his previously traumatised, nothing, little life at that moment and in those circumstances? What was the purpose of the Planter child discovery, and why him and why then? Was it to throw light on his uncle's apparent murder? Why was Tony, of all people, his neighbour? Why was he not somewhere else in the village? What was the point of his meeting up with the famous Jessie MacIntyre? What contrivance dictated that his own divorce lawyer should be none other than Peter Knuckey, the very name associated with that famous case? And how to explain that particular law firm ensconcing itself into his own case by no effort at all of his own doing? This weird encounter had the happy event of his daughter, Sally, gaining entry into her chosen field in most remarkable circumstances. Then there was the unlikely event of the Jessie abduction. Why would that occur right outside his own front door in order for him to be involved? Was that so as he could attain ownership of the Wheatley's place?

To his mind, too many things happened in too ordered an appearance to be random life incidents. His parent's realigned their lives to be near the now reassembled family. Then there was the Renu incident – what was that all about? Now, out of the blue, this aeroplane crash occurred right before his eyes. Why? All this was weird enough, but the mere fact that he was even involved with Cobar at all was disturbingly eerie. That was the most bizarre part of all his strange new life. Why? Now on the horizon was another contribution seemingly innocently inserted into his life – this Ophelia woman – why her and why now?

Graham had a sad moment of reflection. He thought of Jenny. He still often thought of her. He so dearly wished he could be sharing all this weirdness together with her. He still thought of her fondly. He was saddened by the reality check that in no way would she have fitted into his new existence. He knew that as a fact. Was she removed from his life in order for him to fulfil these strange requirements – alone? He still had a feeling of love for her.

Ophelia was looming as a threat to his resolve not to succumb. He wished to honour Jenny's memory and not have any other woman in his life. He wondered why he felt he should honour his late wife so, considering what she did to him and his children, but he did. He still harboured a sense of failing her because of her apparent unhappiness and her deserting her family. He wondered often what he had done to fail her.

CHAPTER SIXTEEN

Graham and Jason ended up staying at Cobar for three weeks. Fiona was most appreciative of their assistance and company. Sid was still housebound but becoming more mobile, and the plaster was to be removed in another week or so, he hoped.

On his return to Captains Flat, Graham tried to reimburse the Faulkners, which he did, but Jackson would not hear of allowing anything like the real amount of the cost of Jason's absence for that time. Jason regaled the entire assembly with Graham's heroics over the aeroplane rescue, embellishing the story way beyond what Graham thought of as accurate. It reinforced in the minds of the Faulkners that their inadvertently acquired normally staid and reserved friend was indeed a remarkable person, seemingly always calm under adversity.

Out along the Shoalhaven River, Graham had become much friendlier over time with the neighbours on the other side of his farm, Will and Moyra Davidson. He always tried to cultivate neighbourly relationships, especially out in the isolated rural scene that he now found himself in. He had been conscious that he could possibly lose his most important mentor in John Wheatley, so ensured that he was on the best of terms with the Davidsons as well, who were of course also most knowledgeable in the sheep industry. He had informed Will that he would be absent for a few weeks and that the Wheatley place was as yet unoccupied, so could they just keep an eye on the place as they drove past. He was at pains not to divulge that he was in fact the new owner of the Wheatley's, a fact that he was reticent to reveal to them, as yet anyway. That was going to be a delicate revelation.

On his return, Graham had several issues which he had to wrestle with and decisions that needed to be made. The main one of concern involved the property in the village of Captains Flat. Its usefulness to him as an abode was greatly diminished now that he had acquired the Wheatley homestead next door to his shearing shed block. He and Richard were now going to be heavily involved with removing all the extraneous material from the village to the farming property proper, finally cleaning up the old cottage completely of any farming equipment.

There was quite a demand for appropriate properties to rent in the village, as many people wished to live there for the convenience of local employment, plus also rents were obviously much cheaper there than in town. Graham did not really wish to sell the cottage, as it was his late aunt's, but he was also reluctant to rent it out.

Another subject that emerged, impacting on his time, was the ramifications of the revelations emanating from his late neighbour, Tony. The further Ian Knuckey and his now growing team of investigators delved into things associated with all those revelations, the more snippets of detail emerged, some going back decades. This was having an impact on the Summers clan, especially an aging John Summers.

The other issue requiring his attention, and one he had not originally contemplated on, was the continuing saga of the Jessie Summers abduction. There were several aspects of this interlude that impacted on Graham. Firstly, of course, was the acquisition of the Wheatley property next door. This had ramifications on him in relation to his immediate neighbours. Graham had made no bones about the fact that he was a new chum in their rural lifestyles, inexperienced, ignorant and untested. He had even volunteered his labours to his neighbours to gain as much knowledge as possible from them. They all realised that he was a complete novice. Explaining his acquisition of the well-established Wheatley property by a man thought to have been a battler without arousing their ire was a matter that was going to require much delicate manoeuvring. This revelation could not wait too long either, as Graham's contact telephone number for matters regarding use of the shearing shed was soon going to become John Wheatley's old number, a fact that needed to be explained sooner rather than later. He might be able to relocate his aunt's old number in Captains Flat out to the homestead located along the river; he would investigate that possibility, or even just get a new number altogether.

Secondly, Graham had established, for some reason, an unplanned and unexpected rapport and affinity with the mysterious and enigmatic Jessie Summers. She was normally extremely reticent to socialise – with anybody – and he knew that. Somehow, however, she developed an empathy with Graham, wholly originating from her own initiative that she could not entirely explain. She acknowledged that he had saved her life and probably an horrific death by his mere presence and then his determined actions on her behalf.

When Graham had inadvertently mentioned during their time together in his Captains Flat cottage, after the abduction, that he had an irrigation licence, it had piqued the interest of Damien, as he was their irrigation guru and supplied the Summers' properties with additional winter and drought silage in the form of his irrigated lucerne crops.

Damien had offered to advise Graham on irrigation matters if he ever felt the need to delve into that form of supplementation. He also volunteered to come up to Graham's place and reconnoitre the layout and suitability of his irrigation site on the river. Graham was tempted to take advantage of so much expertise being freely offered, and tentative arrangements were agreed to for some time in the future.

The opportunity arose inadvertently, and via the hands of the Summers themselves, when, some months after Graham's acquisition of the Wheatley property, Damien contacted

Chapter Sixteen

Graham and offered to come up one Sunday when John Summers was not well enough to attend the usual Sunday family company meeting. He was feeling unwell, so the family company gathering was postponed. Damien, feeling a little at a loose end, decided a trip up to Graham's would be a nice diversion.

Graham was taken aback by the offer but was very eager to partake. During the course of the conversation, Graham asked Damien if he would care to ask if Jessie and Thomas would like to come too, to see over the place she had so kindly acquired for him. He agreed to ask her and get back to him. Graham was a little surprised at her agreeing to come up along with Thomas. It was arranged. Jessie and Thomas would come up along with Damien and his wife, Helen. Graham suggested that they all come up for the day, he would provide some lunch.

Graham was no entertainer and had no experience as a host. He hoped to impose on his wonderful mother to assist with that task. When it was agreed that the four Summers were to come up, Graham contacted his mother.

Dora was enthusiastic to be asked to do such a thing. She was once quite the hostess herself. If so many distinguished visitors were invited, she would be able to prepare quite a feast, despite being slightly unfamiliar with the cooking arrangements and the equipment at the new property.

Jessie was enthusiastic to see the place she had bought for Graham. Despite purchasing it, she had done so sight unseen. Any faults it might possess would be well balanced, she reasoned, by having the homestead next to his shearing shed. The homestead was reputedly magnificent, though not all that grand or old, but nevertheless modern, large and well maintained. She would dearly love to see it.

The Summers arrived by ten o'clock. Jessie drove them up in her Discovery, Damien and Helen cadging a lift with her as he did not own such a good vehicle.

Graham had gone to a lot of trouble – at least, he had arranged for his tireless mother so to do. She organised a large roast dinner for the lot of them, and there were a lot of them. Graham could not keep his enthusiastic father from the excitement and his two boys, being a Sunday, had to be there as well.

On arrival, Jess was given a thorough tour of the house itself. She expressed her satisfaction at its apparent suitability for purpose. Graham had already resurrected the ancient gate opposite the house that led into the shed paddock and replaced the sagging old strainer assemblies and stays, making access to his shed paddock much more convenient and shorter, now not having to go out onto the road to gain access to it. He was keen to advance the irrigation story, so proposed that the inspection occur before lunch. So, after a cup of tea on arrival, it was suggested, as it was not all that far, that they walk the distance to the riverbank where the irrigation site used to be.

Jessie decided that she was not all that interested in that actual aspect of the visit, despite its ostensibly being the reason for the trip, but that she would rather reconnoitre the home paddock and the facilities about the property and check out the country for its suitability. That meant that all but Jessie and Dora wandered off in the direction of the river and its former irrigation site.

Jessie wandered alone about the property, taking in all the facilities and the many aspects of this enterprise. She still held little real interest in anything pertaining to sheep as her preference was always with cattle and the horse side. She did note with some keenness the two ancient, resurrected vehicles that Richard had managed to restore to full running order.

Jess wandered back to the house well after midday, a little surprised to discover that the rest were still not back yet. Graham had warned his mother that Jessie was not much of a conversationalist, and asked her not to question Jess about the acquisition of this new property. To this she had agreed. Jessie was reluctant to enter into any socialising with Dora, especially if they were to be alone together, and Jess found Dora's hard-of-hearing a challenge as Jess had a soft voice and disliked speaking loudly. She had, however, found Dora to be pleasant and rather occupied at the present moment, reminding her slightly of Edna Coniston from Ravymoota Station in the Kimberley.

Jess sidled up to the large kitchen table, asking if she could assist in any way. Dora replied that all was in order; she was just awaiting the return of all the others – soonish, she hoped. Dora chattered about nothing in particular as was her want but was finding it difficult to resist the urge to express her gratitude and perplexity at the turn of events that led to this moment.

Dora was not a sophisticated woman, she was simple and

honest and she had never moved in the circles that Graham had in his previous employment. She was not accustomed to deciphering and navigating the nuances of discretion, at least not at the level Graham had suggested. He had told his mother that there were no secrets about any of his adventures, only that he did not discuss them with anyone and tended to keep them circumspect and guarded, more out of reserve or timidity and diffidence than anything else.

Dora was finding Jessie's detachment and reticence to converse unsettling. She was unsure whether Jess was really just shy or whether her demeanour bordered on aloofness. Dora also found Jessie's piercing stare unsettling. In the end, to ease some of her uncomfortable sense of being alone with this person, Dora ventured, 'I believe we have you to thank for Graham being able to move into here.' Jess did not answer, so Dora continued a little nervously, 'He really has told me nothing about it but said you were involved.'

Jess gazed at the fidgety Dora for some time. Then she finally replied, 'Our paths crossed in a most remarkable way. Let's just say I was able to recompense him in a small manner for his actions for me.'

Dora looked at her still confused but said nothing. In the awkward pause in which Jess sensed a slight vulnerability, Jess decided to venture into a normally forbidden area for her: some personal questions. She was still intrigued by Graham.

She asked, 'Dora, do you know how Graham came to be so friendly with the Faulkners?'

'I don't really know much about that. Apparently, he did

some action or other that saved the life of their daughter from some madman. He has never spoken of it, at least not to me. I only learnt of it from his daughter, Sally, when she found out from the girl's parents somehow.'

'I didn't know about that either,' said a surprised Jess.

Dora thought that she was on surer ground now so, in light of an apparent easing in the atmosphere, she ventured, 'Yes, apparently he took her out to his place at Cobar to get her away from danger.'

'What's at Cobar?'

'Oh, Graham owns a half-interest in an enormous place out at Cobar along with another family member. He inherited it from our aunty along with the farm next door. It is not very valuable and requires a lot of time and money to run, I believe. It's really quite large. He goes out there regularly. In fact,' continued a more animated Dora, 'he was out there only recently. You know, when that plane crashed into the paddocks? Well, he was there. He was the one who saved those six people from being burnt alive. It was really quite amazing.'

'I didn't know that either,' said a surprised Jess.

'Yes, apparently, he risked his life to save them from the flames. I was terribly upset when I was told about it, and not from him either.'

Just then, they heard the distant voices of the returning party from the irrigation site, so Dora got up from the table and started fiddling with the cooking again. The troupe wandered in, still chatting about their stroll and Dora directed them to enter the large dining room. Luckily, the Wheatleys had left behind most of their dining room furniture and crockery as it was designed for ten. Where they were going, they would have no need for that quantity or, for that matter, the room at their new place for all that. Dora asked Graham how it all went. He replied that it was most satisfactory. He and Richard might now go down to Damien's place to see his facilities.

'What did you find out, dear?' she asked.

'Well, Damien is impressed with the area. He said it is twenty-five acres of prime soil. We found where all the old fences were and the pumps and maybe even an old windmill.'

'Good. I'm pleased you were happy. Now all of you come in and have lunch.'

Graham was keen to advance gaining the benefit of all this freely offered learning, so he arranged for himself and an enthusiastic and garrulous Richard to travel down to Damien's property opposite Bridgehead, John's homestead, to learn all he could and be shown the ropes of all the intricacies of irrigation. This he did within a fortnight of their visit. He took copious notes and gave the whole scene deep thought for using this process himself.

*

Graham was aware that cranky old Jacob Cranchovic, who he had heard referred to as "Crankyvich", had had a stroke. It was severe enough to preclude his ever returning to the house in Captains Flat. He was domiciled in an aged-care facility in

Queanbeyan and some months later, the house was put on the market by his semi-estranged daughter. Graham was relieved to see the end of him, at least of his presence in the village. He was not missed by anyone much. Graham severely regretted not managing to ascertain Jacob's involvement in the Planter case and indeed his own uncle's death. As it turned out, that sad state of affairs was about to change dramatically, and in an unlikely way.

The old village house was open for inspection on a Saturday some months after his removal to the city. There were several groups inspecting the house over the time that it was open for inspection and Graham was keen to inspect the place, just to see what was there. He wandered about the property in deep thought, thoroughly checking out each room and its contents. The house was still fully operational and contained all the old man's possessions at this stage. He spent some time in the yard and then inspected the garage.

It was quite a large garage, double-spaced and fairly long, containing some workshop space at the rear, plus a lot of accoutrements associated with the former trade of the retired chemist stacked up on a rear shelving system. It was here that Graham got the shock of his life. He could not believe what he was looking at. There, on the top shelf of an obscure and high sill scattered among similar types of objects, stood a small silver artefact that sent shivers down his spine. It was partly hidden but its most characteristic feature was clearly evident. It would be a meaningless trinket to anybody else sitting in the accumulation of assorted paraphernalia, but not to Graham.

When the body of the small girl had been finally retrieved from the site on his farm out along the Shoalhaven, the Planter family had expressed a desire to inspect the area and its surrounds. Graham agreed readily and the family came out several times. He allowed a small cross to be erected at the rock. The final visit involved the two surviving sisters, one of whom lived interstate, who had travelled down expressly for this purpose. Graham had agreed to accompany them to the site and escort them about the place.

It had been an emotional experience for all involved and the subsequent conversation was a little unsettling for Graham. The two sisters, Leone and Annette, were both younger than Linda. During the course of the moving and poignant episode, the elder of the two sisters, Leone, was quite distraught. She confided in Graham and reminisced about that fateful day. In one of her teary ramblings, she said something to Graham that at the time meant little.

'I never forgave myself for that day.'

Graham countered by saying that she could not blame herself for that tragedy.

She responded with, 'We had a terrible argument that morning. You see, Linda had borrowed from a display cabinet of Beth's – that's the lady we'd come to see – a small silver box, quite ornate but with a small ballerina on the top as a sort of handle to open it with. We told her that was stealing, but she said she just wanted it to put the stones she was looking for in it. She was a stone and rock collector, anything unusual.

As you know, Captains Flat is strewn with unusual stones. Anyway, we parted, angry with her. How little does that matter now. But I never forgave myself. Poor Linda,' she said through bitter tears.

The conversation had remained embedded in Grahams' mind, not for the matter of the box but for the terrible emotional impact that day had on her suffering sisters. He still recalled in vivid detail those draining moments spent with the distraught sisters; it haunted him mildly to seem to be a part of their suffering.

But the description of that small ornamental silver box now aroused considerable fear. He checked that no one was anywhere near this part of the property and quickly grabbed the box down from its shelf and secreted it under his jumper. It was particularly dusty and he tried to remove some of the dust before placing it in his jumper. If it had ever contained anything, that was now gone; it was empty. He wandered in a daze for some minutes in the dingy large garage, then sauntered home in some trepidation. He hoped he was not stealing an object with no connection to the Planters.

Graham spent some time wondering what to do next. He would dearly love to ask the sisters if this were the object. He would also dearly love to confront Jacob. He would seriously consider that objective. He was unsure how cognisant and communicative Jacob now was following his stroke. He would think about that.

A couple of weeks later, Graham decided to try and visit Jacob in his new room at the home. He knew that Jacob had two rare contacts in the village, a fellow Czech couple who lived a few streets away. He visited them and found Jacob's address. They informed him Jacob had suffered some mild brain damage, disrupting his speech and, to some extent, his memory, but he was mildly communicative. Jacob spent most of his time dozing in the home where he was now living. He was of little bother to the staff there and they mostly left him to himself. He received almost no visitors. Graham risked a visit.

Graham found Jacob sitting in a wheelchair in a common room and approached him. He sat for some time chatting about nothing much.

Then Graham said, 'What's going to happen to all your stuff at the house?'

'I don't care now,' he stated. 'It can all go to the dump as far as I concerned.'

'Don't you have anything of value?'

'No, nothing of interest to others.'

'There are some nice things there, Jacob. Do you remember that lovely little ballerina box Linda was carrying that day?'

There was a long pause. Jacob was trying to recall.

Then he finally replied, 'Yes, I think so. Was quite small object with much colour. I thought it much heavy for small girl, no?'

'Yes, I thought that, too. You would have liked her because she collected stones, like you do.'

'Yes, she was lovely. We talk much about rocks and stones. I show her my collection in shed. She very keen.'

'That must have been nice for you, to have someone else interested in rocks.'

'Yes, very nice for me. I show her much of my collection. We have good time together.'

Graham was amazed at Jacob's revelations. The stroke seemed to have loosened his tongue, and also his guard. The old couple in the village said he was more talkative than before. Then Graham ventured another angle.

'You collect mushrooms from the farms, Jacob?'

'Oh, yes. Much mushrooms about the village after rain. Very good.'

'You were kind to give some of them to my aunt and uncle.'

'Yes, they were kind to me and I work sometime on farm for …' He paused. He could not recall Tom's name.

'Tom. My uncle's name was Tom.'

'Yes, that's right. My memory not so good now.'

'Did you collect death caps too?'

'No, they were there too, but I not use them myself. Verry dangerous.'

'Would you pick them by mistake, do you think?'

'No, I know difference.'

'Did you ever give some to Tom as a present?'

'Yes, one time, when he saw me … Hey, you try to catch me out. I not sure now what I say. I think you better go now,' he said, suddenly more alert.

'Well, Jacob, it was lovely to see you still with us,' lied Graham.

Jacob did not answer. He just looked at Graham, then

turned away. Graham sauntered out of the building deep in thought. He would dearly love to ask the sisters if this were the item. He thought of asking this 'Beth' woman, whoever she was, but he would have to locate her, then reveal that he had stolen the item back – if indeed it were the real deal, and where he'd got it from. He drove home contemplating what to do.

*

The farewell party for the departing Ophelia occurred a week after the Summers' visit to Graham's place. He was nervous about attending but always found the people there most pleasant. He usually picked brains for information about farming. It was a Saturday afternoon early evening event, so as not to interrupt activities too much, so Graham decided to attend alone. He did not even mention it to the family.

He arrived there about three o'clock, casually dressed and unsure of the calibre of the attendees. He assumed there would be a consortium of horsey people there, a group with which he was definitely at a disadvantage, he knowing absolutely nothing about that trade other than what he had seen Sophia doing. There were indeed several personalities with apparently some considerable gravitas within the industry, but to Graham they were completely unknown. He noticed that they were almost invariably rather superior types, well dressed and mannered and exhibiting a haughtiness and a slight arrogance commensurate with their supposed talent

Chapter Sixteen

and probable accompanying wealth. Graham was aware that this horse industry required considerable financial backup in order to partake of it. They were also all rather manly and handsome men as he detected. He felt a slight sense of inferiority being in this company.

Graham spent some time with Sophia, her parents and some of the more familiar farm hands that he had got to know. It was a pleasant enough afternoon and the people there were all very amiable. Towards the end of the evening, Ophelia sidled up to him holding a long glass of some strangely coloured liquid that Graham deduced must be some sort of sophisticated concoction that would probably taste horrible, at least to him, he concentrating on the rather generous supply of various beer brands. He was also mindful that he had an awkward drive home in the dark on rough gravel roads.

Ophelia seemed to Graham to be slightly over-familiar towards him – his guard was up. She may have been imbibing liberally over the intervening hours.

She asked, 'And how do you find the company here, Graham?'

'Well, I am unfamiliar with most of your colleagues; I fear they move in different circles to me.'

'Oh, you mustn't feel out of their class, Graham, in fact you are admirably suited to this setting, and I like you being here.'

He looked at her severely. She was staring deeply into his eyes. He felt an unease he had not felt for many years.

She smiled ever so slightly, then said, 'In fact, Graham, I like you. I like you a lot. I'd like to see you again, if I may.

Sophia and her parents speak most highly of you, you know. I will be leaving in a week or so and would love to see you again before I go. Is there any chance that you might be in Sydney in the next week?'

Graham realised that this was nothing short of an open invitation to a continuance, and probably a deepening, of any relationship that Ophelia perceived that they might have, with potential to develop. Sadly, for her, he had zero interest in any form of female association, especially one that he deemed to be a rather artificial one, considering the world in which she moved. He stared at her, wondering how to extricate himself from that unwanted proposal.

He finally replied, 'No, sadly. I can't get to Sydney for a while yet, what with all the labours required about the place.'

'Pity. That is a shame,' she responded, a note of disappointment evident in her voice.

'Yes,' was all he said.

She looked longingly up at him with sad, big, brown eyes, then sauntered off to the others. Graham was a little displeased with that encounter. He must avoid her in future. Then Sophia approached him on seeing Ophelia depart.

She said, 'Hi, Graham, how's it going?'

'Fine thanks, Soph.'

'How do you find Ophie's friends?'

'They are certainly a very interesting group. Most unusual, at least for me.'

'Yes, they are different. I see you were speaking to Ophie just now. I think she likes you a lot.'

'Yes, we had a chat.'

'Do you like her too?'

'She's a lovely lady, Soph. I don't really think we'd have that much in common though, do you?'

'Pity. I thought you two might get on well.'

'Oh, we do, indeed. But her world is much more different from mine than this casual encounter reveals.'

She nodded, he thought, slightly disappointed. Graham had suspected from some previous encounters that the Faulkners might have had thoughts of playing Cupid, and matchmaking between them. He must try to ensure that that did not happen again. He thought momentarily of Jenny and his children. Then reality struck coldly as he relived all the pain and suffering he had encountered over his traumatic separation. He was suddenly very wary and moderately distrustful. He might have to reassess his interactions with the Faulkners.

*

The incident with an old cow was an eye-opener for Graham and exposed him to much valuable insight and knowledge of a different rural nature. Luckily, it happened some years after his arrival into the district and after he had had much exposure to handling cattle on the Johnson's property a few doors and some kilometres down the road from his place on the Shoalhaven.

It all started one morning when he was travelling to

Braidwood from the farm. Nearer to Braidwood were some much smaller acreages that had developed into a community of practitioners of what Graham thought of as alternative and organic methodologies. This was a system that was foreign to him in the sense that he was embroiled only in the sheep industry and in no way involved with any other form of agriculture or horticulture.

He was heading for the stock agency in Braidwood when he was passing a paddock that sloped down from the road gently into a plethora of mostly small-scale agricultural enterprises. He happened to look across to his left as he was always fascinated and intrigued by this form of agriculture, as he deemed it rather labour-intensive.

There, almost beside the road, was a cow sitting in the paddock surrounded by several people in what he surmised was an attempt to get the poor beast to her feet. He slowed to observe the activity when he realised they were in grievous error. So, he stopped the vehicle and walked over to the fence to observe. He could plainly see what was occurring and heard the rather excessive noise accompanying this enterprise. At seeing him, they all stopped their activity and gazed at him.

He yelled out, 'What are you trying to do?'

A young man replied that they were trying to raise the old cow which seemed to be stuck.

Graham yelled out again, 'Well, stop what you're doing. That is all wrong.'

He clambered over the fence and approached the cow. She appeared to be quite old and distressed.

He said rather sternly, 'Stop pulling her by the head.'

They all looked at him confused. He sauntered over to the animal and asked them all to step back away from her while he gently spoke to her in a soft tone.

He then said, 'Who are you people? I thought that you would be familiar with animals from your lifestyle.'

It transpired that they were some young students from town studying this subject and were minding the place for the owner.

Graham explained in some detail their errors. Firstly, the cow did not need a bevy of noisy louts skylarking about her in her distressed state. Secondly, pulling on her head made her task of rising more difficult. Thirdly, her rear end had somehow ended up on the downhill side of her body, not a good position, as cattle rose backside first – or had they not noticed that feature? Fourthly, as cows rose backside first, all their efforts should be directed to assisting her to raise her rear end first, then she could do the rest.

They stared at him in confusion, so he went to the head end and tried to roll her over in one complete turn by her front legs to get her head more downhill and her back legs up on higher ground – not an elegant manoeuvre. He gave her a few minutes to recover then he asked a couple of the boys to come to the rear and help her by pushing, or rather, lifting her backside up as she tried to get up. This she finally did mostly by herself with a little encouragement from the men lifting and pushing from behind.

They were very grateful for his rescue. Graham was most

appreciative of all the hours he had spent with Bert Johnson on his neighbouring cattle property where he had absorbed innumerable facts about cattle and other topics. He stroked the old girl and encouraged her to amble about to regain the circulation in her legs. She was a lovely docile animal but confused with all the strangers about.

Graham began to talk to the group and that was when he realised just what a whole other field of endeavour this was that he knew so little about, but could draw some useful information from them. They stood about talking for some time as Graham asked many questions. He began to realise that, though they might be young and possibly inexperienced, they possessed an awful lot of useful facts and theories relevant to some aspects of his own practices.

One of the young men, seemingly the oldest and possibly a leader, finally asked Graham, 'When you look at this paddock, what do you see?'

Graham thought a bit and gazed around. Then he tentatively replied, 'Well, I see an attractive acreage with a few lovely old trees and a pretty fine pasture, really.'

'Well,' replied the young man, 'this is really a degraded and sterile plot. There are no immature trees here. There is no recruitment, and the biodiversity is almost non-existent. It is a grassy paddock, basically a monoculture.'

'It looks fine to me.' said Graham.

'Yes, well, it's not.'

The young man described what should be there and how to fix it. Graham was intrigued for two reasons: one, that it was maybe not as splendid as it appeared to him and two, that he perceived it to be splendid, despite the fact that it apparently was not. The young people became quite enthusiastic in their appraisal and recommendations to altering this block. Graham jokingly cast a suggestion that they come out to his place and pass judgement on his landholdings. They actually jumped at the idea.

After some socialising with the young people, they invited him down to see their activities as he had shown some interest. He was fascinated by their set-up, especially the milking goats. They tentatively agreed to visit him in the near future.

This they did shortly after. He ended up a little depressed at the appraisal they passed on his paddocks. They pointed out that the overgrown shed paddock was more like the rest of the place should be. All he could counter was to say that 'you can't make an omelette without breaking eggs'. He did, however, gain much insight into how he could improve the biodiversity, and consequently, the productivity, of his country.

*

The issue of the new ownership of the old Wheatley place could be avoided no longer. Besides, Graham suspected that some of the old neighbours of the Wheatleys were still in touch with them in their new location. Graham wished to avoid that complication in his relationship with his erstwhile mentor. He devised and concocted a story that suggested to his neighbours that he had managed to acquire the place with the assistance of a couple of other investors, he, however, being the main partner and the manager of the combined enterprise. This seemed to arouse little antipathy or antagonism from the locals with whom he would still have to work very closely, especially where the use of the shearing shed was involved.

This only left the delicate issue of what to do with the cottage in the village of Captains Flat. He was loathe to part with it as it had been integral to his introduction to this new life and had been a central part of his aunt's life as well. In the end, he just maintained it and used it as an adjunct for accommodation for any family members that wished it.

Two things occurred relating to matters legal during this time. One was rather a shock to Graham, not so much for what happened or to whom it happened, but for the implications that reverberated for him about the action and the potential perpetrator. It involved that scoundrel and suspect lawyer, lately promoted to Judge, one Geoffrey Bales. Graham knew from both a nebulous hint from Jessie, but also some details from Ian Knuckey, that there was bad blood between Jess and Bales. He did not know the full story but just knew there were serious issues. Normally an incident of a tarnished and controversial judicial figure being the subject of a violent episode would not register at all with Graham; it was not that an uncommon occurrence these days and he could fully understand people reacting that way following his own traumatic experience with the legal system. However, this name was very familiar to Graham through his association with the Knuckeys, and in particular with Jessie MacIntyre.

What disturbed him enormously was the issue of its occurring at all, and in particular the timing, so shortly after Jessie's abduction affair. It received enormous media coverage, as it involved the judiciary, but the shocking aspect of the incident was the manner in which the deed was perpetrated and the amount of violence that appeared to be involved, as well as the timing.

It happened such a short time after the attempted abduction of Jessie MacIntyre and the rescuing of her by Graham outside his own property that he suspected her involvement. No one else had any reason to suspect her, but he alone did. He clearly recalled the chilling words expressed by Jessie to no one in particular while she was still dazed and slightly incoherent immediately after her rescue by him. He would normally have taken no notice at all of her rantings, but after witnessing her methods of trying to extract information from her would-be abductors, and the violence she exhibited there, he did not doubt her capability of going further. She did have form in this area, admittedly justified at the times and under the circumstances of those incidents. When Graham raised the issue with Ian Knuckey sometime later, Ian recounted some of the trial evidence that reinforced Graham's fears that she might be capable of more.

The details of Judge Bales' rather vicious death that were revealed to the general public were sketchy at best, but the implication was that he had been rather severely tortured, it was assumed, in order to extract information. This had caused much angst among the criminal fraternity, as no one knew what information had been sought or by whom, and who the would-be targets were – potentially many, according to the police.

Graham recalled frequently, for some reason, some of the musings of Jess, while still wrought with fear and anger after her release by him, of her rambling about Thomas being shot at the Cooma saleyards, news to Graham, and a couple of other incidents. She had mumbled something about eliminating this constant threat to her happiness. Ian Knuckey had also thrown a little light on these incidents after Graham made discreet enquiries of him about it. Though always such a gentle and serene being in his company, Graham sincerely believed that Jessie MacIntyre was more than capable of such a deed. He hoped he was not demeaning her character by these unproven beliefs.

The second legal issue that he decided to follow up was the Planter case before it was too late with the passing of old Jacob. He had finally decided to ask the sister who lived more locally if the silver trinket he had purloined from Jacob's garage was the item that Linda borrowed that day. She had identified it as most likely the very object. Graham decided to confront Jacob with this item and gauge his reaction and try to get some confessions from him before he died.

Graham plucked up the courage to pay him another visit. He took along the ballerina box, and the old penknife that he had cleaned up as much as he could.

Graham went to the place in the early afternoon. After some general chit-chat in which Jacob exhibited some more deterioration of mind and memory, he steered the conversation around to the trinket box and the penknife. Jacob showed an increased degree of animation at the mention of the penknife. He went to great lengths to describe it. It was a gift from an old World War Two digger who had fought in New Guinea. It was rather large and heavy, had one blade, a tin opener and a thing he called a pig-stabber. He became less defensive and more open to revealing things at its revelation. He now could clearly recall the day he lost it. It involved that poor little girl that had died at his hand, and he clearly recalled dropping it somewhere near where he buried her.

Before he had realised what he was saying, Jacob began to stare suspiciously at Graham. Graham quickly reverted back to the penknife as that was a subject Jacob seemed to be able to dwell on in calmness. Graham asked if he remembered running into Tom that day. Jacob did recall, and he thought that Tom might have suspected something, so he thought that he would have to eliminate him, just in case. He fondly remembered the method he used as he was quite familiar with those dangerous mushrooms.

'Clever, don't you think?'

Graham was disgusted. At least he had the answers he craved for himself, if not for anyone else. This confession, if indeed it were such a thing, would carry little weight in any court. He could not really tell the Planters this story, and the mystery of the death of Tom was of interest to only himself in as much as it affected poor Alice, and maybe resulted in his being gifted the last worldly goods of his distant aunt.

He looked at the aging and infirm old man before him. It momentarily crossed his mind that he would dearly like to dispose of him, but he knew that his time would come in due course – God would judge. He suddenly could empathise with Jessie MacIntyre if she had suffered many more times the evils perpetrated on her by others. He knew from her own stories that she had form in dealing out retribution, or at least handling threats. He was not quite so possessed, or capable, or courageous.

CHAPTER SEVENTEEN

It was a mild, calm, sunny afternoon in the late delicate congeniality of early autumn in the high country of southern New South Wales. Graham was again visiting Damien's irrigated lucerne farm opposite John's homestead of Bridgehead for insights into his irrigation set-up. John then invited Graham, who he thought of as an enigmatic and somewhat mysterious personage, over to his place to feel him out about any advancement in the police investigations of any interest to himself. John was fascinated that Graham, this seemingly passive reclusive, had exhibited such unknown bravado in the appropriate circumstances. John wondered what else he did not know about this man.

In the eerie tranquillity of the imposing office, John Summers sat momentarily deep in contented contemplation. Opposite him across the ornate, uncluttered desk sat a now much mellowed entity, the formidable Jessie MacIntyre. He still thought of her in those terms, not as Jessie Summers for some reason, despite the fact that she had married and bore his family name. He still recalled the first time he had ever set eyes on her and how much he had distrusted her – in fact, disliked her. Beside her sat this other person John knew little about, the puzzling Graham Longley who, however, appeared to know a lot about John himself, through his legal connections, and other matters. He was wary of people who might have access to any information about his devious past, despite no one really being able, he hoped, to piece it all together, especially now, after so much time had passed with much muddying of the water. Muddy waters cast no reflections, or images within.

John was content with the way that his life had panned out. He had regrets – the death of his young son Brendan; and fond memories – the departed angelic Livinia, for instance; he often thought of her. John had lived a long life, a blessed one. He regularly contemplated that fact. The phrase, 'only the good die young', often cropped up in his more placid, reflective moments. He hoped that was not a portent; he could cross that bridge when he came to it.

This was a unique and peculiar gathering of three very disparate characters, comfortable in each other's company through common traits of mysteries collected through the life force of their unique conditions and rigid unbending natures. Its occurrence emanated from the strange alignment of unusual circumstances. Graham was here again to dredge the most he could from an accommodating Damien, whose farm was opposite John's, over his proposed irrigation developments along his own spot on the Shoalhaven. Jessie was here on a rare, unplanned visit with John as she happened to be passing through this side of town, not a common occurrence for her as she did not attend the semi-official family shareholders' gatherings on Sundays, she not having a share in the family company. Bridgehead was located at some distance northwest of Cooma in an inconvenient location, being many miles off the highway north to Canberra and Sydney. Auvergne, another of John's properties where Jessie and Thomas lived, was located away the other side to the south of Cooma. She normally had little reason to visit here.

John gazed at them silently for some time. Suddenly, one of his ubiquitous long-case clocks that he had everywhere, the one in his office, struck a long series of strokes in the momentarily silent room. He had muffled its bell; otherwise, it would have knocked them out with the loudness of its chimes.

When it finally finished its sole reason for existence, he said to them, 'You know, that clock is over three hundred years old. It says on it "Smorthwait in Colchester", an English clock that strikes only on the hour. It will run for eight days without a touch. Don't you marvel at the craftsmanship?'

Graham had turned his head towards where the thundering thuds had emanated from the tall, elegant edifice while it completed its routine. In the ensuing moments, he took the opportunity to peruse the contents of this graceful and expansive office. It contained the most ornate and intricate antique furniture, heavily adorned with copious bronze statues and statuettes, some quite large. He noticed that there were no pictures anywhere on the walls. The whole scene was extremely neat and tidy, almost as if it were unused. He knew however, that that was not the case. He was removed from his reverie by John's voice.

John, having turned to Jessie, said in a matter-of-fact way, 'Thomas gave me your latest novels some time ago, Jess, but as you know, I'm not much of a reader.'

Graham looked at Jess. He thought she had finished with writing. She returned his gaze in silence.

'Didn't you know she still writes, Graham?' he said to Graham. 'Here, take a look at these.'

He picked up the two large novels near at hand and slid them across the neat desk. Graham picked them up eagerly in respectful admiration.

'I've never heard of these two authors, Jess. Are they you as well?'

After a long pause, she replied, 'Yes, Graham. One of the few secrets I escaped with from my trials was the name of Kimberley West. I don't do a lot with her now, but still do a little. I try to put my diminishing desire to create into the far more grandiose efforts of Catherine Holbrook Seymour. These names are not connected to me in any way so far; I'd like to keep it that way.' she said in a serious tone, gazing at Graham deeply.

He understood her meaning. She trusted him implicitly.

'You can keep those if you wish,' stated John.

'May I?' enthused an agreeable Graham.

'Yes,' countered Jess. 'I have plenty more.'

Graham took this briefly offered opportunity proffered by her novels to look at Jess through the eyes of an enemy of hers and gauge her potential as a violent assailant. Somehow, he just could not see that in her.

John turned his gaze to Graham. After a slight pause, he said, 'I believe congratulations are in order, Graham, for your bravery award. Most courageous, I'm told.'

'Is that for the plane crash out west, Graham?' asked Jessie.

'Yes,' replied a demure Graham, embarrassed by all the fuss over what he thought of as 'that obscure little episode'.

'Well, I understand you risked your life for those people,' said John.

Graham looked sheepishly at him but said nothing. Jess was recalling his brave efforts in her own abduction. She still recoiled in horror at its possibilities if not for Graham's actions.

In the strange silence that ensured, Jess uncharacteristically said, 'It is indeed well deserved. Graham has done much kind service to others that is little-known. I never knew you owned a place way out at Cobar.'

'It's nothing, Jess. A monster of a place, devouring copious quantities of time and money, but I love it and the four people that live out there. I really contribute very little to it.'

He was mindful that she had just bought and donated the Wheatley's place to him. He did not want her thinking he was richer that he really was. He said little else, a little puzzled as to how she knew that fact. He surmised his talkative mother must have spilled the beans.

John interceded, 'I have done little for others in this world.'

'And I have done even less,' responded Jessie.

'I hope my selfishness and self-indulgence do not weigh too much against me on judgement day,' commented John.

'John, you have been a wonderful father and husband and, I understand, a very good friend to those lucky enough to have engaged your acquaintance,' said Jess.

'Nevertheless, I have secrets that I fear to be judged on.'

'Don't we all?' said Jess.

'Well,' said John, 'I have stored my treasures up in this world. Not, I wager, a good portent. I have not delved too deeply into the interaction of men.'

In the silence that followed, all three sat in deep contemplation. As no one commented, John continued.

'You know, I learnt something from the late minister at our little church some years ago now. It gave me reason for deep thought. If you were asked what the words at the very centre of the Bible are, would you believe they go something like this: "It is better to trust the LORD than to put confidence in man." I particularly remember it for a couple of reasons. It is Psalm 118, verse 8, and it comes after the shortest psalm in the Bible, Psalm 117 and before the longest psalm in the Bible, 119. Don't you think that that is a most significant fact?'

No one replied. Jess knew that John was quite religious; she was not, though she did recall many sayings emanating from the cultured mind of the long-departed Norman Woods from

Milbark days. Graham was thinking much the same. It was news to those two, and possibly of little import.

'Turning to other matters, Graham, I asked if you could come over here while visiting Damien in case you might have come up with anything else from your contacts.'

Graham thought for some time before answering.

'Both of you have opened a huge can of worms for poor old Ian Knuckey. Jessie's connection through this Morangill name from my neighbour Tony, and its apparent connection to a myriad of other possible cases has caused an enormous amount of delving into past events.'

'So, you have made no more advancements, then? Does my name crop up still?' asked John, ever concerned about his own devious past deeds.

'No, John, they have no interest in you other than possibly a connection with the death of your parents. They are still looking into that but, as you know, it was so long ago now.'

He did not mention to John that Ian Knuckey was incidentally fascinated to know how John had managed to accumulate so much wealth, wealth that apparently surpassed exceedingly even Graham's summation of its total.

John remained silent, inwardly content. He really did not wish to drag over the long-dead memories of the loss of his little known parents, or the methods of the acquisition of all he possessed.

'Ian Knuckey assumes that both of you are the victims of the evilness of the wicked among us. He admires that you both managed to avoid that stigma and to have prospered despite the wickedness of others,' said Graham.

'Blessed is the man who walketh not in the counsel of the ungodly,' replied a pious John.

Graham momentarily contemplated mentioning the apparent family connection between his late wife Jenny and John's late wife, Livinia, but he decided better of it, at least for now. He did not need any further complications within his dealings with these people.

The three of them sat in contemplative silence in the serene atmosphere of the elegant office that was the centre of the John Summers' empire.

Graham had briefly tried to read the cover notes on the two books that John had given him, without appearing to be too rude.

Graham turned to Jess and said, 'Do you miss the outback, Jess?'

She took a minute to respond. 'No, not really, it was a hard life, and like most things in life, best endured while young.'

'Where did the name "Milbark" come from?' he asked.

'For many years I thought that it came from the ancient pile of rotting bark, twigs and sawdust that littered the ground about the original site where the old hand timber mill was located, when they first moved there and were building the house and sheds. But I later discovered that it had a much more romantic origin. When Stuart's grandfather moved into the area, the local natives called him M'barc omindin, a sort of term of reverence mixed in with a modicum of fear. The whites just shortened it to Milbark, as they couldn't pronounce the complex Aboriginal words very well.

'It must have been a harsh place to start out from.'

'Yes, it was. Even today it is so far removed from reality that I wonder at the folks that live up there. I did love it, though, but am still pleased to now be living down here in the splendid isolation of the beautiful highlands.'

John asked Graham if he would mind keeping him informed of any developments pertaining to himself that might crop up during any investigations. Graham agreed.

Graham wished to extract himself from this stilted conversation, suspecting that John was merely extending as long as possible the pleasant camaraderie that he so seldom got to indulge in in his isolation. He intimated that he might have to make tracks back to his own place, which he suddenly realised did not even have a name. The original huge undivided property apparently was called 'Wolstongrove', according to the earliest maps and plans, but he had seen no names on any of the other neighbouring subdivisions that he recalled. He and his father simply referred to it as 'the farm'.

He and Jess excused themselves from John's study and exited the house. John sat alone in his aged-induced contentment, contemplating the wonderful, and indeed, full life he had experienced. Graham chatted to Jess for a few minutes at the front door, soaking in her aura and persona. He marvelled at her, her life, her success and her abilities. How blessed he felt just to know her. He was eternally grateful for having met her and for her generous gift to him of the wonderful farmhouse that he now called home. He wandered over to Damien's for the last few words before departing for his own place.

On the long, lonely trip back to his farm, Graham was immersed deeply in the thoughts and experiences of the day, and indeed of the people with whom he had become entangled. He was rather pleased with himself, and he felt his sense of self-worth rising – only now, he felt that it was well justified and earned. He briefly thought of Jenny, then his mind drifted to his late Aunt Alice. He marvelled at the irony of the impact of someone else's decision on the lives of others – the interwoven mixture of random choices influencing the direction of someone else. He hoped he had fulfilled any outcomes she might have desired of him in gifting to him all her treasures.

Then his mind drifted to his own wonderful children. For the first time in his life, he contemplated the need to draft a will for himself. He spent some minutes thinking about the people he knew. The Faulkners had a succession plan centred around their only child, Sophia, but they also had some form of company in place. He had learnt from his interactions with the Summers that they had a complex private family company to avoid the break-up of their most successful mixed enterprises. Graham began to consider the possibility of the division of his assets between his two sons and Sally. Maybe some form of family company would more equitably distribute to all the benefits of his aunt's bequest without breaking up the financially successful entity as it now stood.

His mind drifted back to his aunt. Graham could not help

but feel that his aunt had left to him this lifestyle with some stipulations; it did not come unencumbered. Not only had it lifted him out of his languor, weariness and torpor – in fact, they may have been prerequisites to being gifted this challenging offer – but, as recompense for the achievements along the way, Graham had sequentially introduced into his life, in the appropriate synchronicity, a succession of outstanding events and persons – Sophia and the Faulkners, Jessie and the Summers, for instance, plus many more. Then there were all the little incidences that had occurred along the journey. Each one seemed to be a test, a sort of trial. Pass it and the compensation furthered his own impression and standing within his societal cohort, a sort of intangible growing that was only obtained by dint of effort much more valuable than material gain.

He smiled inwardly, very contented.

Milton Keynes UK
Ingram Content Group UK Ltd.
UKHW040809051024
449151UK00001B/71